MINE ·

A PEAK DISTRICT MYSTERY

Is the abduction of a teenager linked to a deceased serial killer, or are other dark forces at work in the limestone hills of Derbyshire?

Old cases return to haunt DCI Forbes and shadow his attempts to find Debbie. He is acting on instinct, unaware of the race against time that he and his team are in.

Debbie is also acting on instinct, but for her it's a matter of survival – she knows how many days she has left in her terrifying, underground world.

Mary is a city-girl, becoming increasingly uncomfortable after moving from the environment she has always known. Is she being paranoid or has she allowed herself and her daughters to be placed in danger? And is that danger very close to home or not?

MINE TO KILL

Derbyshire Detective DCI Michael Forbes Crime Thriller – Book 3

Sylvia Marsden

Early comment from an **Amazon reviewer**
'Once again the wonderfully imaginative Ms Marsden has excelled herself. A highly original storyline, featuring DCI Forbes and his team, which is riveting from the start. I enjoyed it immensely.'

This novel is entirely a work of fiction.

All names, characters, and events in this publication, other than those clearly in the public domain, are fictitious and the work of the author's imagination. Any resemblance to actual persons, living or dead is entirely coincidental.

Sylvia Marsden was born in Mansfield, Nottinghamshire, but grew up in the centre of the Peak District of Derbyshire – an area she still thinks of as home. She now spends much of the summer in a campervan, touring Derbyshire with her husband and her rescued greyhound – and of course her laptop.

***

Books in the same series by the same author

ORPHAN KILL

SERENE VALLEY KILL

***

Her books are available on Amazon kindle, kindle unlimited and in paperback. Follow on Facebook for news of the novels at Sylvia Marsden Books.

***

This novel is dedicated to all the kind and courteous people out there – the ones who are so often overlooked.

***

PROLOGUE

23rd May 1932
MAWSTONE MINE DISASTER
YOULGREAVE, ENGLAND

'There were acrid fumes like thick fog, making useless the electric lamps; the heat was unbearable and the poisoned atmosphere was death itself,' the surviving rescuers told desperate families and waiting reporters.

*

The second incident to happen that terrible day, however, went unreported beyond the confines of the neighbouring farms and villages. Lilly Saunders and Betty Taylor – seventeen year old dairymaids living and working on the largest farm in the parish of Youlgreave, both vanished.

1
Present day

So far, plans for Cousin Jessica's August Bank Holiday wedding were progressing without too many hitches.

That state of affairs was about to change.

At eight a.m., heat was already sapping the energy from eighteen year old Debbie Thomas's legs. The wide-brimmed hat secured to her golden curls wasn't a fashion accessory – it was necessary to protect her freckled face from burning. Not totally trusting the chemical sunscreen on such a delicate part of her body, she tilted her head slightly until she could feel the full effect of the hat's shade on the back of her neck. The rest of her was well protected, her only worry being the pinpricks of moisture leaching from the skin on her back and soaking into her cotton shirt – stepping into a changing cubicle and dripping sweat onto a polished floor would be so embarrassing.

The faster she walked, the sooner she'd be in the shade.

The greasy tarmac felt soft under the soles of her sensible walking shoes, her heeled pair being in the linen bag she was swinging alongside her. She lengthened her stride, filtering out the intrusive noise from an aeroplane crossing the clear blue sky and replacing the rumble with the low buzz from the hundreds of assorted, flitting insects busy at work along the grass verge, in their miniature, magical, but cruel world.

The first five minutes of her intended ten minute walk from her parent's farmhouse took in views over miles of open countryside and randomly dotted farms and villages. The next five, by total contrast, followed the steeply-sloping narrow road between the closely-packed, listed cottages of the small, limestone, Peak District village of Winster.

Following her normal Saturday morning routine would place her in the centre of the village in plenty of time to catch the first bus into Matlock where her cousin would be waiting. The wedding was six short weeks away and the two of them were under strict instructions to present themselves at the bridal wear shop for their final fittings.

Jessica was always fun to be around, and about the only member of Debbie's immediate family not in a state of near panic over the imminent '*big day*'.

The following few hours promised to have all the hallmarks of an excellent Saturday morning.

At two minutes past eight, on the open stretch of road – not quite single-tracked but narrow enough to cause motorists to slow down when they met, Debbie wasn't too concerned about the blue pick-up truck driving slowly past her, and then driving even more slowly towards the bend in the road up ahead. The waft of exhaust fumes against her sun-screened ankles was only a minor irritant – until she watched him reversing into one of her parents' field gateways.

She shortened her stride.

A dust cloud swirled, the road shimmered, and the irritant merged into the parched-earth landscape.

She began dragging her heels.

"It's nothing... it's nothing... keep walking... it's nothing," she repeated the words like a mantra when the truck materialised for half a second and then vanished again, the roar of its engine obliterating everything but the sound of her own voice.

Her feet felt weighted.

A blackbird flew from a tangle of hawthorn bushes in alarm, its beak opening and closing as if to warn others of danger, and in response a curlew rose from its nest in the adjacent field.

The cloaked vehicle accelerated from the gateway with the dust cloud showing in its rear view mirror and a swirl of fear sent Debbie's right hand scrabbling into the bottom of her bag for her phone.

The driver was looking directly at her, and only at her.

She gasped for breath. It was too late for a full-blooded scream – her right arm was being yanked back and her face smothered by a foul-tasting cloth.

Cousin Jessica would have a long, long wait – the obscure thought flashed through her mind as the road rushed up towards her, and as her face struck the warm, gritty tarmac.

*

Mary Stone's eyes widened as their loaded Toyota Verso Estate left the safety of the tarmacked road and bumped onto the rough, gravelled lane. Not that it was even a proper lane – it was a rutted dirt-track descending in a straight line towards what threatened to be her idea of a '*property-from-hell*'. It didn't even gently wind down the steep slope. Just half a centimetre of frozen snow, or a millimetre of ice, and there would be no way of reaching the council-maintained road in the vehicle they were driving now. They would have to spend money that they didn't have on a Land Rover, or something else equally rugged, if she was to agree to allow Peter his dream of moving the four of them into this – his ancestral Peak District residence.

Her first glimpse of Dale End Farmhouse confirmed the worst of her fears – it was a boarded-up, overgrown, isolated, crumbling dump!

Peter, her husband of less than two years, had brought her, her two young daughters and Zelda the dog to this remote location just because he'd inherited it.

They'd been arguing over it for weeks.

He'd brushed aside her aversion to anything rural and disregarded her pleas for him to do what any normal city-dwelling person would do and sell the property, until eventually he'd worn her down. Finally she'd agreed to allow him to drive them all from London through the early hours of Saturday morning to take a look at the place.

Well she was looking!

The three-bedroomed property, with its four, ten-acre fields had been owned by, and lived in by the Stone family since the early nineteen hundreds. Four generations of Peter's family had lived and died here – a chilling fact which had done nothing to endear Mary to the place. Even floodlit with shafts of orange sunlight on a mid-summer's morning, the neglected property and narrow valley looked more intimidating than inviting.

It wasn't physiologically possible, but she felt sure that her stomach was performing backflips.

The ground-floor windows were covered by sheets of greying timber, and most of the mismatched stone and timber sheds were either missing sections of roof or looked about to crumble into heaps of moss-coated rubble – or both. There were plenty of run-down areas in her native London, but once you knew where they were you gave them a wide berth – as a normal person you didn't harbour any crazy desires to go and live in one of them.

It wasn't as though she'd led a charmed life until now; she'd come from a broken home, been in the care of the council and a couple of foster homes where children weren't the priority of the day, and even spent the odd night in a police cell before she'd met her first husband and fallen pregnant with Amy. The one constant in her life had been her mistrust of anything not centred on clean concrete and smooth tarmac.

She turned to Peter, expecting him to say something profound as he gave his wife her first view of the property. But he remained silent and focused on the scene. That was perhaps for the best – the girls didn't need to be waking to the beginnings of yet another heated discussion.

She turned to face the rear seat. Five year old Amy's eyes were tightly closed and her left arm was draped over Zelda, the grey whippet they'd adopted from Battersea Dog's Home almost two years ago, and beside her, three year old Hannah had her mouth open and was making soft, squeaking sounds with each exhaled breath.

It was only because of the precious contents of the back seat that she had agreed to come to Dale End at all. From the moment she'd learned about the place she'd thought of it as *World's End*.

Peter knew how much she wanted him to use his windfall inheritance to pay off the mortgage on their clean and comfortable London terraced home. Dense woods and wide open fields held no interest for a city girl like her. Just the idea of them would normally send her scurrying to the nearest shopping centre or coffee house. Her main reason, in fact her only reason, for relenting was that she didn't want to be seen, at any point in the future, as the adult who had deprived the girls of the chance of an alternative lifestyle. Only in the last week had she reluctantly conceded that the countryside might be a safer and a healthier place to raise them, and agreed to give Derbyshire's famous Peak District National Park the opportunity to convert her urban ways.

And now, six months after the death of Peter's only blood relative, the moment she'd dreaded had arrived – their Toyota's engine had shuddered into silence on the moss and weed-covered yard at the foot of the deep, tree-lined valley in which sat Dale End Farmhouse. She felt physically sick.

"Well, what do you think?" Peter murmured, breaking the silence and placing his hand over hers.

"I thought you said your uncle had been in a nursing home for nine months – this place looks as though it's been abandoned for closer to nine years." Mary realised her voice sounded pricklier than she'd intended. She placed her free hand over of his. "But never let it be said that I'm not up for a challenge. I'm sure that with a bit of work we'll soon have it looking more respectable."

Peter kissed her cheek and reached into the glove-box for the bunch of large, assorted, rust-coloured keys.

They quietly left the car, and with Zelda at their heels walked towards the house.

"There should still be some tools in uncle's workshop," Peter tugged at one of the boards covering a large window, but without making any impression on it. "I'll go and find a crowbar or something to let some sunlight into the place before we start unloading. We might even get the air-beds blown up and one room comfortable before the girls wake. Then we can have a walk around the neighbourhood, if you'd like. There's a pub at the top of the hill. We can go there for a spot of lunch and spend the rest of the day relaxing. We'll worry about the rest of the place tomorrow."

She looked at him, and then at the building, with continuing scepticism.

Zelda had gently escaped from Amy's grip, as though instinctively trying not to wake the sleeping child, and squeezed her narrow body between the front seats to follow the adults from the car. She angled her head in interest as one by one Peter revealed the windows, and then watched her master heaving his shoulder against the heavy farmhouse door.

An explosive crack of timber echoed along the valley. The door creaked open and the whippet cautiously stepped into unknown territory.

Mary stood, putting off the inevitable a little while longer, reliving the time they'd returned from the solicitors and the sinking feeling she'd had when she'd checked out Dale End Farmhouse on Google Earth. That was when she'd first realised just how isolated the property was. The nearest neighbours were at least half a mile away, and with what looked to her like dense, evergreen woods between them, even their property was permanently out of sight. Her head tilted upwards and she scanned the valley sides. The image on the computer screen that day had sent mild shudders through her, but the satellite picture hadn't done justice to the depth or the unnerving silence of the valley.

The sun's rays skimming across a field of tall, rough grasses stung her eyes. She squinted at what she thought must be their boundary fence, and at the long shadows cast by the trees in the adjacent woods.

The apprehension she'd felt as they'd driven northwards overnight, and as she'd first stepped out onto the driveway, became an intense feeling of foreboding.

From somewhere deep in her sub-conscious came fragments of one of the most quoted lines in film history – something about outer space, and about no one being able to hear you if you screamed.

She could put off stepping through the open doorway for another minute by checking that the girls were both still fast asleep.

They were, so reluctantly she followed Peter into the chilled, musty-smelling house.

There were no dust sheets respectfully covering any of the items of furniture. In fact the interior wasn't at all how she'd pictured it. Ten pounds spent on dustsheets would have been ten pounds wasted. The furniture in the living room all appeared to pre-date World War One, but without being classy or of any value to an antique dealer. At first glance there was nothing art-deco, art-nouveau, or Georgian to get excited about; it was ordinary, working class, bog-standard dark furniture. The carpet was plain brown and threadbare, as were the two fabric sofas, the sideboard appeared to have lost whole sections of its laminated covering years earlier, and the random coffee tables were all of the same dark, muddy-brown colour.

She walked through the next doorway, unable to keep the frown of disappointment off her face. The kitchen was just as bad. With a Formica table as its centrepiece, the property's occupant could simply have popped out to the shops. There was a blackened pan on the rust-streaked electric stove and a plate and some cutlery in the drainer beside the sink, and one stained cup waiting forlornly on the worktop to be washed.

At least the electricity was still connected. It was merely switched off at the main fuse box, they'd been assured by the over-cheerful solicitor, and Peter was in the process of finding it now.

The first light bulb flickered into action.

"I've arranged for an electrician to come out here on Monday to test all the wiring," he shouted from the confines of the cupboard under the stairs in a voice he obviously thought sounded reassuring. "You can't be too careful when a place is as old as this and been empty for as long as this one has. Mice sometimes chew through the old stuff."

Oh great, she wanted to shout back; *dirty, damp, isolated, dodgy wiring, and now mice and goodness knows what other forms of wildlife to contend with.*

This fell so many million miles short of the glare and the glamour of the bright lights that she'd taken for granted all her life. Her world had shifted from colour to black and white.

Was this really Peter's idea of the perfect place for them all to live? Their excursion to the outdoor and camping shop yesterday had filled her with horror, but even after that she'd had no real idea of what to expect.

"Air-beds, a twelve-volt pump in case the electricity won't come on, a camping stove and a whistling kettle," he'd said with a huge grin across his handsome face as he'd pushed the shopping trolley up and down the aisles with her trailing behind him, "and with the duvets and pillows from our own beds, we'll all be comfy enough. You can buy anything else we need when we get up there." He'd sounded so enthusiastic at the checkout that she'd been tempted to slap him. There were shops, and there were shops, and that was one type of shop that she didn't intend going into ever again.

She'd never even seen a camping stove in real life – the idea of clipping metal canisters of gas onto something so flimsy terrified her, and to the best of her knowledge an air-bed had never been a part of her existence. But she'd nodded and smiled as they'd loaded up the car; at least until she'd heard him say, "We'll pick up some bottled water on the way home, just in case the water's been turned off. In any case the system will need a good flushing out."

The one consolation was that it was mid-summer. Mary's work as a part-time teaching assistant at the local junior school meant that she had six weeks of holidays to look forward to, and Peter had taken his four weeks of annual leave in one block and arranged an interview so that if they stayed on he could transfer to a branch of his firm in the Midlands. He was an IT specialist. He installed, updated and repaired computer systems, and split his time between days at home writing software programs and days away from home because he was one of the few people in the country who could handle a particular job. He'd worked in Europe and the Middle East before meeting and falling in love with her, he'd told her, and assured her that his skills would be in demand wherever they lived.

Was it really only ten days since she'd drooled over the plans of two of her colleagues who were off to Benidorm together, and of another colleague with a trip to Thailand booked? She'd responded to their questions by telling them about Peter's inheritance, his reluctance to sell, and his plans for the family's future, fully expecting her fellow city-dwelling, sun-worshipping colleagues to sympathise. But they'd slapped her on her back and told her how envious they all were.

Even that hadn't made her feel guilty for the hours and days that she'd spent arguing with Peter over this place.

"Where's Zelda?" Peter's voice cut into her thoughts.

"She must have gone back out," she hurried to the open doorway. "I'll go and shout her."

"Mummeee..." a tiny voice was coming from inside the car. "Mum, I think Zelda wants to get back in with us. Can we get out now?"

"Come on then, sleepy-heads. Take your pillows into the house to Peter." The girls' biological father had left without warning when Hannah had been just four weeks old, and the following year Peter had come into her life. He was tall, dark, good-looking and intelligent. He'd fallen in love with her two girls but didn't want children of his own, and that was fine by Mary. As far as she was concerned her family was now complete, and as close to perfect as it was ever going to be.

Two girls and one excited dog bounded past her into the house.

She was left standing outside again, this time staring up at the building – at the huge gaps in the stonework where it urgently needed re-pointing, the grass-filled guttering which would need clearing out well before the winter set in, and the peeling paintwork around the cobweb-covered, single-glazed windows. As she examined the roof and counted the cracked and missing tiles, a jackdaw disappeared into one of the four chimneys, carrying with it a length of dead grass.

A mild summer breeze floated down the valley, bringing with it sounds she would never normally have noticed – sounds of twittering birds and rustling leaves.

Despite the rising temperature, she shuddered.

2

Unless he was needed elsewhere, a normal Saturday morning routine for DCI Michael Forbes meant spending an hour or two in his office, in the department of homicide and major crimes, in Leaburn police station. Even when his team wasn't in the middle of a major investigation it was where he felt he ought to be. It was a ritual he'd fallen into over the previous five years, and his preferred way of occupying a chunk of his weekend.

His career was his life, and because of that he'd never had either the time or the inclination to spend hours learning a new skill. His only real hobbies, if he could even call them that, were reading – historical novels were his first choice, and hill walking. And the hill walking he did mainly with the local forensic pathologist, and the woman who had shared his bed for several nights of each week for the past twenty-two years, Alison Ransom. She was his long-term girlfriend, in fact she was the only woman he'd ever had a serious relationship with, but when she wasn't working she preferred spending her Saturday mornings with like-minded female friends, clothes shopping and grabbing a bite to eat in whichever town the gaggle of them descended on for the morning, before spending her Saturday afternoons and evenings with him.

His father, Andrew, with whom he shared the family home, was in his seventy-first year, and other than the usual gripes of men of his age was in good health. He spent most Saturday mornings preparing the family's evening meal, ahead of his walk into the centre of Leaburn, to the White Lion public house, for a few glasses of orange juice and games of dominoes.

The only other occupants of the six-bedroomed family house were his twenty-eight year old sister, Louise, and her two year old daughter, Gemma. Louise had turned her back on her old life of prostitution and alcohol, returned home and enrolled at college, and amazed Michael and their father by becoming a devoted mother with plans to carve out a career before her daughter was old enough to attend school.

Michael struggled to tolerate children of any age, and for as far back as he could remember he always had. Youngsters made him uncomfortable. He couldn't seem to connect with them, and he'd never really understood why. Maybe he'd just never tried hard enough.

It was a flaw in his character that he'd been careful to keep hidden from his superiors at work.

His mother had died suddenly when his sister had been only eight weeks old and he'd helped in her upbringing, but he hadn't done enough. Only when it was too late had he realised just how much he'd failed her. And now the beautiful, dark-haired Gemma was rapidly becoming a miniature version of her mother, though for now at least, only in looks. He loved both of them dearly, but was happier out of their combined company. Most mornings he was out of the house before anyone other than Alison had surfaced.

There was no major investigation needing his attention this weekend, no upcoming court cases to worry about, and his detective sergeant was on a well-earned holiday and not due back at work for another few days. For once it might be a quiet, relaxing Saturday morning. He looked at the box of cold case files on the floor in the corner of his office, broke off a double square of milk chocolate and then casually greeted PC Tracy Wilson, the family liaison officer, as she handed him his post.

"This one's marked *urgent*, sir. There was an e-mail to this station last night, after you'd gone home, from the governor of Wandsworth Prison telling us to expect the registered post and to make sure that you saw the package at the first opportunity."

He opened the padded envelope. Two plastic-covered, handwritten letters and one printed sheet with the prison's logo at the top and the governor's signature at the bottom, slid out onto his desk.

The handwriting demanded to be read and he picked up the wrapped sheets first. Written normally the text would have covered little more than a single page, but this giant scrawl filled both sides of each of the two sheets of A4 paper.

He looked at the last page and scowled.

Now they had his full attention.

Dear Detective Chief Inspector Michael Forbes,

I do hope you remember me – I certainly remember you!

I'm dying. You may or may not have heard – and I really don't give a flying fuck either way!

Are you having a good life? I hope that you are because then what I'm about to commit to paper should really screw things up for you!

Six years ago you helped to put a stop to my fun. Do you remember that day?

You deprived me of the thrill of the hunt – of ever knowing the anticipation, the excitement, and the deliciously sweet moment of the capture of my next victim.

I know I'm bad – I'm bad through and through – I was never able to truly enjoy sex without simultaneously inflicting suffering and I didn't need the so-called experts I've met in here to tell me that isn't normal.

Where you might want your women to cry out with pleasure I only ever wanted mine to scream in terror or in pain!

Or have I read you wrong Detective Chief Inspector Forbes? Are you as screwed up as I am – again I don't give a flying fuck either way!

I've accepted that I'm never again going to have the pleasure of slowly squeezing the life out of another human being – but I've saved one nugget of entertainment – one last laugh, until the end. It's a good, belly-splitting laugh – and it's on you Michael!

Do you remember the names of all ten of the women I confessed to killing?

I expect you do – I hope that you do – but do you know how many of those ten women were actually killed by me – no – then I'll enlighten you!

SIX

That's right – six!

Not ten – six!

Oops – egg on face DCI Forbes!

I had nothing whatsoever to do with the deaths of Zoe Stirling, Christine Wright, Joanne Scott, or Lucy Spencer!

Now I'm not about to make your job simple for you – I'm not going to give you a name – and I'm even going to keep you guessing as to whether or not I knew who did kill them!

I took the credits for someone else's works but now I'm reaching my end I'd like to hand those credits back!

YOU HAVE ANOTHER SERIAL KILLER ON YOUR PATCH MICHAEL!

Just picturing your face as you read this will give me no end of pleasure in my final days!

DID YOU NEVER FOR ONE MOMENT SUSPECT THAT YOU MIGHT HAVE GOT IT WRONG?

I guess that's one question that I'll have to go to my grave without knowing the answer to.

Happy hunting Detective Chief Inspector Michael Forbes!
Happy hunting!
Yours sincerely
Brian Garratt Esquire

He stared at the scrawled letters.

Darkness swirled through him.

His ribcage refused to move — for several seconds he couldn't draw a single breath.

Outside his building was a beautiful summer's morning — that wasn't right — there should at least have been a crack of thunder and sheets of torrential rain or hailstones lashing against his office windows.

He re-read the four handwritten pages.

Boots clonking across his floor, and then the crick in his neck as he looked up to see DC Robert Bell approaching, both confirmed that he was wide awake.

DC Bell was from Buxton, a similarly-sized market town to Leaburn and just fifteen miles to the north. Bell had only been a detective for two years but his career path had never been in doubt. Almost every member of his family, for at least four generations, had been involved in some aspect of policing or security, from working as a code breaker at Bletchley Park during World War Two, to being the newest member of the dog-handling unit at Customs and Excise today. Bell eagerly attended any courses offered to him, and his list of contacts seemed to know no bounds. If sensitive information was needed which was not readily available on the police national computer, it would be a safe bet that DC Bell would know the best person to ask to obtain the information in the shortest possible time. He realised he was an asset to the station, and always willingly dropped whatever he was doing to help out with a query.

"Robert, take a look at these and tell me that they're nothing more than a sick joke. Reassure me that in your expert opinion it's just a dying man's final shot at notoriety." Forbes slid the two letters that the governor had diligently placed into two evidence bags for him, across his desk.

The DC picked them up as eagerly as if they'd been winning lottery tickets on a rollover week. "They're from the serial killer, Brian Garratt. He died a couple of days ago, didn't he?"

Forbes nodded.

His DC's face grew paler as the final sentences hit their mark.

Bell's eyes met his and he felt the dual primal responses of gooseflesh forming on his forearms and hairs on the back of his neck standing to attention. They weren't sensations he experienced very often, but then it wasn't very often that a death-bed confession landed on his desk – or rather – a death-bed retraction.

"This isn't something we can ignore, sir," Bell stated the obvious as he slid the evidence bags back across the desk, "however unlikely his claims may turn out to be."

"I wasn't intending to. We'll have to review the files of all ten victims. Did we really close the cases on four missing persons – on four possible murders, that Garratt didn't commit?"

"I think it's highly unlikely, sir. He's trying to embarrass us; make us look foolish."

"Well let's hope you're right, shall we?"

The bodies of six victims had been recovered, each one yielding indisputable forensic evidence linking Garratt to the killings, but no trace of the other four had ever been found. At the time of his arrest, and during the many interviews since, Garratt had steadfastly maintained that he couldn't remember where he'd buried them. He'd even had the gall to blame the police for his confusion.

Those missing four were the victims abducted from the areas closest to Leaburn, and were the four that Garratt was posthumously claiming had been nothing whatsoever to do with him.

"I remember Garratt's arrest," Bell walked to the first floor window and stared across the road at the Tesco car park. "He confirmed details relating to all ten cases – details not released to the public, and that was why everyone believed him. Do you really think we could have had another killer out there all these years, driving around our streets, shopping in our supermarket, and laughing at us knowing that he'd got away with four separate murders?"

"We have to consider it a possibility. But after thousands of man-hours there were no real reasons to doubt any of Garratt's ten confessions… were there?"

"If four of the murders weren't committed by him, how do we account for his detailed information? Did he know the second killer, or was he in contact with someone on the force? Could one of our officers have been feeding him with information? It makes more sense to believe that he was responsible for all ten, sir."

"Garratt had a half-sister who was a junior reporter on the Manchester Evening Newspaper, and he had a cousin, uniformed police constable Stephen Darcy, stationed here at Leaburn at the time of the investigations. We'll need to contact them both. Darcy requested a transfer shortly after Garratt's arrest, and I believe he ended up in Newcastle. Try to find him first. Tell him we need to establish whether he inadvertently leaked information to

Garratt during the investigations. We need to know how close the two men were."

"Will anyone from this station be attending the funeral?"

"Details of the funeral won't be made public." Forbes stared at the documents as though they might somehow give up more of their secrets. "Unless we're busy I might be attending, but only to witness that monster finally being disposed of."

With Bell on his way back to the incident room and sunlight streaming into his office, he clicked on a file he hadn't expected to ever have to open again. He stared into the blank, grey eyes of Brian Garratt.

Did you never for one moment suspect that you might have got it wrong?

Those words had hit him as forcefully, and almost as painfully as a carefully delivered uppercut to his diaphragm from an experienced boxer. He was thankful he'd been seated. They'd not only taken his breath, they'd left him with a powerful ache in his chest.

Garratt had never shown any remorse. His killings had spanned a twelve year period, and as the Chief Investigating Officer at Leaburn station for the last five of those, and working closely with the Greater Manchester force's major crimes unit, he couldn't remember ever experiencing any niggling doubts over any of Garratt's confessions.

But should he have…?

Neither was he aware of anyone on any of the many teams involved in the investigations having any misgivings. Certainly no one had voiced any to him at the time, or since, but it wouldn't hurt to contact one or two of them to ask for their off-the-record opinions now.

Once the press got wind of the letters, Garratt's face would be almost impossible to avoid, but for now it was happily within his power to reduce the man to a stored file. He clicked the close button and his computer returned to its screensaver setting.

The two letters found in Garratt's few personal effects were both dated the day following his diagnosis. If only they'd been found and forwarded to this station a week or two earlier, then maybe one final interview could have been arranged. If nothing else, at least he would have had the dubious pleasure of witnessing Brian Garratt on his death-bed.

"PC Stephen Darcy is still stationed in Newcastle," DC Bell announced as he returned to Forbes's office. "I've spoken with him and he isn't intending coming down to Derbyshire for the funeral. However he is due some leave and if his sergeant will allow him to take it next week he still has close relatives in Buxton that he can stay with. I told him I'd check with you that next week would be all right."

"Next week will be fine. The sooner we can prove that these letters are nothing more than a work of bullshit fiction, the better it will be for everyone. Tell him to contact me directly as soon as he arrives in Derbyshire. Have you located Garratt's half-sister?"

"Yes sir… that is… I know where she is. She's on maternity leave from the same newspaper she worked on at the time of the murders. I have her home address."

"Give her a call.   Then while I inform the assistant chief constable of what's happening, could you find the up-to-date contact numbers of all ten of the victims' families? I want my officers paying the families of the four named girls a visit before news of these letters leaks out. We're about to shatter their worlds for a second time, and they're about to feel the need to see justice done all over again. This time they deserve final closure, so let's get on and give it to them."

"I've already got DC Green searching for those. It's just a thought, sir, but are we certain that Garratt himself wrote those letters?"

"The prison governor confirmed the handwriting as Garratt's – unfortunately."

*

Debbie wanted to wake. She wanted to move, but couldn't.   Something was holding back her consciousness, something sweet-tasting and oddly chemical. Nothing made any sense. Her limbs could have been stuck down by thick treacle, her head throbbed as if held tight in a blacksmith's vice, and her fractured thoughts were battling dense swirls of fog.

Slowly... painfully... the seriousness of her situation was dawning on her. Tears began to pour from underneath her closed eyelids – hot, wet, and silent tears. They trickled down into her ears.

She remembered struggling – her hair being pulled back – a knee bearing down on her chest – being forced to drink something – having to swallow because she was choking – all the time staring up into the face of a man.

And then a needle – a needle jabbed into her arm.

She remembered abject terror.

He'd drugged her. The bastard had chased her down and drugged her.

She opened her eyes, but only for a second. The blackness was intense, almost as intense as her headache.

She wiggled her wrists and then her ankles – no restraints – but maybe it was safest to lie still. Listening was probably the safest thing to do, listening and fighting off wave after wave of panic, straining her ears for any familiar sound.

The roar of her heartbeat grew louder.

A tsunami of panic...

She gulped air into her lungs – dirty-tasting air – not of soil but of something similar.

She needed to calm herself – to take stock of where she was – the fact that she couldn't hear anyone didn't mean that she wasn't alone.

Her breathing steadied.

She was on her back, covered by a scratchy blanket as far up as her neck, and with whatever was underneath her cold but softer. Her hands slowly moved across the lower fabric, then back towards her until they were touching her bare flesh. She was cold and she was naked.

Her senses were returning, accompanied by a wave of nausea. She rolled onto her side to vomit – onto what – she'd no idea. Fear stopped her. She swallowed down bile and slowly rolled back. She opened her eyes again and raised her right hand to her face. Her fingertips touched her forehead but nothing came into focus – nothing but oppressive, all-enveloping blackness.

Had he blinded her? Some drugs had horrific side-effects, didn't they – was that what had happened to her?

Maybe she wasn't a prisoner at all. Maybe she'd been hit by a car and was hallucinating. That was it – she'd been found and was now lying in a hospital bed – in the middle of the night. But then hospitals were never totally silent, and always smelled of either disinfectant or cooked meals, never of mouldy linen and damp soil.

She forced her confused brain to think – to rationalise her thoughts and remember more. She'd been knocked out by something and then taken somewhere. Being comatose while moved was the only thing she felt certain of, but where the hell had she been moved to?

There was a muffled noise; something other than the roar of her heartbeat. Unless her senses were fooling her, or the drugs still affecting her, a grating sound somewhere in the distance had grown louder and then quieter.

Her headache was easing slightly, but nausea was taking its place. She needed to move.

She'd managed to suppress the idea of being buried beneath mounds of earth, in a box perhaps, or a coffin, but suddenly her need to know outweighed her fear. She moved one hand upwards into the unknown, but it met empty space. When she lowered it her fingers touched the edge of what felt like a wooden frame. She quickly pulled her arm back under the cover. It was ice-cold against her side.

Another thought surfaced without warning, and again the need to know one way or the other was too urgent not to respond to it. Her skin tingled as her cold hands moved over her breasts and her stomach and down towards her thighs. There was no soreness. She wriggled and then reluctantly touched the tops of her thighs. Neither was there much moisture. The bedcover, or whatever it was, was cold and wet, and so was her backside. She'd urinated, she was fairly certain, but if she'd been raped wouldn't there be other signs, more moisture on her legs – from blood or semen – or both? And wouldn't she be bruised and sore?

But then she'd never been intimate with anyone – so how could she be sure? She was naked and that meant she'd been abducted for one thing and one thing only.

Weren't girls regularly being sold into the sex industry?

She batted the thought away.

If there wasn't a sexual motive for her capture, was she being held for ransom? Her parents weren't poor, but they weren't exactly rolling in money, either. They were an ordinary working family. Her mother was a local councillor, but she had no real powers.

Another wave of nausea washed over her, accompanied by another wave of panic. The side of her face throbbed and her breathing was too fast and too shallow. It was making her light-headed. She had to get a grip. And she had to stop herself from shivering. She wasn't cold – she was in shock.

She was alive, but in serious trouble.

Whoever had taken her could have raped and killed her and left her in a ditch. That hadn't happened.

For whatever reason, she'd been taken somewhere and covered with a blanket. Those two facts might just mean that there was a slim chance of her surviving whatever ordeal lay ahead.

She had to hold onto that thought.

3

"First of all, thank you to those of you who have voluntarily abandoned your plans in favour of spending your Saturday afternoon at the station with me." Forbes counted five, eager, off-duty officers swelling the numbers in the incident room. "This may prove to be a time-wasting exercise, so for that reason we'll name it ourselves for now and call it Operation Fantasy."

The names allocated to police operations and major incidents were normally randomly generated by the police computer. He was still hoping it wouldn't come to that.

DC Harry Green wasn't sounding downhearted at the prospect of a huge manhunt. "If there is another serial killer in this area then we're all looking at plenty of overtime." The Liverpool-born detective who had moved to Leaburn five years ago was the father of four young girls and his finances were permanently stretched.

"That's still an if... Harry, and I don't want to hear those words used outside this room until we have solid evidence to support them." Forbes glanced at the four pictures lined up across the top of the first of the three whiteboards in the room. "You've all read this morning's two letters, and some of you have had a chance to refresh your memories by looking through one or two of Garratt's original confessions. None of us expected to see any of these faces on an incident board again, and what we need to discover, as quickly as possible, is whether these four young women looked into the eyes of a killer other than Brian Garratt."

"If they did, and if he's still in our area, it might only be a matter of time before he strikes again." DC Bell looked around the room and a few heads nodded.

Again Bell had stated the obvious and so Forbes didn't respond. He turned to the board. "Zoe Stirling, Christine Wright, Joanne Scott, and Lucy Spencer, all disappeared from the Buxton and Bakewell areas between eight and sixteen years ago, and while the six women whose deaths can definitely be attributed to Garratt all went missing during the same time frame, they were all abducted from the Manchester and Stockport areas."

He turned back to face the room, desperately hoping that Harry Green wasn't about to get his overtime wish. As a small rural police station, their budgets were always under scrutiny. He didn't want to see his workplace reduced to another part-time station as had happened with so many others. "The locations and the fact that the bodies of these four women have never been found are so far the only proven differences between the two groups. I need you to find more, however slight they might be: the methods of the abductions, dates, days of the week, times, weather conditions, anything you can come up with to differentiate the four from the six, or to link the four together. Did they have friends or associates in common, or did they visit the same places?"

"Sir," DC Jade Sharpe, the newest member of his team spoke from the back of the room. "Garratt was arrested six years ago, but just under two years ago, when I was stationed at Buxton, I worked on a missing person's case which I think might be relevant. Faith Crispin was originally believed to be just another runaway, but she's been an official misper for twenty-two months now. I've checked and there have still been no sightings of her. It's as if she vanished into thin air. She had fair, shoulder-length hair, just like the rest of those on our board, and she was a very pretty eighteen year old. Do you think we should provisionally add her to that list?"

"I'm familiar with that case, Jade. I'll go along with your suggestion; well spotted. Add her picture and details, and then trawl the databases for any other potential victims in the Derbyshire, Cheshire, and Staffordshire areas. If we have had a killer operating under our radar for the last sixteen years, then we have a lot of backtracking to do."

As he finished speaking his phone began to ring.

*

Debbie wasn't sure whether she'd slept again or not. Time was worthless. All she knew was that her headache had eased slightly and she was wide awake. She almost wished she wasn't.

The covers underneath her had retained the cold and wet from her *accident*. From somewhere she'd found the courage to move from the worst of that, and at some point she'd vomited over the side of the bed, but since then she hadn't dared to move anything other than her arms.

The scraping sound wasn't in her head – she'd heard it more than once, though how long apart the sounds had been she'd no idea, and twice she'd thought she'd heard an almost human cry.

She stifled a sob and wrapped her arms around her chest.

Someone was out there – wherever there might be, but the darkness remained absolute and she was too terrified to call and find out.

*

Forbes scribbled down lines of notes while listening to the call from the civilian dispatcher in the force control room. The ache in his chest was spreading. "Leave what may turn out to be nothing more than a fanciful story, everyone," he switched off his phone and walked over to a blank whiteboard. "As from this moment we have a live investigation. Deborah

Thomas, aged eighteen, from Shining Bank Farm on Bonsall Moor, has just been reported by her parents as missing. A few minutes ago her smashed phone was found by her father at the side of the road, about five hundred metres from their home. She was last seen just before eight a.m. this morning, walking from her home just outside the village of Winster. From there she should have walked into the village, a ten minute walk at the most, and caught the bus into Matlock where her cousin was to meet her for a dress fitting. From what her parents have been able to establish by phoning friends and neighbours, Debbie, as she's known, never got on that bus and so far no one has been found who can say that they definitely saw her in the village this morning."

He was transferring details from his notebook onto the board as he spoke. "I want an immediate, full-scale search organising, of the route between Shining Bank Farm and the village, and then extending outwards into the surrounding area. Scenes of crimes officers and air support are being alerted. I'll put in a request for dog handlers. Given the terrain of the area, Buxton and Edale mountain rescue teams are also being alerted and will be called upon if Debbie doesn't reappear during the next hour. The first twenty-four hours of these types of investigations are always the most vital, and we've already lost six. I want a press conference organising in time to catch the early evening local news – there's still a slim chance that she's had some sort of a meltdown and is holed up with a friend somewhere with no idea of the fuss that she's causing, despite her parents insisting that she's a very sensible and reliable girl who would never have missed the final fitting of her dress for her cousin's wedding."

DC Jackson held up her phone. "Debbie's friends have been posting her picture on Facebook for the last two hours. It may be that she's with someone who doesn't have internet access or a phone…"

"How likely is that these days?" DC Bell added the subdued comment.

"Every bit of publicity helps." Forbes turned to the board now displaying the faces of five girls. The last thing that anyone needed was another face adding to that first board.

*

Debbie blinked hard. Her left hand touched her nose and her fingers spread out across her face, but however close they were made no difference. Her eyes stung, only now she was too terrified to close them.

That sound had definitely occurred again. Someone was out there; wherever there was. To shout out might mean alerting her captor, but to stay quiet could mean missing her one chance of rescue.

She seemed to have been awake for hours and no one had come to her. She couldn't just lie here forever, doing nothing. And besides, she needed the toilet again. Shouting out was a risk she was going to have to take. Whoever had abducted her would return sooner or later, but help might only come along once. "Hello... is there anyone there? Help... please help me... I'm Debbie Thomas and I need help." Her voice sounded unfamiliar as it left her throat. It echoed back, again and again, each echo fainter than the last. Fear squeezed her chest even tighter. Where the hell was she?

But someone must have heard her.

Cooler air drifted across her face, tangy and smelling faintly of ammonia, and of putrid earth and rotting animal manure. It was noticeably different to the air she'd been getting used to. The sensation lasted only seconds, closely followed by another sound, this time more metallic. Now she knew the noise wasn't from her own frazzled brain. People had to be out there looking for her – help could be one more shout away. "Hello... is there anyone there?" Stabbing pains shot across her ribs. "Help me... please help me... I'm here... help." More tears trickled across her cheeks.

Her body felt stiff and bruised, as though she'd been in the same position for hours. It could be well into Saturday by now – or even Sunday. Would Jessica have raised the alarm, or would her parents have called the police? It didn't matter, as long as someone was searching for her.

She blinked. It wasn't her imagination – a soft light was appearing high above her. Maybe it was the first of Sunday's morning light filtering through a roof window.

No, it was changing too rapidly. Some sort of artificial light was slowly becoming brighter. Someone was coming for her. She felt a surge of relief, immediately chased away by a pang of terror as she realised it didn't necessarily mean she was about to be rescued.

The overhead light was growing stronger and the unclear sounds louder. She drew in a painful breath, about to shout out again, but fear stopped her.

Her surroundings were slowly coming into focus. She turned her head one way, and then another. All around were dark stone walls and shadows.

She was alone in the space, but where was the door? Why couldn't she see the door?

She hugged the coarse blanket to her chest, sat up, and swung her legs to the ground, ignoring the fact that she'd thrown up there earlier. Her feet met a cold, damp, uneven floor.

Every inch of her body trembled. Trying to stand up and squeeze the cover to her body, she staggered. Her nakedness was an embarrassment, but it was nothing compared to her terror.

A rescuer would be shouting her name by now – letting her know that she'd been found.

Whoever was approaching wasn't bringing help.

The light was growing stronger by the second, but still nothing anywhere around her resembled a door. She had nowhere to run to, and nothing to defend herself with. She was trapped like a wild rabbit in a cage, waiting for the inevitable.

Her teeth chattered and her knees buckled, collapsing her back onto the bed.

Stay calm and try to bond with your kidnapper – isn't that what they say? How the hell was that even possible with a totally dry mouth, trembling innards, and a heart that wanted to leap from your chest?

Her abductor was about to show himself and there was nothing she could do to alter that fact. Whatever happened she would try to be brave. Calmness might be her only tool in a battle for survival.

A louder clang of metal on metal startled her and she cried out.

Calmness – who was she kidding?

All the sounds were coming from high above, from where the light was still growing stronger and closer, and where she could now see a dark shadow bearing down on her.

There were no walls, not in the ordinary sense. Whichever way she looked only rock and more rock came more sharply into focus; dark slabs of stone dotted with pick-marks and natural fissures, and shadows – so many dark shadows. She was in a cave – a cave with access only from above.

The realisation ploughed into her with a sickening jolt.

The bastard had placed her inside an enclosed cave, like a pet goldfish in a circular bowl, with nowhere to go and no hope of escape.

There were no doors because the only entrance was twenty or thirty feet above her head, and the steady clang, clang, clang, was from someone descending a metal ladder before they even reached the entrance to her prison.

Black shadows danced across the floor but she only glanced at them. She couldn't help but look upwards. The figure with the lantern had reached the foot of the metal ladder. He was walking across something, carrying the light. What looked and sounded like metal frames went part of the way around the roof of the cave. The man was on some sort of gantry, far above where she could have hoped to climb to.

She was right; there was no other way in or out of her prison.

*

DS Adam Ross had just lifted the last suitcase from the boot of the taxi when his phone rang. He'd arrived back at Jane's house with his son, Ryan, and Jane Goodwin and her daughter, Lucy, after a five day break in Wales. The holiday had been relaxing – as relaxing as it could be with two young children, but the meter was ticking.

He let his phone ring out, paid the driver, and then carried the cases into the house.

Jane had been his unofficial fiancée for six months and the holiday had been intended to mark that milestone. They'd discussed buying a ring to make it official but looking into jewellers' windows were as close as they'd come to actually choosing one, and the few tentative plans they'd had for the wedding had stalled. Jane hadn't been feeling well for several months and her doctor had blamed her mystery illness on the previous year's trauma of finding her mother dead in her kitchen, and then more recently being caught up in a police investigation and almost killed in a house fire. He'd recommended therapy but Jane had refused.

"Kettle's nearly boiling," he shouted as his phone sprung into life again. "Do you want tea or coffee?" This time he looked at the screen and the name displayed there made him accept the call and press the loudspeaker icon.

"Adam, are you home yet?" It was his boss, DCI Michael Forbes, and he wasn't likely to be calling to request a peek at their holiday snaps. "Did you have a good holiday?"

"We've just this minute arrived home, sir. The break was good, thank you." Good described it accurately enough – one part of it had actually been quite wonderful, but overall, it had been good. "Did you want something, sir? I've brought you that bottle you asked for."

"No time for that, I'm afraid – now I know you're not due back at the station for another few days, but we have two on-going incidents, both of them serious, and I could really use your assistance. We have a missing eighteen year old girl and a reopened case that you'll have to see for yourself to believe. The whole thing is giving me the willies, I don't mind telling you."

"A missing local girl...?"

Jane walked into the kitchen and nodded to him.

"She's only been missing for a few hours but the early signs aren't good. If she doesn't turn up safe and well could you come in tomorrow morning?"

"I'll be with you first thing, sir."

*

With a plastic mug of lukewarm coffee in his hand, Forbes walked back into the small, and the only incident room in Leaburn police station. There would be no relaxing Saturday evening family meal to look forward to today. The only chance he was likely to have of a hot meal would be courtesy of the microwave. He'd already texted Alison and asked her to plate something up for him.

Things were moving fast: James Haig, his crime scene manager, was controlling activity around the area Debbie had possibly been abducted from, Tracy Wilson, the family liaison officer, was with the parents, and when Forbes left the search area DI

Lang and the mountain rescue teams were in joint control of volunteers from the village and uniformed and off-duty police officers.

Six pictures of Debbie, all family photographs and all showing her smiling, were lined up along the top of the second of the three whiteboards. He hated times like these. With every passing hour hopes of finding a missing, attractive young woman alive, were dwindling. He knew it, his team knew it, and deep down the missing girl's family knew it.

But this was only day one and it was a part of his job to maintain optimism for as long as possible. "Good afternoon, everyone, it's Saturday, six-thirty p.m., and this is the first official briefing of Operation Barley, the search for missing teenager, Deborah Thomas, known to everyone as Debbie. She's known to walk the same route at the same time every fine Saturday morning, so it's possible that someone she knew pulled up to offer her a lift. Her damaged phone was found under a hedge by the side of the road, quite close to the farm track leading up to her home. That is now with the forensics team, and so far we only know that she hadn't phoned home or anywhere else for help."

"So we're certain now that she's been abducted?" DC Harry Green asked in his strong scouse accent. "She's small, fair-haired, and slim, and with her looks is there a chance that she could be another victim to go on that first whiteboard? Is the serial killer that we didn't realise we had in our area, still at work?"

Forbes hesitated for a moment, "Let's hope not, Harry, let's hope not. But that's what we're intending to find out."

4

Every sinew in Debbie's body screamed at her to take flight.

Dark soles clanged along the gantry. They halted. Two bare light bulbs, suspended from the metal framework, flickered into life.

And there he was, staring down at her, his face lit from below and looking grotesque. She couldn't help but stare back.

He was the one from the lane. His was the last face she remembered seeing.

She felt desperate to look anywhere other than upwards – upwards at the black soles and the leering face peering over the top of them. From her position there seemed to be nothing of substance between his feet and his face.

Her whole body was trembling.

Feet and face... face and feet...

She forced her eyes downwards. She needed a first proper look at her surroundings. Fight or flight – isn't that what they say that the body prepares itself for? Flight wasn't an option. She needed something to defend herself with.

A white, folding plastic table and two matching folding chairs, the kind that most gardening stores sold throughout the summer stood closest to her bed, pressed against the rock face. Beside that was a bench stacked with towels, cushions, and more bedding. And opposite them was another pair of the same type of chairs, and a plastic bucket. That was it – there was nothing more.

Keep calm, she told herself, but in that same instant remembering he'd seen her naked. He'd touched her.

The whimpering sound was coming from deep in her chest. She had to stop that and force herself to speak. Her tongue stuck to the roof of her mouth. "Please... let me go... don't hurt me... please..."

"Shush, Debbie, shush, I don't want to hurt you; really I don't." She remembered that voice – it was the last thing she'd heard before passing out. "There's a good girl. You've no need to be afraid of me, no need at all."

"What do you want...?" Her words sound slurred.

He stood against the gantry railings, staring down at her, but not answering.

Fall you bastard, she wished she had the courage to shout out. *Fall and break your sodding neck, why don't you?*

Maybe she could win him over – convince him that although he'd done wrong it wasn't too late to set it right. If he wanted her to beg, then she'd beg – but not just yet.

She drew in a ragged breath and forced herself to look up and speak out again. "You won't be in trouble if you let me go now. I won't say anything to anyone."

"I'm sorry Debbie," he spoke slowly and deliberately, "but I don't know you well enough yet to think that you might not cause trouble for me."

"Who are you?" Despite the distorted shadows his build and clumsy movements told her he was much older than her. He looked vaguely familiar.

"I'm your new friend," he answered her in a soft, patronising voice. "You never answered me this morning, Debbie, when I asked you how you were. That was very rude of you. I'd told you I only wanted to talk with you. There was no need for you to run like that. But I'll ask you again... how are you?"

"I'm scared witless, but I'm all right," humour him, she thought; humour the bastard. "Let me go home now... please."

"But you are home, Debbie. Take another look around you. Let me switch on more of these lights ... there... that's better, isn't it?"

Two more dusty light bulbs shone a stronger, harsher, yellow light onto the damp-looking stone walls.

"I'm sorry about leaving you in the dark, that was very remiss of me and it won't happen again."

"What time is it?" So far she'd seen no sign of her bag or her phone.

"It's Saturday evening, my darling. That's all you need to know."

"I was going to meet someone. My parents will be worried. I should be back in my room now."

"But this is your room… your bedroom… our bedroom, at least for a short while, and I just know that we're going to be blissfully happy here. I've admired you for a long while, and you will grow to love me in this room, Debbie, just as a dutiful girlfriend should. And when I'm convinced your feelings for me are genuine you can become my wife. I realise our courtship will be somewhat unconventional, but once you've passed each of the tests I have planned for you, and once you've proved your love for me beyond any doubt, then we can leave here together and be married properly, in the eyes of the law."

"Married…?" She shuddered when she ought to be laughing in his face.

"We'll be known as the unconventional couple, and be proud of it, and be so much in love that people will envy us. Your parents will see how happy you are – how happy we both are, and they'll be pleased for us."

He was crazy – she'd been abducted by a loony-tunes!

She'd been right to consider that whoever had taken her might not be a killer, but the thought that he might be stir-crazy hadn't crossed her mind. "If you care for someone you don't keep them as a prisoner. You can't force someone to love you by doing that. Why don't you let me go home, and now I know how you feel about me, maybe we could go out together on proper dates and get to know each other."

"I knew you'd say something like that, but really I've nothing to lose by doing it my way. I've tried normal relationships but they've always been on the woman's terms, and I've found myself being used and then dumped. None of them stayed with me long enough to really get to know me."

You mean they were with you just long enough to get to know you; she wanted to yell upwards at him.

"None of them bothered to try to love me like I know that you will. And you will fall in love with me because your future depends on it. But please don't be afraid. Look upon today as the first day of your new life – of your life of love with me."

She was thinking hard. He'd mentioned getting out of here, but that could be his way of taunting her, of putting her on the back foot. He was unbalanced, but he didn't speak like a complete idiot. She was going to have to be extremely careful, and play along with his games for as long as she was in his underground playpen. "I don't know your name; perhaps if I did I'd feel less threatened."

"That's good; that's very good; you're inviting me into your life at last. Craig will do for now – Craig Osborne – that sounds like a good, trustworthy name, don't you think? I'll give you my real name when we leave here together."

He bent down and began gathering up a bundle from the floor of the gantry.

She watched as a rope ladder tumbled over the edge of the metal framework and stifled an instinctive murmur of terror as he stepped off the gantry onto the swinging rungs. Her heart was pounding.

Not once while he was climbing down did he look at anything other than her. His polished shoes kept missing the flexible rungs; he wasn't finding it easy. This had to be his only access point into her prison. Now she knew why her ribs and her back were so sore – she'd been lowered down like a lump of meat on the end of a sodding rope.

Traumatic events occurred in slow motion; she'd heard about that phenomenon but until now dismissed the idea as unlikely. But that was what was happening right in front of her – he was walking at an excruciating pace, taking forever to cross from the foot of the rope ladder to where she was sitting. And she'd guessed right about his age. His hairline was receding and what remained of his hair was gelled back. He was well under six foot tall, perhaps three or four inches taller than her, thin, and with a lined face. And as he gave her a toothy smile crow's feet spread almost to his ears.

He appeared calm, and almost nervous of her. Maybe his speed across the floor wasn't an illusion.

If he was expecting a smile back he was going to be disappointed.

At first glance he'd looked reasonably smart, but only while she discounted the rucksack lodged on his back. He was wearing a grey suit and white shirt, and a grey and silver tie was hanging loosely around his neck. The collar of his shirt seemed to be fitting the tie rather than his neck. He'd either made an effort for her or he was going on somewhere afterwards – probably the latter, but he was a long way from being trendy. Everything except his shoes looked at least one size too large for him. Thirty years earlier he might have been expecting to grow into the outfit. Now it matched the colour of his hair.

"Please don't stand up for me. I know you won't be feeling too good at the moment. And relax – I told you, I'm not going to hurt you."

He sat on the edge of what appeared to be a home-made wooden bed, leaving a gap of about a foot between them. She clenched her jaw to stop it chattering.

"I wish you wouldn't look so scared, my darling. You're quite safe down here." Beads of sweat were following the contours of his face and trickling down his cheeks, and a droplet of something had formed on the end of his nose, but he made no attempt at wiping anything away. "I've brought you food and drinks, Debbie, and some clean clothes and today's newspaper. And I've brought clean bedding. I thought you might need it after the drugs I was forced to give you, but please don't worry because I anticipated the problem and placed a plastic sheet over the mattress. I'll take any dirty bedding away on my next visit."

So she'd remembered correctly, he had drugged her.

He still seemed unable to look anywhere other than directly into her eyes.

Returning his gaze repulsed her. It was making her feel physically sick, but she forced herself to do it. Building some sort of a relationship with him could prove vital to her survival. "Thank you," she pushed out the words in as clear and as steady a voice as she could manage, but even so she could barely identify them.

"I've brought cheese and tomato sandwiches, fruit juice and bottled water, and an apple and a banana to keep you healthy. I don't know what you like to eat, but that's part of the fun of getting to know another person, isn't it? We've so much to learn about each other. We have such exciting times ahead of us."

"Where am I?"

"You're not too far from your parents' house, Debbie, not too far at all. But don't go getting your hopes up because no one will find you. You're at the very bottom of a long-abandoned spar mine which belonged to my father and grandfather, and now belongs to me. It isn't on any official records anywhere. One day I'll explain to you how these mines were worked in distant, dangerous times, but you're safe enough down here today. This is a natural cave that my family discovered many, many decades ago. In my father's day it was dug out and made larger in the search for spar. He mined and sold the mineral until the vein was exhausted, then returned it to its other, more pleasurable use."

The corners of his mouth twitched slightly. If he was proud of his family, then maybe they were his weak spot. She ignored the more terrifying part of his statement and risked asking. "Is your father still alive?"

"Enough with the questions," he raised his voice for the first time and she flinched. "We'll have plenty of time for small talk. Now take a look at the clothes I've brought for you. They should fit. It's all right – you can get dressed after I've gone. I've already seen and approved of what you have to offer." He held out a blue floral dress and a pink cardigan. "Now what do you say?"

"Thank you." This time she really did have to force out the words. The idea of him ogling her body and touching her had brought bile up into the back her throat.

"Good girl."

"For your toilet there's a natural fissure in the rocks over by the other table, and you can keep refilling the bucket from the hosepipe I've installed for you at the side of it. We're a long way below ground but this cave has never flooded. I know it's not ideal for a young lady of your refinement, but it won't be forever."

Panic rippled through her again. "I really don't like it down here." She tried not to sound as though she was whining, but tears were already forming.

"Enough with the small talk; I've already told you, we'll have plenty of time for all that in the coming days."

He looked away from her for the first time as he rummaged around in the bottom of his rucksack. Tempting as it was, without a weapon in her hand she didn't make a move. She had to build his trust, get him to relax, and wait for a cast-iron opportunity to disable him and make her escape. If she was going to go up against him she was going to have to be absolutely certain of not leaving him standing.

"Here… I've brought you two torches just in case the electricity fails. It can be a bit unpredictable, I'm afraid. I don't much like the dark, either."

Her fingers folded around the largest of the torches and it felt good in her hand. It felt balanced and heavy, and given the opportunity would make a decent weapon. One or two more mistakes like this on his part and her chances of escaping would improve greatly, but now he was watching her again.

"And I've brought you some coloured, solar fairy lights so that you can decorate the room. You can put them wherever you like to make this place feel more homely. Look…"

He lifted the coloured box and pulled a string of tiny lights from it, beaming at her as though he'd done something which ought to please her. "I bought two sets so I can charge them up for you and swop them when they fade. They're supposed to last for up to eight hours. Aren't they pretty?"

Seeing them gave her a jolt. Only two days earlier she'd bought some exactly the same for her south-facing bedroom window, but they were still in their box on her dressing table. She'd paid three pounds and ninety-nine pence at the bargain store in Matlock for the length of cable with sixty tiny bulbs dotted along it. They'd been on special offer.

So he could have been telling the truth – he could be a local man whose family worked these mines. The police looked at local residents first, didn't they? If she could just hang on, maybe there was a strong chance of being found.

"I'll leave you in a minute. I don't want to take advantage of your good nature. But before I go would you do something for me?"

Her stomach clenched. "What…?"

He reached back into his bag and this time pulled out the newspaper. "I've always loved the sound of a woman's voice when she's reading. Will you read something out loud to me from the front page of today's paper? You choose. I don't mind what it is."

She scanned the page for something unconnected with sex or violence and settled on a political article in the small column down the side.

Her voice faltered but she managed to read the whole article. At least while she was doing that nothing else was happening.

"That was wonderful. You have a beautiful speaking voice. Now then... your clothes... I'll bring yours back over the coming days, but I've had to wash out the dirt and grass stains from when we met." He smiled. To him it was obviously a good memory. "You'll find that the temperature doesn't alter much down here. And there are some magazines and female toiletries with those towels over there. See – I've been busy preparing for you. I wanted everything to be just right."

"But what if something happens to you? I'll starve down here."

"That, my darling, is a risk we are both going to have to take. Now eat your food and then you can play with your lights. I'll be back to see you again tomorrow. And please don't look so frightened, you're quite safe here. Sweet dreams my angel."

She focused on the soles of his polished shoes as they returned with him to his life in the outside world. Finally they disappeared.

There was nothing she could do to stop her tears from falling.

5

DCI Forbes happened to glance out of his first-floor window as DS Adam Ross was arriving at the station. There was no mistaking that little blue, split-windscreen, Morris Minor that had belonged Adam's late wife. He only hoped Adam would have the good sense to park it round the back, well out of sight of the general public. The DS's usual parking space had been occupied by whoever was lucky enough to see the space first while Adam had been on holiday, and as most officers hadn't been expecting him back just yet, this Sunday morning was no different.

With a missing teenager taking priority over everything else, Forbes had placed DC Bell in charge of Operation Fantasy and the death-bed retractions. The families of the four girls named in Garratt's letters had all been assured that the claims were being fully investigated and were not being treated as the dying man's hoax that they most probably were.

But before he could give Debbie his full attention he wanted his detective sergeant's opinion on the letters. A fresh pair of eyes was always good and he didn't want anyone in the station speaking to Adam and colouring his judgement.

There was just enough time to get a cup of coffee from the temperamental vending machine in the corridor before Adam reached his office – anything to delay looking at a copy of those letters again.

When he returned to his desk he placed the offending items at its centre and stared at them. Not that he needed his memory refreshing – every word of them was seared into his brain.

Did you never for one moment suspect that you might have got it wrong?

The ache in his chest had been there when he'd woken this morning and it was still throbbing away.

His suntanned detective sergeant strode into his office carrying the thinly disguised bottle of single malt Welsh whisky that he'd been looking forward to sampling.

"I thought it did nothing but rain in Wales?"

"There wasn't a drop of the stuff while we were there, sir, unlike this," the bottle hovered over the centre of the desk, but only for a second.

"Wonderful, thank you; I see you've not invested in a new car yet. The insurance is all sorted, isn't it?"

Adam's car had been written off during a high-speed car chase a few weeks earlier when it had been forced off the road and had landed in a field full of potatoes. Jokes about the incident were still rattling around the station.

"If anyone else asks whether I'm going to buy something more *appealing* next time, or if I've fully recovered from the *smash*, I will be seriously tempted to clobber them. I was intending to look at a car in Leaburn this morning. It's less than two years old, doesn't have many miles on the clock, and the price is reasonable. My local garage phoned to tell me that the owner had passed away and the family were looking for a quick sale. But your call sounded as though I was needed here."

"I wanted to put you in the picture as soon as possible but I can spare you for an hour if you think it might be the car for you. But before you disappear, read these letters and give me your initial impression."

Adam's brow creased as he read them. "I'd say that they were time-wasting, literary farces." He didn't seem as affected as DC Bell had been. "We investigated these four disappearances thoroughly at the time, and we were able to link them all to Garratt. I remember we didn't take his confessions at face value."

"I've got Bell looking over the cases now, but I can't throw any more man-hours at the problem while we have a missing girl on our patch. Do you recall the Faith Crispin case?"

"Yes sir, I helped in the search but no trace of her was ever found."

"If... and it is a very big if... those letters are factual, there could be a chance that Faith was victim number five of our unknown killer, and I hope that I'm wrong, but if I'm not, then I'd say that would increase the chances of Debbie Thomas being victim number six."

Adam frowned at the idea. "Are we taking statements from the villagers and neighbouring farmers? We're slap bang in the middle of the tourist season but someone behaving suspiciously may have been noticed."

"We're making door-to-door enquiries now, and we're appealing for anyone who used the road up to Bonsall Moor yesterday morning to get in touch with this station. And we're waiting for forensic results from the area we believe she was abducted from."

"There are miles of rough pastures and rocky scrubland around Shining Bank Farm and the area's riddled with old mine shafts. If she's been killed and dumped there it could take a while to find her."

"Let's hope that isn't going to be the case. The National Park Rangers are checking and marking all the known mines and ventilation shafts. We don't need anyone else disappearing, and yesterday a helicopter with thermal imaging scoured the hillside while search and rescue dogs covered the ground around the farm. The same is happening today, but covering a wider area. If she is anywhere up on that hillside, we'll find her. Now go and take a look at that car, and then report back to me."

*

Mary Stone stood in the front doorway of Dale End Farmhouse. Before the knock on the door she'd been cleaning out cupboards and unpacking cardboard boxes of groceries in the kitchen. It was obvious that this hadn't been a woman's domain for a long, long time. Deciding where best to store her pots and pans if they were ever brought up from London maybe wasn't the best use of her time, but she'd been listening to the local radio with interest as she worked. She'd also been trying to ignore the noise of the helicopter alternately circling the farm and following the contours of the valley.

And Peter had said that the peace and quiet would take some getting used to!

She wasn't alone at the open doorway. Hannah was clinging to her right leg while Amy was holding onto the dog's collar as though the skinny whippet might at any moment lunge at the stranger in an attempt to rip him to shreds. The four of them were staring at a wiry-looking man who appeared to be in his late fifties or early sixties, as he removed his cap to reveal a thick mane of shoulder-length white hair.

"My name is Ben Allsop, ma'am. I've just walked down from the village." He held out his hand, obviously expecting a ritual handshake. "I'm pleased to finally meet you and your two lovely young ladies. I looked after the grounds here for your husband's late uncle, and also for your husband's late grandfather. There's not much I don't know about the soil in this garden. I was wondering whether, if you're moving in here, you'd require my services at all."

There was a low rumble and Mary looked down to see Zelda's lips drawn back slightly. In the two years that they'd had her she'd never shown any sort of aggression, but she was in strange surroundings and facing an unfamiliar male. "It's all right, Zelda, good girl."

"Only I used to come here a couple of days a week," the man continued without acknowledging the dog. "I kept the lawns and the bushes tidy, and weeded the flower-beds. I could soon have the old place looking a lot more welcoming for you. I could even resurrect the vegetable plots, if you'd like. Old Mr Stone used to enjoy fresh produce from his own garden and it seems a shame to let all that good fertile ground go to waste."

Maybe she imagined it, but for a second she could have sworn that the man's last statement was accompanied by a slightly lewd expression. She shuddered.

The noise from the helicopter was growing louder. It sounded as though it was about to pass directly over Dale End – again. "I'm not sure," she shouted. "We've only just arrived. I haven't even looked over the place properly yet. I'll talk to my husband. He's just gone to the village shop for some milk."

"Then I must have only just missed him. I walked past the shop not ten minutes ago, but the street's full of police asking questions..."

"Daddy," Amy yelled and released her grip on Zelda. Mary flinched as the pair raced across the yard to the foot of the driveway. The grip on her right leg loosened slightly, but the three year old wasn't quite brave enough to follow her sister's lead.

Or maybe she was picking up on her mother's tension.

Mary watched the white-haired man turn and begin striding out to meet their car. Her heart sank.

"Peter, I've not seen you since the funeral," she heard him shouting. "Your uncle was a fine man. He was always talking about you."

Damn, Peter was bound to invite the creep into the house now.

"Ben, it's so good to see you again," her husband shouted back with a grin as wide as on the day they'd shopped at the outdoor and camping shop. "It seems a lifetime since you were showing me where the woodland birds were nesting, and since you caught me when I fell from that old oak tree over there. Tell me, did your back ever fully recover?" Peter was laughing as he scooped Amy up into his arms and began striding towards the house. "Won't you come inside for a drink?"

"My back's never been better, thanks for asking." Ben fell into step with her husband. "I was just asking your wife whether you might need my services in your garden. I can offer you one or two mornings each week. Your uncle was always very happy with my work."

"We need to get our finances sorted. Uncle left us this property but no money. We can sell our London home, but before you go thinking that we're loaded I'll let you into a little secret. Like millions of other people we have a hefty mortgage to pay off. We've got to find work up here quickly because we won't be leaving the city with very much change. This has all been a bit of a whirlwind – I didn't know until after the funeral that I was to inherit the place. But I'm sure we'll be able to afford you for one morning a week."

"I can start straight away, if you'd like, and you can pay me when you get straightened out."

"Thanks Ben; that's good of you. Now come on through to the kitchen and you can fill me in on what's been happening around here since my last visit."

Mary watched the forceful little man pulling out the only comfortable-looking chair in the kitchen, dusting off the cushion, and then plonking himself down as if he didn't intend moving from there until he was asked to leave. Inwardly she screamed.

"Well," Ben leaned towards her as he spoke, "have you heard about the missing teenager?"

*

The gleaming Morris Minor swerved around the patrol cars in the yard of Shining Bank Farm and came to rest in the only available space, in the gateway to a field full of sheep. Forbes had to give it its due – it was a nippy little motor – just not the type anyone would expect a detective to arrive on their property in. After all, Adam was no Lieutenant Columbo, and this was Derbyshire, not America. But the fact that his detective sergeant was finally doing something with his late wife's car could only be a good thing.

Forbes walked over to the Morris Minor, resisting the urge to comment on it. "Did you make an offer on the car?"

"I did, and it's been accepted. The garage is giving it a quick once-over and then delivering it to Jane's sometime this afternoon. Is there any news?"

"I'm afraid not; Debbie's an only child and the family's distraught. The father's blaming himself for not driving her down to the village and the mother's had to be sedated. We still haven't found anyone who might have seen Debbie after she left her home yesterday. Come to the house, Adam. I'd like you to meet the father."

They walked between the parked cars, back towards the front door of the farmhouse.

"Have we ruled him out?"

"Yes, he was using the landline for five minutes after Debbie left the house and his wife says that neither of them went outside for at least an hour after they'd waved her off."

"Does she have a boyfriend?"

"Her close friendship with a local youth called Wayne Soames is a relatively new development, apparently. He was due to go on holiday to Greece tomorrow with some friends, but he's said that unless she's found safe and well he won't be going. We'll find out a little more about him, and about his friends. While we're here we'll take another look in Debbie's room. All her electronic equipment went to the high tech crime lab yesterday, but we might find something else of interest."

Telling parents there were no new developments in the case of their missing child was almost as bad as giving them the worst possible news. The family still had hope, but set against that was the knowledge that their missing loved one could be going through hell while they were sitting waiting, helpless, drinking endless cups of tea or coffee. Fortunately he hadn't been placed in this situation too often his career. He'd dealt with the parents of runaways, and in a handful of those cases thought that if he'd been that teenager; he too would have been tempted to leave the family home.

But this case had felt unhealthy from the first phone call.

*

Mary Stone placed the two mugs of coffee onto the coasters in the centre of the kitchen table with exaggerated precision. Then she cupped her own mug in both hands and leaned back against the kitchen worktop, facing the two men. Her girls had lost interest in the white-haired stranger and were unpacking their toys on the living room floor, accompanied by Zelda. She would have preferred to have been upstairs with them, unpacking their possessions in their bedroom, but the need to be involved in whatever Peter was arranging with this man was the stronger emotion.

"Leave the gardens to me, Peter, and I'll sort them out for you. Half a day won't be enough time for me to grow much in the way of vegetables, and it's a bit late in the season for planting, but I'll put in a few lettuce plants and some spring cabbages for next year for you. Your uncle set up ventilation and self-watering systems in the greenhouses, and if I can get them up and running they will practically look after themselves. Keeping down the rats and mice will be your biggest problem – these hills are full of rodents."

Mice again – Mary shuddered.

"When Thomasine died a couple of years ago," the man droned on, "I wanted to replace her but your uncle wouldn't hear of it. I don't like having to put poison down. I'm a great believer in the laws of nature, but your uncle seemed to think poison was cheaper than cat food. He was a grand old man, and deaf as a post, but believe me he could hear a pound note rustle," he laughed. "Anyway, I could soon get hold of a kitten for you if you'd like me to, and I'm sure those two girls of yours would love one."

"Maybe when we're living here permanently, Mr Allsop," she wasn't about to have this creepy little man organising her life for her.

"Please, call me Ben. I want you to feel as though you're a part of our little community, and one of the reasons I came down here today was to welcome you to the district. I know a few of the more hysterical local females are reluctant to stroll down into this valley, but you mustn't take too much notice of the gossip. This house is in an idyllic spot and you should all feel privileged to live here."

It was Peter who asked the obvious question. She wasn't even sure she wanted to hear the man's answer. She'd been all-but dragged here under protest and didn't need anything else to add to the long list of negatives in her head.

"Well it's all to do with the lead mines and spar mines in these hills and along this valley." He leaned back into his chair to begin what sounded like his well-practiced story. "The lead mines and their ventilation shafts are all supposed to be capped off, but some of them date back to Roman times and every now and again, usually after heavy rains, an unknown one opens up in the ground or an old one collapses. But that can happen just about anywhere in the Peak District, as a few ramblers and farm animals have found to their cost over the years. Are you both sure that you want to hear this story on your first weekend here?"

Peter glanced at her, but then answered for both of them without bothering to wait for her to voice her opinion. "I expect we'll hear it at some time; it may as well be now."

"Very well; until about forty years ago the spar mines under these hills were still being worked, and were very lucrative."

"Spar mines...?" She'd heard about them but that was all.

"It was a thriving industry in these parts – mining for fluorspar and calcite. It was bread and butter for many of the young men in the area, but in the days before Health and Safety it was hazardous work. It's still being dug out of some areas today by a few of the locals, although the only large firm to be mining it around here stopped digging it out about forty years ago. Anyway, my story begins in one of the lead mines – Mawstone Mine, back in nineteen-thirty two. Every so often, so I've been told, the miners would use what they called 'dets'. They were small charges that they actually threw at the roofs of the mines and the tunnels to release any loose shale. It wouldn't be allowed today of course but I've spoken with men who've actually done that. That may not have been the cause of the explosion that day, we'll never know, but six men were supposed to have been working on a ventilation fan and only one made it out alive. There must have a gas build-up in the tunnels when something went terribly wrong. Three rescue workers were subsequently killed by fumes, taking the number of dead to eight. The coroner said that the men knew the risks and took them every day. That statement didn't sit very well with the local people. Anyway, Mawstone Mine was never worked again, although some have tried, and the site now lies derelict and out of bounds to the public."

"What has that got to do with our property," Mary asked, "are the abandoned mines right under our feet?" Was this yet another negative for that list?

"No, no, it's nothing like that, the tragedy happened over the next hill, a good five miles from here."

"Then I don't understand."

"You need to appreciate the history and the topography of this area, Mrs Stone. These limestone hills have more mines and tunnels running under them than are marked on any maps or recorded by any Miners Historical Societies. After being worked out the mines were capped by metal or stone slabs, and even occasionally by lumps of timber, and over the centuries those covers have grown over and some have rotted. Only a few years ago a farmer not many miles from here was digging out foundations for new cattle sheds when he opened up a shaft and at the bottom of it found the remains of his great uncle who'd gone missing about seventy years earlier. Now whether he'd had an accident all those years ago, or whether someone got away with a murder, we'll never know."

"This is all new to Mary," Peter explained, "but I've always known about them. There are two capped ventilation shafts just inside our boundary. They're both fenced off but I was intending to check them before Zelda and the girls went exploring. And I was going to take advice about looking into them and recapping them one day."

"That's your decision of course, but some things are best left undisturbed."

Mary shuddered for no good reason when Ben looked at her.

"Are you sure you want to hear the rest of this story Mrs Stone?"

"Now we're really intrigued," Peter answered for her again.

"Very well, but you must remember that people have disappeared from their homes for all sorts of reasons over the centuries, and until fifty or so years ago, if a girl got herself in the family way around here and couldn't get the father to marry her, it brought shame on her family. Some young girls would leave home rather than do that. What I'm coming to is the tale that on the day of that explosion, two young dairymaids from a farm quite close to the site disappeared together. They were both seventeen, and both good girls, by all accounts. Their parents and friends were adamant that neither of them had a boyfriend, and neither of them took any money or clothing. There was a search, but at that time people were more concerned about the miners and their families. Rumours spread about the girls wanting to see the city, and people assumed that because they were together they would be safe enough and would return one day. Everyone stopped looking for them – until about a fortnight after the explosion."

Ben seemed to have paused for effect and Mary looked through the open doorway into the living room. Toys and books were scattered across the floor and poor Zelda was having trouble finding a large enough clear space to lie in. The mess didn't matter. Tomorrow would be soon enough to start worrying about such inconsequential things.

Ben placed his half-empty mug down, ready to pick up the story. "That was when people reported hearing sounds coming from the collapsed tunnel. Apparently they'd sounded like weak cries for help, from females, so before the disaster site was sealed it was searched again, along with all the known surrounding mine shafts. Farmers and teams of rescuers scoured the fields around the site for unmarked or newly collapsed shafts, and the sounds were apparently even heard by some of those who were out in the fields searching, but it all came to nothing and the noises were eventually attributed to changes of wind directions in the tunnels as a direct result of the explosion."

The helicopter rattled over the farmhouse again. For a minute no one spoke.

"All four parents passed away without ever knowing what had happened to their daughters." Ben continued as though the disturbance was an everyday occurrence. "What you need to know is that those same noises are still sometimes heard, but only in the mine shafts in and around this valley. They've been heard in all types of weather, and when the wind has been from different directions. Your uncle had a dozen or more home-helps in the last couple of years of his life, sent in by social services, but sooner or later each one of them refused to return after dark to help him get settled for the night."

"That's known as mass hysteria," Peter was appearing to find the story amusing. "Surely you're not trying to tell us that this area is haunted by the ghosts of two girls from the nineteen-thirties?"

"I only come here in daylight, and then only when I know someone else is on the property. Mass hysteria or not, those ungodly sounds began after the explosion, and I have heard them – on several occasions – and to me they sounded like young women. Your grandfather and your uncle both said it was superstitious claptrap, but I know your uncle never went outside after dark. You can make your own minds up, and maybe I shouldn't have told you the story yet, but forewarned is forearmed, as they say."

"So what have the spar mines got to do with the rumours?" Mary tried not to sound too critical.

"It was around the spar mines that the sounds were most frequently heard. That was why everyone at the time was confused. The two workings aren't connected, you see, although both lead mines and spar mines run underneath these hills. Where you find one mineral you usually find the other close-by. Some folks claim that they've heard the spirits of the dead men, while others say they've heard the young women. It's been known to cause quite a heated argument in the pub late at night."

It wouldn't be dark for another eight hours at least. She fully intended being tucked up in bed long before then.

6

Debbie had slept, but not solidly. She'd woken either shivering or crying, or maybe both, she wasn't sure. It had to be the unused adrenaline in her body playing havoc with her system. Sleep had come, but only hours after her captor had disappeared, and without her phone she had no way of knowing how long she'd been alone. In any case – time was irrelevant.

Some gentle exercise might help; it was worth a try.

The cave was roughly circular, about four times the width of her bedroom at home, and from about ten feet above her head it curved inwards, rather like the shape of a bell.

So far it seemed devoid of any insect other than her captor, and no moving shadows other than those of human origin.

She walked the circular route, all the time clutching the heaviest of the torches. The idea that the lights might fail and plunge her back into that absolute blackness, causing her to lose her bearings in the small space, had set her heart pounding.

It was a long shot, she knew, but there might be something – anything – that she could use to her advantage. At the furthest point from the bed she kicked at some loose rocks and shale on the floor. Until she'd disturbed them they'd been hidden by a layer of dirt, and presumably they'd fallen from the wall years earlier, but some of them looked a useful size. She gathered up those that she hoped might make the best defensive weapons, and after placing a dozen fist-sized rocks and sharp wedges of grey shale far enough under her bed that they couldn't be seen without lying on the floor, she lay back down.

There was little else to do. She closed her eyes and pictured being back in her safe, warm, comfortable bedroom, surrounded by the many bookshelves her father had installed for her over the years, most of which were now groaning under the weight of natural history and science books and magazines.

She'd had dreams of becoming a zoologist, or an entomologist. *Those were crushed dreams now – crushed beneath the man's feet in the same way as any insect would be if he chose to tread on it.*

No; she couldn't think like that. That was the road to compliance and eventual madness and she wasn't going to give him that satisfaction. Holding on to her sanity was part of the process of staying alive long enough to be found. She had to be able to think clearly if she was to outwit her captor.

One of her favourite childhood hiding places had been the small, dark cupboard underneath the stairs. She remembered a childhood game of taking in a cushion, a torch, and several books to pass the time until people pretended to stop looking for her and she could come out.

She opened her eyes again, and this time looked up.

As a treat for her fifteenth birthday she'd been up in the London Eye and loved every second of it. But how different was this – gazing up through a cavernous roof space into a black tunnel, unable to even see the roof of her prison?

She fought off the dizzying sensation and shone a torch upwards into the opening. She could have been upside down – upside down and about to fall into a deep hole, like Alice from Alice in Wonderland – about to tumble down a black hole after a white rabbit. If only she could reach out to the shelves on her bedroom wall for that book right now.

There was no point in wasting the battery. She switched off the torch, sat up, and looped the string of lights around the table, but only to pacify the creep when he eventually returned.

She'd led a fairly sheltered life, she recognised that, but then nothing in anyone's upbringing should be so bad as to prepare them for this.

She lay back down and waited.

The scraping sound she'd dreaded echoed down the tunnel, followed by a dull thud, possibly a door. Someone was out there but this time there was no point in shouting for help. Her body began to tremble and her heart rate soared.

The string of lights would look so much better wrapped around the creep's neck, his face turning purple as she pulled them tighter and tighter, but that wasn't likely to happen. She had to take as few risks as she could hope to get away with. She had to act carefully, not react instinctively. He was possibly a man of many layers and she had to work out the best ways of getting along with him.

A short burst of cooler air brushed her face, and with it this time came a familiar smell from the outside world – of mown grass and cattle. It was hay and silage making season, but there were thousands of acres of farmland in Derbyshire, and that fact alone had to reduce her chances of being found alive.

The same clang, clang, began again.

Despite what he'd said about setting tests and marrying her, he was unlikely to let her live for too long. The creep was unbalanced and she was going to have to play along with his fantasy, but not too willingly. She couldn't risk him seeing through her one plan of making him overconfident and trusting of her.

She began counting. The slightest scrap of knowledge about where she was might come in useful at some point.

She counted the sounds of shoes hitting metal – eighty rungs down to the gantry. If they were six inches apart, that would mean he was now about forty feet below ground.

"Hello, my lovely."

Her stomach clenched and her teeth grated at the sound of his voice.

"I'm sorry I'm so late but I've had a very busy morning."

She didn't answer.

Again he descended the rope ladder without looking away from her. He didn't trust her any more than she trusted him.

"I've brought you more solar lights – oh my goodness – you've decorated that table nicely. There's nothing like the touch of a woman for brightening up a place, I always say."

Forty more rungs to the rope ladder meant she was about sixty feet underground. What was that in real terms – about half a dozen stories of a normal building? She was in one hell of a deep cave.

"Well aren't you going to say hello to me? I've brought presents."

It was time to take a deep breath and choose her words carefully, but she wasn't going to stand up.

"Hello Craig, the only present I need from you is my freedom, but at least you haven't abandoned me."

He walked towards her and dumped his rucksack on the bed beside her. Despite her resolve not to, she flinched, and then fidgeted to disguise her reaction.

"I've brought some of your own clothes, you'll be pleased to see, and I must say that I admire your taste in matching underwear – very sexy – very sexy indeed."

They were her best ones. She'd only been wearing them on Saturday because they were what she'd intended having underneath her dress on Jessica's big day.

His hands hovered over them.

"They all smell so much nicer now than they did."

She had been feeling better, but suddenly she wanted to vomit. The image of him pressing her used underwear into his face and breathing it in before placing it into his washing machine was now firmly fixed in her head, and there would be nothing she could do to remove it. He was violating her without touching her.

But did he have a washing machine?

Did he even have a house, and if so, did he live with anyone?

"Thank you, did you wash them yourself?" She hoped she wasn't being too obvious.

"I've got my own place and that's all you need to know for now. Allow me to sit down beside you. I've brought cheese sandwiches and fruit juice; you do like cheese don't you, and an apple and a strawberry yogurt? I chose strawberry because of the pink lid. All young ladies like the colour pink, don't they? I'm right aren't I?"

"Yes, thank you, I like everything you've brought." She forced the words out although they weren't the ones on the tip of her tongue.

She was holding herself together incredibly well.

"And as an apology for leaving you for so long I've brought you two gifts." He lifted two newspaper-wrapped parcels from the bottom of his bag. "Today feels special, my darling. It feels as though we're meant to be together. It's manic above ground with so many out there searching for you, and that's why I was a little late. But don't worry, we're safe down here. Now open your gifts."

If people really were *'out there searching'*, then maybe she wasn't too far from home after all. Her fingers trembled but she pulled at the brown wrapping tape and managed to rip the newspaper apart. "A clock, thank you, it will be a comfort to know the time."

"I knew you'd be pleased. That's eleven-thirty in the morning, by the way. And it's Sunday so I suppose that's why so many people are milling about. Now open your other gift."

Two books fell onto her lap. They were at least a sign that he didn't intend to kill her today. "I know these books – they're classics, thank you."

"Little Women by Louisa May Alcott, and Black Beauty by Anna Sewell, they are two wonderful books, aren't they? They belonged to my mother but I don't believe that she truly appreciated them. I, on the other hand, have read and reread them. Black Beauty never fails to make me cry. I thought we could discuss the storylines when you'd had time to study them. It would be like having our own private little book club."

"I..."

"Because I can only imagine how boring it must be for you down here, my darling," he'd paused for breath but that was all, "and I want to fill the hours for you as pleasurably as I can. I really am a gentle, caring man, and very soon you'll come to realise that. You'll come to look forward to my visits over the next few days. You'll come to depend on me, and then... and then, you'll come to fall in love with me. Oh my sweetheart," he lightly stroked her cheek with his dirt-engrained fingertips.

The odour of cattle manure seemed to be all around her.

"My own sweet Debbie, I can hardly wait for that exquisite moment."

His bloodshot eyes were gazing into hers, and suddenly, out of nowhere, she pictured an article she'd read in a magazine not too long ago. There was a syndrome, the name of it didn't instantly spring to mind, but it was a condition which caused feelings of trust, or even affection to develop in a hostage towards their captor. The term had been coined at the end of a six-day bank siege, somewhere in Europe. Could that be what he was working on? Had he even read the same article? If so, it would make it easier for her to play along with his sick fantasies. She needed to interact with him. "Is that today's newspaper that you have there? Would you like me to read to you again?"

"Are you trying to trick me?" His brow wrinkled and he leaned back.

She would have to be more careful; he didn't like being questioned. He obviously wasn't comfortable with her taking the initiative. "I was only trying to make conversation. I thought you'd like it, I'm sorry."

"No, I'm sorry; I couldn't live with myself if I upset you. Please, I'd love you to read something to me now." He handed her the paper. "Read it out loud and clear, my sweetheart."

She picked an article about rare tiger cubs appearing for the first time in their enclosure and read it as steadily as her trembling ribcage would allow.

"That was wonderfully read, my darling. And now I have something to tell you – something exciting. Today is just your settling in day. Tomorrow will be the first day of our real courtship, and I've set a time limit for you to complete your tasks and then finally convince me that you truly, truly love me. Tomorrow will be day one of nine. There... what do you think of that?"

"Nine days...?"

"Nine wonderful days, yes."

"What tasks...?"

"The tasks are nothing that you won't enjoy. Rest assured that I would never do anything to hurt you, so be a good girl and eat up your food." He stuffed the paper back into his bag, stood up, and hoisted the bag onto his shoulder. "I'm afraid I have to go now in case I'm missed. We can't have people becoming suspicious of my movements, can we? I'll see you again tomorrow."

He leaned towards her and seemed about to kiss her. If he was, he changed his mind. He stood up and walked to the rope ladder, all the time looking over his shoulder at her until he'd climbed almost to the top.

He hadn't said what would happen after nine days if she failed any or all of his tasks, and she'd been too afraid to ask.

"Stockholm syndrome," she muttered as he rattled the rungs of the metal ladder and as a trail of dust and the odd fragment of gravel landed on the gantry. "That's what it's called. I read the article in a newspaper magazine not many weeks ago. Well if the sick bastard thinks that this hostage is ever going to bond with him, he's in for one hell of a shock."

He'd left her with the prospect of counting down her nine remaining days. Her previous fear of being stuck down here for months, all the time clinging to the hope that people were still searching for her, had been bad enough. This new fear was more intense – more urgent – he'd set a time limit on her life.

The silence wrapped itself around her like a blanket and she allowed her tears to fall again.

7

Thirty hours after Debbie had last been seen there was information flooding into both the large white Major Incident Vehicle parked in the village street and the incident room back at the station. Data was appearing from all directions: from the forensics teams, from the general public who were keen to help, and from time-wasters with nothing better to do. Officers were at times shoulder to shoulder manning the phones.

And PC Darcy had arrived in Leaburn from Newcastle and was on his way up the station's stairway.

DCI Forbes waited at his desk, reading over a transcript of an interview with Brian Garratt which he had taken part in six years earlier in a Greater Manchester police station. Without moving his head he switched his gaze to the officer cautiously approaching him. He had no problems disciplining officers for negligence when the lapse in professional behaviour was a recent one, but PC Darcy's was not. Darcy had been a young recruit during the height of the manhunt for Garratt, and wasn't even one of his own officers any more, yet he had been good enough to catch the first available train down from Newcastle and present himself for questioning on a Sunday afternoon.

He swivelled his computer screen to enable Darcy to see exactly what he'd been reading. "All I'm asking from you is the truth of how close you were to this man."

"Yes sir, I'm here to help in any way that I can."

"Data protection is one of the first subjects all officers are expected to understand," Forbes frowned at the dejected-looking constable and tried not to feel any sympathy towards him. "What I need to know is whether you flaunted those rules in favour of your cousin while you were working at this station."

"I think I may have done, sir."

"I appreciate you're honesty. I had a lengthy telephone conversation with your duty sergeant yesterday and he assured me that you are one of his most diligent and trustworthy officers, always willing to go that extra mile to help your colleagues, and that you are a well-liked and respected officer. That said – if my assumptions are correct, nothing that you've done since can excuse your behaviour while you were at this station. I can't keep your name out of my reports and I doubt it will take the press very long to locate you once the story becomes public. It's possible that a serial killer has gone undetected in our area because of your thoughtless actions."

"That's one of the reasons I've always worked so hard, sir, to try and make amends for leaking information to my cousin and possibly delaying his arrest. But I promise you, on my life and on the life of my infant son, that I truly believed Garratt was responsible for every one of the ten murders that he confessed to. If I'd thought differently for as much as one second, then I would have said something."

"I'm glad to hear that. But I'd still like to hear an off the record account of what passed between the two of you."

"Other than delaying his arrest by a few months, during which time there were no more victims, I didn't believe that I'd caused any damage. I was as shocked as the rest of my family when he was charged, and those closest to him were in bits. People who'd known us for years shunned us in the streets, as though they thought my family must have known about the slaughter and done nothing to stop him. The woman I'm married to now was my fiancée at the time. It would have shattered her and her family if they'd thought I was somehow involved. It was to protect her and any children that we might have had in the future that I moved out of this area."

"If you'd come to me at the time I would have understood and supported your request for a transfer without prejudice. We might still have accepted all ten of his confessions, but at the very least we would have examined them more closely."

"I was being selfish. I realised that but once my cousin had been arrested, and after I'd got over the shock, I felt such a fool. Brian Garratt originally approached me with a story that he was doing research for a novel – a fictional thriller, and that he wanted plausible ideas and background information on how a murder enquiry was conducted. The irony of it is that if he hadn't been family I would never have talked to him about an on-going investigation. I've tried to put the episode behind me but it's always been in the back of my mind. In many ways I'm glad that Garratt confessed to his lies before he died, even though it may mean the end of my career."

"I'll do what I can to protect your career, but don't go expecting sympathy from officers in this station. In return for my support I want to know everything you and Garratt talked about – every snippet of information you remember passing on to him."

"Since I got the call yesterday I've been putting down everything I can remember talking to him about, sir." He handed over a thin file.

Forbes read the first four of the eight printed pages. "This reads as though you doubt that all his confessions were genuine."

"That's only in hindsight, sir, you have to believe that. I know that document puts me in a bad light, but I really don't care. I'll do anything to help put this right."

"A killer we haven't even been looking for has almost certainly killed again, and now we have another missing girl on our patch. There's nothing you or anyone else can do to put that right."

"I realise that, sir. I put my own family's shame ahead of doing the right thing and I deeply regret that."

Forbes could empathise a little with that. His wayward sister, Louise, had been a drunk, been involved in prostitution, and had been beaten senseless on one occasion while he'd been studying hard to become a detective. He'd done his level best to keep her name well away from his. And more recently he'd begun discussing active cases with her to encourage her in her newly chosen career as a pathology technician. Two years ago she'd been caught up in an investigation and had to jump from a first floor window to save her own life, and that had made him more cautious, but his actions hadn't endangered anyone other than his sister. He hoped he would never have chosen the course of action that PC Darcy had. He didn't think he'd ever have been able to live with such a secret, not without driving himself mad.

*

From his seat in the darkest corner of the tap room of the Nag's Head public house, in the heart of the village, Craig peered through the doorway into the crowded main bar and studied the perspiring faces. It wasn't so much a search party he was looking at as a group of nosey old farts mingling with a gaggle of yuppies who in turn were doing their best to fit in without losing their air of superiority.

"As you can see, concern for a much-loved local girl is uniting our community." Mrs Cotter, the landlady, was using her telephone voice to address the reporter and camera crew.

"You're right there, duck," old Mr Marshall, normally a once-a-week customer, leaned in towards the young, female reporter. The sound engineer and the camera operator turned their equipment towards him. He puffed out his chest and continued speaking. "She's a lovely young girl and a credit to her hard-working, community-minded parents – she is that. It'll completely bugger them if they don't find her alive and well."

The microphone quickly swung back towards the bar.

"Hypocrites, every last one of you," Craig muttered, "hypocrites and losers; how many of you stuck-up females actually bothered to turn out and vote for Mrs Thomas, the councillor, and how many of your sweaty men would pass up the chance of having a beautiful young woman fall in love with them? Success in life is for those who get on out there and grab it, not those who stand about wittering."

"Is it true that they've found evidence she's been abducted?" Local man, Frank Seal's gruff voice cut through the chatter and the reporter turned towards the new voice. "I've heard the search is to be scaled down after this afternoon and that our group will be the last to be led out there by the police. Has anyone else heard that?"

A few heads nodded but no one seemed certain enough to commit themselves to a live broadcast.

"Hypocrites, losers, and idiots," Craig continued his quiet tirade, "every last one of you. You can search all you like but you won't find her. She's mine and you lot aren't getting her back."

"Aren't those dogs brilliant?" Deidre Rose's shrill voice was the next to rise above the low rumble of conversation. She was a leading light in the local dog rescue and rehoming charity. "I heard that at one point they thought the dogs were onto the girl's trail, but that it turned out to be the remains of a sheep at the entrance to a foxhole up on the hillside."

"Again... idiots, the lot of them," he'd staged that for them to find. He'd anticipated them bringing in dogs. He'd planned well. The 'foxhole' the searchers had thought their dogs had found was actually a ventilation shaft, and it was slap bang in the centre of his land. It wasn't marked on any documents other than his personal land deeds, and even on those it was recorded as being fifteen feet deep and unsafe. In reality it was much deeper, perfectly clear, and drawing stale air from the labyrinth of tunnels where his Debbie was hidden. He couldn't risk blocking it but he'd had to disguise her scent somehow. He'd dug soil from the entrance of the nearby fox's lair and made the vent appear to be the home of another family of foxes. The smell was pungent, even to someone used to mucking out cattle sheds and calving cows, and he'd even ripped up a lamb carcass he'd found and placed that in the soil. It would take an expert in wildlife to recognise that the whole thing was staged.

He afforded himself a smug smile. His hours of hard work had paid off.

And he'd spent an enjoyable day, soaking up the atmosphere and pretending to take part in the search while keeping a watchful eye on his deception. His heart had pounded when he'd witnessed the dogs rushing towards his handiwork, dragging their handlers behind them, only to be pulled away minutes later to shouts of: *"Sorry... no... distracted by foxes... all clear..."*

"Idiots... your dogs are brighter than you," he'd been tempted to shout from behind the safety of the hawthorn hedge, but instead he'd muttered the words into his cupped hands.

And Debbie was too far below ground for the heat-seeking equipment of the helicopter to find her. He'd been proved right about that as well.

No, she was his for as long as he wanted – for the next nine days – and then beyond.

*

Peter Stone raised his head from the pillow. They were having another early night – it was only just turning ten o'clock and not totally dark. He waited. Mary was breathing steadily and quietly beside him and the bedroom door was opening. But instead of the tousled infant he'd expected to see he found himself staring into the dark, soulful eyes of Zelda. "It's all right girl, we're all here. There's nothing to be afraid of," he murmured.

Mary stirred. "I heard her coming up the stairs not long after we came to bed." She propped herself up on one elbow while Peter switched on the bedside lamp. "You were out like a light so I went to check on her and she was curled up on Amy's bed. Both girls were asleep so I left her. That was only half an hour ago."

"It must be the unfamiliar surroundings. Dogs don't like changes to their routine; it unsettles them. Just give her a couple more days and it will be as if she's been here forever. In the meantime it might be a good idea to bring her basket upstairs at night and let her sleep on the landing, so she feels closer to us all."

"You do realise you spoil that dog?"

"Yes, but not as much as I intend to spoil you if you'll agree to give life in the Peak District a real try. And you shouldn't take too much notice of old Ben Allsop's stories. He used to tell me that there were gold coins in the magpie's nest at the top of the oak tree at the far end of the garden. That's how I came to fall out of a tree and injure his back – sweet justice or what?"

"He sounded convincing to me."

"He makes up stuff – he always has. He bases his tales on at least one true fact, and that way people are more inclined to believe him, but basically he talks a load of rubbish. Just remember that the next time he's waffling on."

"So the missing girls and the fatal mine explosion were true events…?"

He nodded.

"And what about the unearthly noises…?"

"Wind in the old mine shafts – nothing more sinister than that. People often hear what they expect to hear, don't you think? The parents of those girls wanted to believe they were somewhere close by, and alive, and the whole thing got out of hand."

"I suppose that's possible. And I promise I'll make a definite decision tomorrow about relocating here, after I've had a proper look around the district and enquired about the nearest schools."

Zelda snuggled between them.

Mary turned her pillow over and settled down, and Peter reached to switch off the bedside lamp. Neither of them noticed the distinct tremor in their dog's skinny body.

8

Debbie turned onto her side and pulled the blanket up under her chin. It felt cold and clammy.

Why was her bedroom damp in the middle of summer?

Her eyes opened and her stomach cramped. She wretched over the edge of the bed but only vile-tasting froth dribbled past her lips to the floor.

She reached out to the table for a drink of water. Her hands shook but she pulled the plastic beaker to her lips and drew in just enough water to swill around her teeth and spit out onto the slime she'd just brought up. She allowed her second gulp of the stale-tasting liquid to slip down her throat and shuddered. Three more large gulps emptied the beaker.

Again she hadn't slept well, but she'd been able to count the hours. According to the clock he'd brought her it was six o'clock in the morning – Monday morning if what he'd told her was correct.

Her mother and father would be in bits by now. This was bad for her, but for them it would be torture.   And what about Jessica – would her wedding go ahead without its one and only bridesmaid?

Yesterday her father would normally have been working in the garden while her mother prepared the Sunday lunch. Later they'd have gone for a walk or a drive while she caught up with her studies and prepared her books for the coming week.

Not this weekend.

This weekend, she guessed, the police would have been at the house and friends and neighbours would have been calling round asking if there was anything they could do to help.

No, there was nothing anyone could do to alter the situation they'd found themselves in – nothing was going to change for any of them unless Craig had an epiphany and decided to release her.

What would they be doing today – other than going out of their minds?

Tears rolled down her cheeks and her stomach churned over again. Despite everything she was feeling hungry. After his first visit she'd only eaten the packaged food – determined not to eat anything his fingers had touched. He'd wanted to know why she'd left the food and she'd told him she still felt ill. He'd appeared to believe her.

But she didn't want to risk making him angry, nor did she want to grow weak through lack of food, so she'd eaten all the food he'd brought to her on Sunday. Whatever he'd got planned for her, however degrading it might be, the most sensible thing to do was to play along in the hope that a half-decent chance to escape would present itself.

There was that sound again; someone was up there. But what if it wasn't him? Her heart hammered at her chest wall. She held her breath and strained her ears for the slightest difference in the sounds.

If the clock was right the outside world would be bathed in early morning light by now.

Supposing what she was hearing was her only chance of rescue? "Hello, I'm down here," she cupped her hands to her mouth and yelled upwards. "Hello, please help me. I'm trapped down here, help."

Surely people would still be out there looking for her.

They couldn't have given up yet.

"Shut your racket, you stupid bitch. Didn't I tell you that no one will find you down here?" The familiar, grating voice came back at her again and again, echoing around her prison until the words merged into one incomprehensible sound.

Pacify him, creep to him, do what you need to do to quell his anger.

She closed her eyes and counted his steps down until she heard him on the gantry. "I'm sorry," she said, "but I thought something might have happened to you. I'm so afraid of dying alone down here. Please don't be mad with me. I'm scared. I panicked for a moment."

Stop gabbling, you know he doesn't like it when you ask for anything.

The slightly different sound must have been because of his boots. Over the weekend he'd worn polished shoes. This morning he was in work boots, with mud and straw embedded in the treads, and he was wearing a shirt, a thick checked shirt, not the kind worn to an office, and no tie. The creased shirt looked as though it had come straight from a washing line, or had been worn under something much heavier.

He'd been in overalls on Saturday morning.

He had to be a farmer – a cattle farmer judging by the manure on his boots and the odour from his hands yesterday. He was a local man who either owned or worked on a farm. If she could just hang on, and if the police were checking local people, then she'd soon be found. She had to hold on to that thought.

He reached the foot of the rope ladder and this time strode towards her while unburdening his wiry frame of the rucksack that from below made his silhouette look so grotesque. She braced herself, expecting him to strike her. But he stopped just short of the bed and smiled as he placed the bag down on the floor.

"I'm so sorry, my beautiful, beautiful angel."

Was that pride that she heard in his voice? Her face muscles wanted to tighten in disgust but she fought with them to hold steady.

"I'm afraid I'll only be able to visit you once a day. There are police everywhere, questioning everyone and looking for you. I daren't risk giving away the location of our little love-nest, but I've been thinking of you constantly. It's Monday morning and you must be famished, you poor darling."

She saw him scanning the empty food packaging and chose her words to please him, "I'm feeling much better now I've eaten."

"And because I'm here...? You're actually pleased to see me, aren't you? Tell me that you're pleased to see me."

She barely suppressed the shudder running through her insides. "Yes, I'm pleased."

He smiled. Two of his front teeth were missing, but he didn't seem conscious of the fact. It was a wide, full, stupid-looking grin and it made her want to look away, but she held his gaze as he sat down beside her. There was barely an inch between his leg and her thigh and his body heat began filterlng through the thin fabric of her skirt.

She was determined not to flinch.

"Really pleased... you're not just saying that?"

"I'm really pleased."

"Then there's no need for you to shout out like that again. Shush, my angel," he leaned closer and placed his right index finger vertically to her lips. "I listened to your concerns yesterday. I'm a sensitive man, as you'll find out. I've written a letter explaining where you are and I've put it in an envelope at the side of my bed. I will kiss that letter every night before I go to sleep, and if anything should happen to me it will be read by the first person to enter my bedroom and you will be rescued. There... does that make you feel better?" He moved his finger from her face.

"Yes... yes it does, thank you." *I can hardly believe my luck;* she'd wanted to sarcastically add. She couldn't make another mistake now, but she didn't want him to realise she was simply humouring him.

"But it might take days, even weeks before anyone went into your room – I couldn't survive without food, and supposing the hosepipe stopped working?"

"You're deep underground, my angel," his right hand landed on her left knee. "I can see that I'll have to educate you. There is always water down here. Have you not noticed it dripping from all those stalactites clinging to the roof? I positioned your bed and your tables in the few places where there are no drips so that you'd remain dry. See how I look after you?"

"I've been sleeping a lot, but I can see them now." Of course she'd seen them, and heard the damn drips.

He stared at her as if reading her mind, but finally he smiled and spoke. "Men have survived far more hardship in far less comfortable places than this. I know an awful lot about the history of the mines all around this area. For instance, in 1879, a Dennis Bagshaw of Hucklow was trapped by a massive rock fall in the Black Engine Mine when a roof caved in. Lead miners from surrounding villages worked non-stop, not changing clothes, and having food taken down the mine to them, for a week. Finally they dragged him out. He'd made a cup from a lump of clay and caught dripping water in order to stay alive. What do you think about that?"

"It must have been terrible."

"Then think no more about it – you're quite safe here. From tomorrow I'll bring extra cartons of food, just in case I can't get to you for any reason. Look what I've brought for you today – sandwiches, fruit juice, and boxed cakes. They're a few days out of date but they'll be all right, and some more lady stuff."

He held the box of own brand tampons in front of her face and her jaw clenched. But if he'd bought those locally, might someone not think that it was suspicious? Hopefully that was big mistake he'd made.

"Have you read any of those books I brought you?"

"Not yet. I wasn't feeling up to it. I wanted to be able to enjoy them…" She stopped herself. It wasn't sensible to overdo the creeping.

"Never mind; it's too early for the shops so I've brought another page of yesterday's newspaper for you. Now read something from the main story. Read it loud and clear."

It was a tabloid paper and the story was all about a celebrity being caught out having an affair with a politician – or the other way around, depending on how the reader wanted to interpret it.

She had no choice but to read it. He was forcing her to think about and talk about sex, and they both knew it.

"Regrettably I can't stay for too long, but I did say that today would be the first day of our courtship and so I expect to be able to kiss you. I won't make any other demands, because I want to take this nice and slowly. I want you to enjoy the thrill and the anticipation of the build-up to our union just as much as I do."

He leaned in towards her, gripped her shoulders, and then slowly increased the pressure of his wet, flabby lips against hers. She was an animal in a trap. Her eyes involuntarily closed and her lungs froze. His tongue touched her lips and she clamped her teeth tightly shut.

Then it was over.

The need to instantly wipe her mouth almost overpowered her. Instead she opened her eyes and took a few short breaths. She hadn't noticed it before, but his hair smelled unusual. His short grey hair was slicked back with something she didn't imagine too many cattle farmers used.

"That, my angel, is a moment I will always treasure. I don't expect that you enjoyed it as much as I did – I'm not a fool. I know that in your eyes it won't have transformed me from a frog to prince, but over the next few days you'll come to appreciate me. And very soon you'll desire me, and yearn for me as I yearn for you."

Well he got one part of that right, but the only thing she was yearning for was an opportunity to slam a lump of rock into the side of his head and hammer down onto his distorted features until there was nothing left of his ugly, lined face.

"But that one kiss, my sweet angel, will have to sustain me over the long hours until we can be together again. It will be tomorrow morning – day two of our courtship, and I can scarcely wait."

He stood, placed the sheet of newspaper into his empty bag, hoisted it onto his shoulders and walked away, again not removing his gaze from her until he was over half-way up the rope ladder.

"Some animals can smell traps." Out of nowhere came a memory of home. They were the words of the man her mother employed in the winter and early spring to set the mole traps in the pastures.

Craig had washed very recently; there was no doubt about that. As well as the unusual hair preparation she'd detected scented soap and cattle dung – and he'd left another unmistakable odour behind him.

About four months ago she'd been walking the collies through the woods and brushed against undergrowth newly scent-marked by a dog fox. Her trousers had reeked. She'd intended putting them in the wash as soon as she got home, but by that time the smell had grown so strong that she'd decided the only thing to do was to throw the old pair of jeans away, and then she'd had to scrub at her legs to obliterate the musky odour.

Craig had been around foxes – she was certain of that.

*

Mary Stone opened her eyes and blinked, but with the heavy bedroom curtains tightly closed the room was a blur of still unfamiliar shapes and shadows. Amy was standing at the side of the bed and telling her something. She raised the edge of the bedcovers and moved over a few inches to allow her daughter to wriggle into the warm space.

Peter was either still fast asleep or doing a very good impression, because now she was tightly sandwiched in the middle of the bed with him at one side and Amy pressed against her on the other as though her little life depended on it.

"Is daddy Peter asleep?" She always called him that when she was worried about something.

"I think so, sweetheart. What's wrong? Tell me again."

Zelda was circling in her own bed and Amy waited while she settled down. "I woke up and Zelda was on my bed. I like it when she does that. She didn't wake me and I think she'd been there for ages because my bed was warm where she was sleeping. Something else woke me, and it woke Zelda as well. She was frightened. She jumped off my bed and crawled underneath it, and that made me frightened as well. I wanted to shout for you but Hannah was asleep and I didn't want to wake her because I knew she would start crying. So I got out of bed, and Zelda followed me."

"That was very thoughtful of you not to wake your sister." Mary cupped her hand under the girl's chin and tilted the trusting face upwards until their eyes met. In the half-light she marvelled at the child's physical likeness to herself. There could never be any doubt about her parentage, and she liked to believe her daughter's reserved mannerisms, and her quiet and considerate nature had also been inherited from her. "Can you describe what it was that you think woke you and Zelda?" She didn't want to dismiss the child's fears as a dream – not yet.

Amy shook her head in annoyance. "I didn't think that it woke us, mummy. It did wake us."

Peter was still showing no signs of being awake and Mary suddenly, and irrationally, felt sick with apprehension. "I'm not doubting you, sweetheart. Tell me all about it."

"It was a sort of a voice, but it didn't say nothing."

"Didn't say anything...," she automatically corrected her daughter and then mentally chastised herself. "What did you think it sounded like... can you describe it?"

"It sounded a bit like someone trying to shout something, and then it sounded more like the noise Zelda makes when you shut her out of the kitchen because you're baking and taking stuff out of the oven. Only it definitely wasn't Zelda because she was with me." Amy's large blue eyes looked straight into her mother's, willing her to believe her story.

Mary gently stroked her daughter's head. "Sweetheart, this is the countryside. Do you remember when we watched those nature programs together on the television – Springwatch and Autumnwatch?"

Amy nodded.

"And do you remember all those animals coming out at night and early in the mornings when no one was around, in the woods and the fields, and the strange noises that some of them made? I'll bet that what you heard was Mr Fox, or Mr Badger."

Amy nodded again, but this time her blue eyes were narrowed with suspicion.

9

Forbes looked up from his notes and saw a sea of tired, but eager faces in the packed incident room. Not one of his team had taken their allotted Sunday off and everyone had worked on into the night. "The time is seven-thirty on Monday morning and this is the fourth briefing of Operation Barley." The room was unusually quiet. "You all came in yesterday in the hope of finding Debbie Thomas alive, and I'm sure her family will appreciate that."

"Time's running out for her though..." DI Lang's voice tailed off.

"Quite; but we did gain some useful information yesterday which gives us cause for hope. Scenes of crimes officers have isolated tyre tracks found in a field gateway two hundred meters from where Debbie's phone was found." He indicated a marker on the wall map. "The owner of the field used a tractor to enter and leave by that gateway well after nine o'clock on Friday night and the tyre tracks of another vehicle can clearly be seen over them. The ground is hard and dry, so the tracks aren't deep, but we know they were made after nine p.m. Friday and before midday Saturday when the alarm was raised. A dark coloured pick-up was observed from two fields away by a dog walker. It was seen parked beside the road close to the area of

Debbie's broken phone, shortly after eight a.m. The walker was unfortunately too distant to see what was happening, and neither did he notice anyone on foot. One other witness reported seeing a vehicle pulling away from there at a similar time, probably dark blue in colour but he couldn't be certain about that. As it was ahead of him he couldn't see the occupants. We think it's possible that what they both saw was the kidnapper's vehicle."

"Do we know if she ever accepted lifts?" DC Emily Jackson asked.

"Her father said not, and we don't believe that she'd arranged to meet anyone. She'd counted out the correct change for the bus before leaving her home. All indications are that she is in the early stages of a relationship with a local boy who should have been setting off on holiday today with a group of his friends. His friends have gone but he's voluntarily remained at home. We'll continue appealing for anyone who used that road between seven and nine to come forward. Did anyone see a dark-coloured pick-up in that area at any time on Saturday morning? Someone may have been suspicious enough to take more detailed notice of the vehicle. Extend the search for private CCTV footage to a seven mile radius, and remember that we're not necessarily looking for a sole-occupied vehicle."

Forbes turned to the whiteboard furthest from the door and pointed to the spot on the map where

Debbie's phone had been found. "The way the grass was flattened in the roadside ditch beside the grass verge here not only indicates a struggle, it also suggests that Debbie was placed face downwards, in the recovery position. Forensic analysis of the soil has shown diazepam mixed in with her saliva. The prescription drug causes drowsiness, but in the strength that we think Debbie ingested it, if she was given enough, it would have resulted in unconsciousness fairly quickly, or at least an inability to move. We believe she could have been left there either while her attacker collected his vehicle, or while he waited for the dog walker to move out of sight. The fact that he drugged her may indicate that he wanted her kept alive for a while."

"Do we need the public in a continued search today?" DC Jackson asked.

"No, but we need their help in finding this vehicle. Unfortunately we don't have a make, model, or even a definite colour. Ask whether anyone has been noticed hanging around Debbie or her family's home, or noticeably watching any girls in the area. I realise it's a popular tourist area but I want descriptions of anyone unusual in the nearby public houses on any day during the last week. We also want the names and addresses of all the people in the holiday homes in the village last week and this weekend, in the bed-and-breakfasts, and on the camping and caravan sites. Someone may have noticed something suspicious."

"The weekend campers will have already gone home, sir. They may be more difficult to trace."

"Good point, Rawlings, but do your best. Every name that you do find needs to be run through the police national computer, and followed up with a contact of some sort."

He walked over to the first whiteboard. "Operation Fantasy with Brian Garratt, deceased, is something we unfortunately have to keep in mind. DC Bell is in charge of that for the moment. Last night I had a lengthy conversation with the governor of Wandsworth Prison and he informed me that Garratt used to brag to prison officers about writing thrillers and horror novels, insisting that the murders he'd committed had been done in the name of research."

"We now believe it's highly probable that he killed six women, and not ten," DC Bell added, "as he intimated in his letter."

"And we now know where he got some of his information from," Forbes continued, "information which helped to convict him of all ten murders. The prison governor agrees that the more notorious Garratt believed that he was, the more likely he thought it was going to be for his name to live on after his death."

"He's managed that," DC Green added, "but has anyone seen anything that he's written – other than those letters?"

"His claims to be a writer were apparently as worthless as his confessions," Forbes answered. "He had an unnerving knack of being able to convince people of his sincerity of just about anything, as we now know to our cost."

"It's just a thought, sir," DC Bell was suddenly sounding pleased with himself, "but if we assume that Garratt covered for a serial killer by taking the blame for four murders he didn't commit, could the timing of Debbie Thomas's abduction be significant? Is it possible that she could have been taken as some sort of a tribute to the man?"

"Have you been talking to that forensic psychologist cousin of yours again?" DC Emily Jackson never missed an opportunity to tease Bell about his seemingly endless number of family members working away somewhere within the legal system.

Forbes held up his hand to put a stop the banter. "Unfortunately, DC Bell, you could have a valid point there. Garratt's death was announced on the national news on Thursday morning and Debbie was abducted only forty-eight hours later."

"Should I put in a request for a psychological profiler," DI Lang enquired.

"That might be a sensible idea. There's certainly plenty of material for a profiler to work with and we're going to need all the help we can get. But today, identifying that vehicle and finding Debbie Thomas alive both take priority over everything else.

Emily, how's the intelligence on the local sex offenders coming along?"

"It was the weekend, sir, but we've questioned three of the four in our area who are on the sex offenders list and they have alibis. The forth is in hospital so we've ruled him out. We haven't had time to check the alibis out yet, of course."

"Then get on with it." The room fell silent and Forbes remembered his own unshakable feelings of dread when his sister had completely disappeared for six months. Louise had chosen to cut herself off from her family, and then chosen to return. That wasn't the case with Debbie Thomas. Now though, his own private concerns were more for his ageing father, but they were worries which could wait.

*

"Good day to you, Mary," Ben Allsop shouted through the kitchen window at her. She tried not to scowl. Did this odd-job man have a permanent sneer fixed on his weathered face, or did he turn it on just for her because he sensed how much she disliked him?

"Your Peter said to come over for a couple of hours on Monday to cut back some of the overgrown bushes. So here I am, and I've brought my own loppers and a handsaw. I'll have a cup of tea in about an hour, if that's all right?"

It was an uncomfortably hot morning, one of the hottest of the year so far, with a deep blue, almost cloudless sky. There was talk of thunder on the weather forecast. She hadn't been planning on using the kettle. "I'll bring it out to you," she looked away from his sneering face, picturing him dripping sweat over her new vinyl tablecloth. "Come on Zelda, back to work for us."

The dog had been unusually subdued and shown no interest in in the outside world since this morning. She'd assured her girls that Zelda didn't enjoy the heat, but she wasn't quite so sure that the weather was the only thing bothering the little dog.

Peter had taken the girls, both smothered in sunscreen, to the local park – one set of swings, one roundabout, and one battered slide, while she got on with some serious cleaning and clearing out of the dead man's clothes. She'd had to admit that in summer, if you enjoyed the truly rural life, you'd have to go a long way to find a more peaceful and beautiful location for a family home.

The property was the perfect size for them, with three good-sized double bedrooms, one more than they had in London, and a range of sheds and garages which needed work and would no doubt keep Peter occupied for hours on end. The girls and Zelda had plenty of room to play and to explore, and with anyone coming down the drive easily visible from the front of the house well before they reached it, she was feeling more relaxed than on the first day. Even the village shop was only a quarter of a mile away – a ten minute steady walk up the hill and a five minute brisk walk back down it. It was a walk that she was actually looking forward to.

She was a city girl in the country, and unlike the proverbial fish out of water, if she set her mind to it she had the ability to adapt and evolve.

Ben Allsop was her greatest bugbear. She felt sure that he already had his claws half-way into Peter and she was damn-well going to make sure that he didn't sink them in any deeper. If, and the way she'd felt after Amy's early morning whisperings it was a big if, her little family settled at Dale End Farmhouse, she would jolly well learn how to manage the vegetable garden herself. There was something about having that man poring over and handling her food before it reached her kitchen sink that she found extremely distasteful.

She retreated upstairs and tipped the remaining black plastic bag out onto the girls' beds. "Just your summer clothes, two teddy-bears and one warm coat each," she'd told them both, just over a week ago, "and we'll come back for more things if we need them." But they were typical girls, and neither had been satisfied until every bag had been so full that it wouldn't hold even one more pair of tiny socks.

"Zelda, these girls have more clothes than I have." She'd been constantly talking to the dog, which was watching her from the corner of the room as though she understood and approved of every word. She'd invited Zelda into each room with her as she worked, not just to acclimatise the dog to her new surroundings, but to give herself the reassurance of another heartbeat in the room. Her uneasiness was slowly fading, but it remained something she couldn't discuss with Peter. He'd only make fun of her, and it was a feeling that she hoped would soon leave her altogether.

Far outweighing her worries, the advantages to her family, including herself, of moving to where they could all have a fresh start, were going to win the day. She would be in a neighbourhood where no one would remember her as the out-of-control teenager from the care home that she'd once been.

After watching two of her friends die in agony from a rogue batch of heroine laced with cyanide, she had been taken in by a probation officer and his wife. Their daughter had died from an overdose two years earlier, and their determination to help her, together with their shared feelings of guilt, had worked to change Mary's life. Their influences had somehow transcended all the previously bad stuff in her life. They'd each done what they could to help the other, and she would always be grateful to them.

They were God parents to Amy and Hannah and were the two people she would miss the most when they moved from London for good.

In a matter of a few minutes her thoughts had turned from if, to when, she realised. She smiled to herself. That new beginning in her life had worked out for the best, and maybe this one would too.

The clothes were still in a heap. She'd been daydreaming. She lifted two teddy-bears from the floor, placed them onto the pillows and then set about sorting the clothes and hanging them up in one of the few decent items of furniture in the house – the 1930's, inlaid mahogany wardrobe.

Zelda pricked up her ears and whined.

"What is it, Zelda?" She walked to the window and breathed a sigh of relief. Her little family was back.

"We're home," three cheerful voices echoed through the house and Mary clattered down the stairs to meet them.

Hannah ran to her and flung her arms around her legs while Amy ran to ran to the dog, plonked a kiss on top of the long nose, and then followed her sister to Mary's hips for a cuddle.

"Lunch is almost ready," she squeezed the dishevelled, dusty infants to her legs, "we're just having sandwiches and salad. And Ben's in the garden, Peter, if you'd like to take him a cup of tea. Have you all had a good time?"

Peter was looking at the three of them as though he was privileged to be a part of the little group. "We certainly have, haven't we girls?"

"Yes thank you, mummy," Amy said quite solemnly. "And we've made two best friends. If we do all live here, when I start school I will be in the same class as Sarah, and then Hannah will be in the same class as Sarah's little sister when they're both old enough to go. If it's sunny tomorrow, can we go again? Sara's gran takes them to the park most days, but sometimes they have no one to play with. I can play with them, can't I mummy?"

"Tomorrow, as long as it's not raining, we'll all go. Then I can meet your new best friends." She smiled as she stroked the girls' heads and looked at Peter. She was aware that her blue eyes could have told the whole world what she was thinking.

The missing local girl, Ben Allsop, and the unidentified noises were insignificant. She could live without the city – and the city certainly wouldn't miss her.

*

"News of Garratt's letters has reached the ears of the media," Forbes began the impromptu mid-morning briefing, "so I've called a press conference for one o'clock and two detectives from Manchester who worked on the case should be with us by that time. I expect the media will have some awkward questions for us about our handling of the case six years ago, but I've spoken at length with the chief constable and for now I will take whatever flack the press want to throw at this station. I expect the rest of you to keep your heads down and get on with whatever action you've been assigned to. Our primary task is still to find Debbie Thomas." He looked across at PC Danny Grant, a traffic officer. "Have there been any more sightings of the dark pick-up, at or around the time of the abduction, Danny?"

"No, just the two so far, and both witnesses have made their statements. One thought that it was a Land Rover type of vehicle, and the other said he thought it was a pick-up. Either way, what they saw wasn't a regular family-sized car. We've cross-checked the descriptions with the wheels of known sex offenders in the area but found no matches. The descriptions are too vague at the moment to start checking the general public."

"Nevertheless, keep looking; someone else may have seen that vehicle, or Debbie, sometime between eight and half-past that morning."

"Do I keep searching for a link between the five missing girls on the board, and Debbie?" DC Bell asked.

"For now, yes, although that isn't public knowledge yet. Two detectives from Buxton are expected here this afternoon to discuss the case of missing teenager, Faith Crispin, but until we have evidence to the contrary, Debbie's case will remain a separate enquiry."

"Have the Crispin family been notified that Faith could be about to make the news again?"

"Buxton officers are doing that today."

The door of the incident room opened and two unfamiliar detectives entered the room, each carrying a box file and a laptop.

It was ninety minutes before they were all due in the press conference room and he felt the pressure of every single one of them.

10

Debbie woke and looked at the clock. At least the lights were still on. It was ten past six – Tuesday morning – the beginning of her fourth day in captivity and day two of the idiot's sick scheme to make her fall in love with him. She couldn't think of him by his first name, real or not, he was a nothing to her, as thick as the walls of her prison and just as dangerous.

What did she actually know about him? What could she use to her advantage? She'd formed an outline of a Peak District resident with family roots in the area; one who worked with cattle and shopped locally, and who could have been speaking the truth when he'd said that he hadn't taken her far. His weathered complexion and his Monday early-morning visit in soiled work boots could signify that as a farmhand he was out checking the livestock in the fields when he visited her. So maybe she was being held close to his place of work. Today's boots might confirm that. And he never stayed for long, thankfully, so maybe people were checking on him.

She'd seen the tiny beads of perspiration on his brow and the tremors in his fingers when he'd handled the solar lights – and his demeanour slipping from confident to nervous, and then back again, all in a matter of seconds. He was possibly a man very close to the edge of sanity. His warped mind hadn't seen fit to rape or to kill her, but that could change in a heartbeat.

His dreams of a happy-ever-after life for the two of them were never going to happen, but the longer she could keep those crazy dreams alive the greater her chances of survival were likely to be. Sooner or later someone out there had to become suspicious of him.

Escape from the bell-shaped cave was, in theory, possible. She could stack the tables on top of each other, rip up the sheets and towels to create something long enough to reach the gantry when she threw it, and make some sort of grappling hook from pieces of chair legs or pieces of bed frame, either tied together or held with the wing-nuts she'd seen on the frame. But that would take hours, or even days to put together, and if he caught her trying it she'd be dead meat. And what would she even find if she reached the top of the ladder before he found her; more obstacles and locked doors?

That could only ever be a back-up plan in case he abandoned her totally.

Those metal rungs might just lead to where her shouts for help could be heard, but there was only one way to find that out.

She opened the carton of fruit juice, ate the last of the out-of-date cakes, and then she lay back and closed her eyes. A few days ago she'd been in a comfortable home with loving parents fussing round her – sometimes to the point of making her feel smothered, loads of friends of her own age, and if her exams had gone as well as she'd hoped, university to look forward to. Now she had out-of-date cakes to eat and an occasional visit from a creep who was most likely going to turn violent sometime in the next few days, to look forward to.

A dozen bloodthirsty ways of defending herself and overpowering him were rattling around in her head, but again, she'd only get one shot at it.

She'd tried to read the books he'd left but her fear level was such that she couldn't concentrate. It was taking every ounce of her mental energy to reign in her imagination as she waited... for what... she could only guess.

The intermittent noises she'd heard since the first day had sounded different this morning. When she'd allowed her imagination a long lead it had come back telling her of the soft sounds of someone crying. She'd called it to heel. That was too much to cope with... besides... it was survival time again.

He was moving rapidly towards her this morning – more rapidly than normal, slithering and clanging down the metal ladder. He could have been an overweight boa constrictor, clinging to the metal framework, coiling and uncoiling his way towards her. She pictured his face on the front of a huge snake, slithering down from its sleeping position in a metal tree, hunting for prey.

Maybe that was an insult to snakes.

He landed on the gantry and she listened for a hiss.

None came.

Instead he slithered silently over the side of the metal framework and descended the rope ladder at his normal speed. Her snake was wearing soiled work boots.

"Debbie, my angel, I see that you've eaten everything I brought for you yesterday. I'm so relieved. I really regret having made you poorly, but I had to get your undivided attention. Please tell me that you'll eventually forgive me."

She couldn't risk sounding patronising. Just because he had some vital parts of his brain missing didn't mean that he was a complete fool. "I think I understand how you feel, and when we both get out of here safely, I promise I'll try to forgive you." Her mouth was still dry but she was finding it easier to talk to him.

He smiled. "That's all I have any right to ask for. Today... oh I can hardly wait for this... look... today I've brought music."

The tremor returned his hands as he lifted a dusty and scuffed portable DVD player from the top of his bag and placed it on the plastic table.

He pressed the play button while giving her his sickliest smile yet, and then held out his hands to her.

"Please stand... Miss Thomas, this is day two of our courtship, so for your task today, would you do me the great honour of dancing with me?"

What choice did she have?

She raised both hands slightly but before she could stand he was pulling her towards him. His left arm slid around her waist.

The likeness to a boa constrictor had been an accurate one.

The music was classical; other than that she'd no idea and didn't risk asking. It felt like a waltz – she'd seen her parents dancing to a waltz a few times. She did her best to follow Mr Boa Constrictor's lead, without breathing too deeply, as he whirled her around the dirt floor to the longest piece of music that she'd ever heard. Finally it stopped.

"I hope you enjoyed that," he leaned back and looked into her eyes. "I certainly did." Then he moved in for his expected kiss.

The fruit juice she'd drunk not too long ago rose to the back of her throat. She forced it back down, closed her eyes, and accepted his cold, wet lips on hers. It took a supreme effort not to shudder.

He leaned back again, apparently overcome with emotion. There was more liquid than normal in his eyes. "I was imagining that we were the only couple on a massive, polished, wooden dance floor, with everyone watching and admiring us. Oh I can't wait for our wedding day. I have it all planned, but I don't want to spoil the surprise for you."

"I'm not a good dancer…"

"You were good enough, my darling, and with a little more practice and coaching from me, you'll be sensational. Now sit down. I want you to read to me from yesterday's morning paper."

She sensed the end of his visit. It never lasted too long after the newspaper reading. And as usual he would leave behind an aroma of stale sweat, soap, cattle dung, and eau de fox.

*

Forbes stood beside the flame-haired young forensic profiler that the Greater Manchester Force had sent over to them at DI Lang's request. She appeared to be in her late twenties, or maybe thirty at a push. Only one member of his team, DC Jackson, would have a problem taking this young woman seriously, and he'd already given her several consecutive seconds of his death-stare. Emily Jackson was the eldest of a large, down-to-earth family who believed in calling a spade a spade, not in looking for hidden meanings, and 'psychological clap-trap' as she called the art of profiling.

In the interests of covering every possible aspect of the Garratt case and the potential link to Debbie's abduction, he was doing his best to make the visitor welcome. He was giving her space to work, both physically with her own work station in the incident room, and mentally by instructing all his officers to give her their full co-operation. "This is the Tuesday morning, sixth briefing of Operation Barley," he began. "Victoria Stenson is a forensic profiler who has been studying the late Brian Garratt's crimes, and his death-bed retraction. She's also here to assist in the case of Debbie Thomas. Over to you, Ms Stenson."

"Thank you, Michael. Brian Garratt was a confirmed sociopath who craved publicity, and because of this I originally had my doubts that his letters to DCI Forbes were anything other than a last ditch attempt at grabbing the nation's attention. However, after several long discussions with detectives over the weekend I've concluded that these letters should probably be taken at face value. I also think it's possible that Faith Crispin and Debbie Thomas could have been taken by whoever took the four girls mentioned in Garratt's letters. In total one man could be responsible for at least six abductions, most of them occurring at between twenty-two and twenty-four month intervals. The longer gap between the last girl that Garratt's was convicted of abducting and Faith Crispin's disappearance may mean that there is at least one other, as yet unidentified victim. Serial killers, after their first successful killing, tend to accelerate the frequency of their atrocities. They are encouraged by their own successes. This man is more controlled. Because of this I think there is a strong possibility that Debbie is still alive. All six were taken from very close to their homes and this man selects his victims carefully. They are all slim, fair-haired, attractive and in their late teens. I believe he spent time researching them, because with the exception of Debbie, none of the girls had boyfriends. Debbie's relationship was only in its infancy and he may not have been aware of it. We are probably looking for a man between thirty and fifty years of age who knows the Bakewell, Buxton, and Leaburn areas well. It isn't easy to dispose of a body and he's managed to do that at least five times already, and in my opinion will continue to do so. This man fits into society. He may be a farmer with sufficient ground to bury bodies without arousing suspicion, or he may be in the construction industry with access to building sites and poured concrete. Your man leads a normal life in every other aspect. Serial killers and sociopaths often have an above average IQ, but as he doesn't seem to conform to the usual patterns of these types of offenders, I don't think that necessarily applies in this case, rather you're looking for a Mr Average."

"Do you think he could have been in contact with Garratt?" Adam asked.

Forbes answered for her. "Not unless Garratt had access to a phone which hasn't yet been traced. In six years the man never had any visitors and his family disowned him. We have to hope that Ms Stenson is correct in thinking Debbie is still alive, and that some new development will come out of the reconstruction we're arranging for this coming Saturday morning – one week from the time she was last seen. If we can jog just one person's memory it will be a worthwhile exercise. The publicity surrounding Garratt's letters should also be making local people think about the other missing girls, so let's capitalise on that and appeal for any fresh information on those. I want it widely publicised that anyone can come and speak to us, or telephone us, in complete confidence."

*

He was breathless from waltzing much of his way home —around the cow pats, the mole hills, the thistles and the ankle-spraining clumps of old, tough rye grass – he hadn't cared about being seen.

This woman made him so happy.

The surge of excitement and hope when she'd fallen into his arms had thrilled him. He'd tried to play down his belief that something wonderful was occurring between them, but it hadn't been easy.

Across the fields, through his front door, and into his kitchen he imagined that she was still in his arms, that the warm swell of her breasts was still pressing into his chest and that he was still battling with his inner demons to maintain control as her short, gasping breaths lit up his entire body.

He flicked the kettle on and side-stepped on his toes around the kitchen. On the only available space on his table, he placed his previous evening's copy of the local paper before finally sitting down with his mug of coffee. Last night he'd had to deal with a calving cow and by the time he'd arrived home he'd been too tired to even glance at the edition. His boss wouldn't have to mind if he was an hour or so late this morning; he'd had his money's worth out of him in the shape of a strong healthy bull calf.

The headline on the front page screamed out at him.

"My Debbie has a boyfriend… no… that can't be right… it has to be a trick… someone's lying… they're taking me for an idiot."

He looked up. The half-empty bottle of whisky was just sitting there on the table, staring at him, mocking him, and with shaking hands he grabbed it and tipped several good measures of the fiery liquid between his chattering teeth and into the back of his throat.

It didn't help.

"Nooo… I've watched her for days. But why didn't I know… why didn't she tell me about this when I talked to her about marriage?"

The whisky was slowly taking effect. His teeth had stopped chattering. He took another deep gulp, slammed the bottle down, and then read the first lines of the article out loud. "Wayne Soames, aged twenty, cancelled his holiday today in order to help with the search for his missing girlfriend, Deborah Thomas."

He reached for the bottle again and felt his throat protesting. "They tell lies…" He coughed. "The newspapers are famous for printing lies… everyone knows that. The papers will print anything to juice up a story." Tears trickled down his burning cheeks.

He'd been so lucky to find Debbie. She was his soul mate, the good luck charm that he'd search so long and so hard for. She couldn't belong to someone else – she just couldn't.

But there, slap-bang in the centre of the page, was a picture of a solemn-looking, dark haired youth, claiming that she was his.

The magic of his morning had vaporised. The precious moments he'd intended to treasure forever were instead tainted forever. He wanted to rush back and confront her – to beg her to tell him the truth, good or bad. He needed to know. How was he going to get through the remainder of his day and night without knowing how she felt about this boy?

But too many people were still out there, looking for evidence of who had taken her and where she might be. He had to behave normally. Somehow, as excruciating as it was going to be, he would have to restrain himself until tomorrow morning.

11

Boa Constrictor was back. He'd descended the ladder even faster than yesterday. Something had changed. His face looked twitchy and a scowl was replacing his usual sickly smile on his lined and weathered features. He slithered across the damp floor to her bed without speaking and sat down. His thigh urgently pressed against hers.

This was new territory.

She waited for him to speak after allowing him to take both of her hands in his own dirt-ingrained serpent-fingers. His hands felt limp and moist, and cold from their grip on the metal ladder, exactly how a snake ought to feel. His eyes blazed. Suspicion and anger were written there. Maintaining eye-contact was almost painful.

When he finally spoke it was slowly and calmly. "Why, my sweet Debbie, didn't you tell me that you had a boyfriend?" His eyes were half covered by drooping eyelids now as he almost begged her to tell him what he wanted to hear. "I wouldn't have been angry with you, only with myself. I want to know everything there is to know about you. I thought we were growing to trust each other. Please tell me that what the newspapers are reporting isn't true."

His tone sent the chill from her hands rippling up her arms and into her chest. After a moment of hesitation she decided on telling the truth, trusting that it would be her safest option. There was no telling what Wayne had been saying to the media. "If you mean Wayne, we've been friends for years, his parents buy some of our lambs each year, but we've only been out together once. We went out the week before he was due to go on holiday… a week ago yesterday… for the first time… just for a drive round and a burger at a McDonalds… it's nothing serious."

"Have you slept with him? I need to hear the truth from your lips." His now wide-open eyes were scanning her face at an alarming rate."

"No… no… I promise… I'm not like that… I've never had a proper boyfriend." She banked on that being the answer he wanted. She held her gaze on his face and her tactic worked. His eyeballs were steadying.

"No, I didn't think you were, and that's exactly why I chose you. You're such a sensible girl. And once you've fallen in love with me as deeply as I've fallen for you, we will have such a wonderful life together." His eyes glazed and he looked past her – to Hell and back for all she cared.

She waited.

"The others were merely steps along the road I had to travel to get to this point. They were all insignificant, I can see that now, and it was my fault for choosing badly."

"The others…?" She didn't really want to know. Instinct alone was telling her she ought to be showing an interest in his conversation. "You can tell me anything and I won't judge you. I'd like to know more about you."

"Enough now… forget about them," he released her hands, stood up and took a step back from her bed. He'd switched to his confused setting.

He'd flicked from confidence to insecurity because she'd said too much. *You have to let him lead*, she reminded herself and stayed silent.

"This is our day three... our first Wednesday morning as a couple. It's a day for us, and only us. Forget about the others."

"For us..."

"Before you read to me today I need to feel reassured. I want us to lie on the bed together for a little while, wrapped in each other's arms and imagining that we're an old married couple. Would you like to do that?"

"I think so," she'd been trying to prepare herself for far worse – as much as anyone could prepare themselves for the unknown. If he stopped at imagining they were an old married couple it would be little short of a miracle.

"I want to be able to whisper into your ear and caress your delicate throat, and I want to feel your body moulding into mine. My body craves you, but first I need to feel that you trust me completely."

"I want to trust you."

She let him push her shoulders down into the bed. Then she closed her eyes as lay down beside her and tried not to breathe too deeply.

*

Mary Stone lifted four plates from the kitchen cupboard, placed them on the worktop next to the freshly-scrubbed cooker, and froze. Alongside the angry squawks from a pair of squabbling blackbirds in the garden she'd heard a rustling sound. Her breath caught in her throat as she turned. "Ben..."

"Ah, good morning ma'am, I was trying not to distract you while you had your hands full. I'm sorry if I startled you, but the back door was open."

She looked down at his feet, and with a jolt of horror realised that his wellington boots were already lined up beside hers in the rear porch. And he was as casually-as-you-like striding into her kitchen and reaching for a chair.

"Peter and the girls are out walking with Zelda while I prepare breakfast," she said without smiling, hoping he wasn't too stupid or too insensitive to take a hint.

"Ah that's very generous of you, ma'am, but I'll break bread with you all on some other occasion, if that's all right. I'm an early riser in the summer. I had breakfast hours ago and I've got mine and mother's lunches all prepared and ready to pop into the microwave when I get home."

That hadn't been what she'd meant and she felt certain that he knew it. He was deliberately making her feel like a small child being humoured. "Can I help you with anything else?" She didn't bother trying to disgulse her sarcasm.

"No missus; I just wanted you to know that all those sprouting potatoes that you brought up from London have gone into the rows at the far end of the garden. You should get a late crop of small tatties off them. I never buy seed potatoes – they're a waste of money in my opinion. I'll get some in the ground a lot earlier for you next year. I've rigged the hosepipe up so if you'll just ask your husband to keep them well watered you should have a good few meals off them."

"Thank you; I'll tell him."

"While I was at that end of the garden I couldn't help noticing that he's not yet strengthened the fencing around the old mine shafts. They should be securely capped off, but with two kiddies and a dog running around you can't be too careful. Would you like me to get some fence posts and barbed wire from the farmer and sort it for you the next time I'm down here?"

"I think Peter intends to work on it this weekend, but I'll tell him you've offered in case he needs a hand." She began cracking eggs into a bowl, still hoping he'd take the hint.

"They've not found any trace of young Debbie Thomas yet. And if she's anything like the others they never will do. Have you been following the news since you arrived?"

"Yes of course, and it must be agonising for her poor parents." She was beating the eggs longer than necessary as a way of avoiding having to turn and look at him as she spoke. "According to this morning's news the police seem to think that a serial killer's been stalking the Peak District. But they say they're not yet linking Debbie's disappearance to five others."

"They'll change their tune if she's not found in a day or two, and they'll find there's been a few more gone missing if they do their jobs right, lass. You can ask any of the local folks and they'll tell you the same – there have been young lassies going missing from this area for almost a hundred years. And you mark my words now – all those disappearances are linked."

Now she had to turn and face him, if only to check that he wasn't sitting there grinning at her – pulling her leg. "But people go missing all the time for all sorts of reasons. You said that yourself." She pictured some of the youngsters she'd seen sleeping rough in London.

"Aye lass, and that's exactly what whoever... or whatever is behind these disappearances, is counting on. My own mother's best friend vanished completely – almost sixty years ago. Mum doesn't like to talk about it because it still upsets her, but I've heard some of her friends describing this here area as the Bermuda Triangle of the Peaks."

"Now I know that you're teasing me."

"I wish I was. No lass, honestly, and even as I'm telling you this I can feel a chill coming over me. Your property is slap bang in the centre of the supposed triangle, and that's another reason why no women would come to settle Peter's uncle or grandfather down after dark."

She felt her brow wrinkling. "But Peter's family have lived here for generations."

"I can see you're sceptical, and coming from the city I can follow that, but if you do decide to live here you need to take good care of yourself, and especially good care of those two little girls as they grow into young ladies."

"You're surely not suggesting that the people who lived here had anything to do with... with whatever it is you're talking about?"

"Who knows? But Peter's grandmother left with her two boys when they were just toddlers. She went back to live with her own family and never returned to Dale End. Peter's father passed away quite young, so I understand, and Dale End was left to his uncle who never married, on the understanding that the property would one day pass to Peter. No woman has lived here for as long as I can remember – not until your good self this week."

She sighed; the man was becoming tedious. "If there was any truth to your stories I'm sure my husband would have said something. I'm sorry Ben, but you're talking rubbish. I'd like you to leave my kitchen now."

She watched the old man's posture change.

His back straightened and he raised his chin until his neck was at full stretch and his eyes were looking deep into hers. "Then answer me this – why do you think the villagers have refused to come down here after dark for so many years; why did your husband never tell you about that, and why is he so dismissive of the unidentified noises that so many people, myself included, have heard coming from this valley?"

Her face was burning. "Because he has more sense than to believe in your superstitious rubbish," she snapped back at him.

He frowned at her and shook his head. "Have it your way, for now at least, but I'm only putting you in the picture because I don't want to see any harm come to you or your lovely girls. Superstition and brutality live hand-in-hand, and whether you believe me right now or not, I'm telling you that evil lives in these hills around your valley."

He got up from his chair but continued talking as he did so. "Until it's stopped, young women will continue to vanish from this area, and until those who are already lost can be found and given a proper burial, the noises will continue. Debbie Thomas's disappearance isn't superstitious rubbish, it's as real as I am standing here, and I do hope that she's found safe and well, but I very much doubt that she ever will be."

*

DCI Forbes had been in his office since six a.m. and Adam had followed him into the building less than ten minutes later. A coffee break was needed. "Adam, I never thanked you properly for cutting your holiday short. Did you all have a good time?"

"Excellent sir, thank you. We had two days of windy weather, but that's Wales for you, and it didn't prevent us getting out and about."

"From what I've seen of those two youngsters it will take more than a bit of blustery weather to hold them back. You and Jane are doing a fine job of raising them. I realise it's not been easy for either of you."

Adam shrugged off the compliment. "Jane's a natural mother. Ryan already thinks of her as his mum. I talk to him about his birth mother sometimes, but it's not easy. It still chokes me up to think of Erin holding him as she was dying."

"He's lucky to have you both."

"I do have one piece of news though, sir. I've been saving it for when we had a quieter moment. Do you remember last January that after I thought I'd lost Jane in that fire at Oakwell I proposed to her in her hospital bed?"

"Everyone in the station remembers that, you cheapskate, a bunch of flowers from Tesco's and a ring borrowed from a nurse."

"It was a spur of the moment thing, but one I've never regretted. I've been waiting for an opportunity to put my clumsiness right and propose properly." He grinned.

"This is the best news we've had in this station for days. How did you do it?"

"The four of us had packed up a day's food and were taking the easiest route to the summit of Mount Snowdon. Picture this, sir, if you will: we were close to the summit and resting in a sheltered gully – whichever way we looked the views were spectacular and the children were tired enough to be sitting quietly on the picnic rug – the wind was blowing through Jane's hair and all our faces were reddened from the air currents and the exertion – and for the first time that day the sun had come out and there was no one within fifty metres of us."

"That's quite a picture, but I've got it," he leaned back in his chair.

"I went down on one knee, told her how much I loved her, and then offered her the ring I'd been carrying in my jacket pocket for almost a month. The couple nearest to us saw what I was doing and recorded it on their phones. We exchanged numbers and they sent recordings to us in e-mails. It couldn't have worked out any better."

Forbes leaned across his desk for a vigorous handshake. "It took you long enough to do the job properly. Congratulations. Have you set a date yet?"

"That was the second surprise I had for Jane that day. I've arranged everything for three weeks from Saturday. She doesn't have to do a thing except choose her outfit and turn up at the Bakewell Register Office for eleven o'clock that morning. We'd already discussed what we both wanted for the day, so it wasn't too difficult."

"You crafty old dog you. Jane's a lucky woman and I'll tell her that when I next see her. But on a serious note, I wish the four of you all the luck in the world. You both deserve it and congratulations again."

"We're not making a song and dance about it, so I'd appreciate it if you'd keep it to yourself for now, sir. I'm only inviting a dozen guests – my parents and a few from this station, and we'd be honoured if you'd join us for the day. It's nothing fancy so there's no need to go buying a new suit or anything. After the service we're all going for a meal at Rowsley and then if it's fine we're going on to Chatsworth Estate for a stroll by the river to let the children run free for a while. Then we're intending going back to Jane's for a few drinks and some cake, and if anyone wishes to stay over we'll have room. We'll set the tent up in the back garden and there are two spare bedrooms in the house."

He refrained from commenting, but he knew why Jane wanted a low-key wedding. Her domineering ex-husband was constantly interfering in her life. She would be hoping to keep the news from him until the event was over. "It sounds as though you've got everything organised except the weather. It also sounds like my kind of thing. Thank you, I'd be delighted to witness Jane and you cementing your family unit. May I bring a guest?"

"Yes of course; I presume you mean Alison? What's the state of play between you two these days? Have you any plans for marriage?"

"We ruled that out years ago. She wanted to focus on her career as a forensic pathologist and neither of us had any desire to procreate, so staying single was by mutual agreement. But you've reminded me that a wedding needn't be a traumatic affair, and she does spend more nights with me than in her own flat these days, so who knows, maybe I'll surprise her and ask her again one of these days."

"Well good luck with that, sir."

"We're far too busy at the moment for anything like that, but one way or another I'll make time for your wedding, Adam."

"Thank you, sir."

"Right now we need to find Debbie. We know that Brian Garratt used his own, fifteen-year-old red Ford Escort Estate to transport three of his victims, and that he hired white Ford Escort vans to move the other three. There was solid forensic evidence to that effect. But white vans were also linked to the abductions of Christine Wright and Lucy Spencer, and Garratt claimed he'd borrowed those vehicles from friends he refused to name. Those vans were never identified and his claims were presumably a part of his web of lies, fuelled by information gleaned from PC Darcy. Added to that is the fact that one of the main lines of enquiry in the Faith Crispin case was centred around a white van which witnesses claimed to have seen Faith standing close to on the day that she disappeared."

"We're looking for a dark coloured farm vehicle or pick-up in connection with Debbie's disappearance. If it's the same man then he's changed vehicles during the last twenty-two months."

"Or he owns two. Find out whether the DVLA can supply a list of multiple ownerships of those types of vehicles in our area."

*

He wasn't going to be fooled by his Debbie any more than he'd been fooled by any of the others. He wanted to believe her – oh how he wanted that, but for his own sake he had to remain cautious. There was only so much disappointment that one man could take in a lifetime, and since Saturday he'd been praying hard that he wasn't setting himself up for more. Debbie had a reserved manner, she was pure and honest and he'd sensed those qualities in her the moment he'd first noticed her waiting for the school bus with her friends. Those were the features which had set her apart for him – those and her beautiful blonde hair.

The others hadn't been right for him; they hadn't been truthful with him, and that look of fear when he'd uncovered their lies – that look that they'd all tried so hard to disguise was one that he'd become an expert in spotting. That look turned him on, sexually, emotionally, and violently, and it was the look which had ultimately sealed their fates.

His skill in manipulating and extracting the truth from young women was one of his greatest assets. He'd enjoyed perfecting it over the years, and until the last few snatched hours he'd spent in Debbie's company, he'd found nothing quite as exhilarating as the final hours spent in the company of those young, but deceitful women.

These last few days had opened his eyes. He really had tasted true love. Nothing else had come even close. He realised that now.

Sitting in his late father's rocking chair he pictured Debbie sitting contentedly on the sofa opposite him. She would be wearing an elegant, not too short skirt, a white frilly blouse hinting at the cleavage beneath it, and with bare, tanned legs seductively crossed and showing just enough of her thighs to excite him – prim yet seductive. "My beautiful Debbie, how I long for you to be the one; to be my soul mate."

Such a blissfully married couple, everyone who knew them would say.

She just needed to get to know him a little better; that was all. She could be trying to outwit him, he knew that, he wasn't stupid, and he was happy to play along for another day or two, but at some point it had to become serious between them – love just had to happen for her as it had for him.

The one stumbling block might be her boyfriend. She'd played down their relationship, but if it was so casual then why was the boy talking to the media and boasting about never giving up the search?

Could it be that the seriousness of their relationship was all in the youth's head, or was he just craving the limelight and the publicity?

Or had Debbie actually lied to him?

That thought made him push forward out of the chair and stumble to the kitchen. He screwed up the whole of Monday's edition of the local paper and pushed it down into the pedal bin between the microwave meal wrappers and the soggy tea bags. He didn't want to feel anger towards her – he wanted to feel love and trust, and he wanted to cocoon her and shield her from the rest of the world – and from self-centred, over-sexed, sultry-looking youths.

If only he could get rid of that boy as easily as he'd disposed of his picture.

That was it. He'd hit on the only option open to him. He was going to have to dispose of pretty-boy Wayne Soames. He was going to have to plan. He enjoyed making plans. Suicide – yes that was the way – he'd make it appear as though Wayne had taken his own life. Then when he told Debbie, instead of her possibly blaming him, she'd turn to him for comfort. Yes it was a good plan. She'd fall into his arms for solace and then she'd be his for the taking.

And how much better would it be if the police thought that Wayne had killed Debbie and then killed himself in a fit of remorse? Maybe then they'd stop searching for her quite so desperately and begin looking for a body.

Tomorrow would be day four of their courtship – almost the half-way point. Wayne's body would have to found fairly quickly.

He liked that idea; it was by far his best idea yet.

12

He'd hardly slept. At least a dozen ways of disposing of Wayne Soames had rattled around his head until he'd come up with a short-list, and then at two a.m., the winning idea. By four a.m. sun was filtering through his bedroom curtains and birds were singing love songs to each other as though nothing else in their tiny, feathered worlds mattered. He kicked off the duvet and headed for the bathroom.

By five a.m. he was crossing dew soaked fields with a half-full sack of calf feed over one shoulder and a half-full rucksack of food for Debbie over the other and disturbing hoards of horseflies from damp cowpats as he walked. Swallows soared and swooped ahead of him and then behind him, all making the most of the sudden glut of food flitting through the air. It really was an excellent morning to be alive.

*

The clang, clang of the metal ladder woke her. Heaven-help-her, she must be getting used to being down here if she was sleeping that much better. She looked at the clock – ten past five, and she needed a pee.

"Good morning my sweet Debbie, I know I'm a little early this fine and sunny Thursday morning, but I was concerned that the isolation might be becoming too much for you. I would spend more time with you if I could, you must believe that."

He was descending the rope ladder in a more cheerful, relaxed manner than she'd seen before. She sat still on the tatty excuse for a bed. If this was another of his moods she would have to gauge it carefully.

"Instead of yesterday's daily national," he continued as he walked towards her, "I've brought Wednesday's local evening paper for you to read. The front page is dedicated to us – take a look. Your parents are distraught at the moment, but think how relieved they'll be when they realise that all that's happened is that you've discovered true love. They'll soon forgive you – they'll forgive us both."

His clammy hand rested on hers as he sat down and she made the usual effort not to flinch. He continued looking into her eyes as he unfolded the newspaper onto her lap and as she lowered her gaze and gasped.

Instant tears splashed the newsprint.

"I thought you'd be pleased to see a picture of your parents?"

Seriously... did he think he'd given her something which might make her feel better?

She needed to stall for a few moments, to gather her thoughts. She reached for a tissue and wiped her face. "It… it's just upsetting for me to see them both crying like that. I miss them so much. I desperately, desperately wish that there was some way I could let them know that I'm all right." Seeing their anguished faces had been a shock, but she'd been praying for just a chink of an opportunity to drop the suggestion of a letter into Mr Boa Constrictor's slow brain. She silently prayed that she hadn't been too obvious.

"And look," he continued as if he hadn't heard her, "there's a smaller picture of your friend, Wayne Soames, showing off to all and sundry, bragging that he's never going to stop looking for you. Now why would he be saying something like that if he's just a casual friend, do you think?"

"You said that lots of people were out there looking for me. And you're right about Wayne – he always did enjoy being the centre of attention. Do you think people might stop looking if they thought I'd just left home to be with someone and was intending to return home? Would that make it easier for you to keep me company? I am finding the isolation a bit much." Now she was pushing her luck, but she'd been presented with the perfect opportunity to suggest contact with the outside world. Fate had presented her with a stroke of luck worth grabbing and squeezing for all it was worth. "It would be comforting for them to know I'm being well taken care of." She'd loaded her suggestion with a compliment before falling silent. Now she just had to wait and give his warped brain time to digest the idea.

She'd silenced his grating voice for a few moments at least.

Her suggestion was obviously running around in his head, bumping into obstacles and objections, changing direction and then running on again. How many circuits of his brain would the idea need to complete before what few little grey cells he had up there could come to a decision?

"Soon, very soon, my darling, I might let you make contact."

He hadn't dismissed the idea and that was progress of sorts. "I'd appreciate that." The next time she suggested it she'd have a go at making him believe the idea had been his. That was a nugget of psychology she'd picked up from listening to her mother. Her father never really stood a chance when her mother wanted something that he was against. Tears pricked her eyes. Mr Constrictor wasn't anything like her father, but it had to be worth a try.

"Please don't fret, my angel; if you do as I ask everything will be all right. Now I expect you've been wondering how far our courtship will progress today. Firstly, I want you to read something from the newspaper for me, and then I'm going to blindfold you. Today's exercise is one of trust."

Her stomach lurched.

"I don't think I'm ready..." Who was she kidding that she could manipulate him – had he seen through her half-formed plan?

Her short protest got her nowhere.

"When I've blindfolded you I'm going to remove some of my clothes – not all of them, not until we know each other better." He gave what he must have thought was a reassuring, toothy smile. "Then I want you to stand in front of me and caress my body, starting at the top of my head, moving slowly down over my shoulders and my chest to my waist and hips. Then I want you to fall to your knees and caress my thighs, and then slowly, very slowly, work your way back up my body to the top of my head. I'll tell you if you're moving too quickly."

I can do this, she steeled herself.

For the chance of another day and an opportunity to get a letter out, I can do this. I can stomach the smell of his stale sweat and cattle dung and foxes to gain one more day. I can even touch his putrid body if I imagine that I'm somewhere warm and sunny with Wayne. I can do this. I know that I can.

"Now read to me while I prepare."

*

Mary Stone had spent much of the last twenty-four hours mulling over her last contentious conversation with Ben Allsop. She hadn't mentioned it to Peter because she knew he'd have viewed her concerns as being second thoughts about giving country life a real try. He'd only have preached to her again about the merits of life in this secluded valley – as though, like a child, she needed reminding.

Not for one moment had she believed Ben's story while he'd been sitting at her kitchen table, but in the early hours of the morning, lying next to her sleeping husband, some of Ben's dark phrases had wormed their way into the thinking part of her brain. And they'd evoked some very unwelcome emotions.

Was it remotely possible that Peter's family had been involved in the abduction of young women – had generations of them been kidnappers and murderers – and if so, where did that leave Peter? He must have known. He was a male – a Stone – had he been expected to carry on the family tradition? Debbie had been abducted the morning they'd arrived. Did that mean Peter had an accomplice – someone who'd prepared for her husband's arrival?

Were young women being kidnapped to order?

She'd watched him sleeping and wondered how many people really, truly knew everything there was to know about their partner's character, let alone that of their partner's family?

She'd sat through American television reality shows where the killers had come from ordinary families, and where their nearest and dearest had lived in blissful ignorance of the monsters in their midst. She'd smugly thought that they must have seen signs, or at the very least suspected that their other half wasn't the loving person that they'd once longed to share their life with.

For a long while this morning guilt had washed over her for having such dark thoughts. Peter was her gentle, loving husband and a good step-father to her two girls, so how and why had she allowed the ramblings of a man she'd only recently met to affect her in this way? But as much as she'd tried to dismiss her night demons, the doubts were lingering. They were intruding into every aspect of her morning to the point where she was having difficulty concentrating on simple household tasks.

There was only one thing for it — she was going to have to make some investigations of her own. If she really had brought her girls into the centre of some sort of a nightmare she intended to either get the hell out of it as fast as possible or meet it head on. She had no intentions of ever being featured on the television news as the dumb little wife who was the last to know.

But before she could make a start on that it was time for lunch. Peter and the girls were singing something together, all totally out of tune, and all walking up the path to the front door. Her heart melted for two of them.

She dished out the cottage pie, with baked beans on the top for the girls, and waited while they all took their places at the table.

"Now that we're settling in for the summer," she spoke without looking at Peter, "I think I'd like to try my hand at some genealogy." The girls looked at her as though she was speaking in some new, unknown language. "I'd like to find out more about daddy's family, especially those who lived here at Dale End."

"What's brought this on?" Peter sounded casual enough.

"I'm growing to like it here, and I can see what an improvement it will be in the quality of life for all of us, but I think I'd feel more settled if I knew more of your family's history, and the history of this house. When the girls are in bed, perhaps you'd tell me what you know about both subjects so that I've got a starting point."

Amy was still looking into her eyes. "We do history at school now. People used to wear really funny clothes."

"And I promise I'll tell you about any interesting bits," she nodded towards their plates, "but only if you both eat up all your food."

"I can go back two generations," Peter added, "but that's about it I'm afraid. I've never taken much interest in the past. But I'll help with your on-line research if you'd like me to."

"Thanks, but it's only a whim that I'm thinking of working on in any spare moments I might have. Besides, we haven't even got the internet set up yet. I just thought that if you told me what you knew then when I next went into the village I could take a look around the graveyard – and at the church register if

I'm allowed. And when the internet is set up I'll research further into the past." The girls had both pulled a face at the mention of the graveyard. "You never know – you might even have some distant relatives still living in this area."

"As long as they don't expect a Christmas present I don't mind." He winked at the girls and they giggled back at him.

A copy of the property deeds lay in an upstairs drawer, and she'd briefly studied it while she'd been alone. She had a rough idea of who had owned Dale End and when, and whose land and property was adjacent to it now, but for the moment she was keeping that information to herself.

As soon as she could she also intended learning more about the mining disaster and the two missing girls from the nineteen-thirties.

*

"Bring my car round to the front… quick as you can..." Forbes slid his keys across Adam's work station, then retrieved his jacket from a hook on the wall and loosened his shirt collar. "A fisherman has just landed a body in the river Wye. It's hot out there so let's just hope the body hasn't been in the water for too long."

After submersion in water for two or three days, especially after being bounced along the bottom of a river bed, sometimes the sex of a cadaver wasn't obvious without getting up close.

There was a chance that Debbie had surfaced.

Only one patrol car was at the scene, but that would change over the next few minutes, and the following few hours if the death was at all suspicious.

"The fisherman is claiming to know the deceased, sir." The uniformed officer at the scene greeted them and handed Forbes and Adam their shoe covers.

"Are you from scenes of crimes?" Forbes hadn't expected to be greeted by protective footwear. A leather holdall and a large plastic tub with his own crime scene kit were in the boot of his car – something similar would be in the car of every detective in the country. But he accepted the offered overshoes.

"Yes sir, I was in the area when I heard the call. I figured that if it was Debbie in the water there was no point in driving any further just to be called back to the scene. It seems it isn't Debbie though, sir. If the fisherman's correct we can be certain the body hasn't been in the water for long. I haven't been that close yet, I was waiting for you, but he thinks the body is that of Wayne Soames. He also says he thinks it looks like either a murder or a suicide – definitely not an accident."

"How far into the river was the body when he first saw it"

"Only about a metre; he stumbled over it. It was face down in the water and level with the surface, but jammed against the river bank. He rolled it over out of the water in case the youth was unconscious rather than dead."

"Let's take a look then."

The middle-aged man, still dressed in full waders and sitting on the ground with his back pressed against a large oak tree, looked as though he probably wouldn't be going fishing again for a while.

It was Wayne Soames all right, right down to the clothes he'd been wearing in the interview room yesterday afternoon. The difference now being that his ankles were tied together with a length of blue nylon rope, his wrists were loosely tied in front of him, and both his wrists and ankles were attached by another length of rope to a concrete building block which was still half-submerged in the flowing water.

Alison Ransom had been called out to certify that life was extinct and she was making her way down the bank towards him. For once he'd beaten her to the scene. It was only six hours since they'd been sitting opposite each other at the breakfast table, eating porridge and mentally preparing to go their separate ways for the day. Minutes from now they would be facing each other again, only this time instead of a pot of jam resting between them it would be a body. These were the careers that they'd pursued rather than settling for a more tradition family life and two-point-four children. They acknowledged each other with forced smiles.

"Murder or suicide?" he asked as she knelt down, but she ignored his premature question.

After a minute of silence she looked up. "The answer to that question is yes. The only thing I can tell you with any degree of certainty is that he was alive when he was submerged in water. There is water in his lungs and he died from heart failure, most probably as a direct result of inhaling the stuff. He could of course have been drowned elsewhere and then dumped here. Take a closer look at that concrete block, Michael. From here it looks as though there could be letters scratched into it."

He stepped onto the mats put down for him by the scenes of crimes officer, and bent down. There were indeed letters scratched into the block; angular letters formed by small straight lines, not terribly deep and possibly made by a narrow chisel, or the edge of a sharp stone. They were childishly formed letters, totally at odds with the body on the bank. "*Debbie – sorry*," he read the words slowly. They could mean any number of things.

"Is there anything on the other side?"

"No, nothing, just those eleven letters."

"Not what you'd call a conventional suicide note is it? We're not going to need a handwriting sample. I'd say that it looks a tad suspicious, wouldn't you?" Alison could find humour in the most unlikely of places. Maybe that was why she enjoyed her work, or possibly that was what helped her to cope with it, either way she could always lift his mood and the mood of those around her, and that was just one of the things he loved about her.

He stood up and stepped back to allow the photographer to work. "What do you think, Adam? Could he have tied those knots himself before jumping into the river?"

"His wrists are tied quite loosely and about two inches apart, but look at those red marks. I'd say that he struggled. It's the middle of summer, and although the river's fast flowing it's only deep enough in a few places to drown a person, and even then it would have taken a while. I think he was forcibly held under the water. He could have been killed anywhere along here and then pushed in."

"A lot of people walk these river banks at this time of the year, and the concrete was never going to allow the body to move far. I think you're right, Adam, and I also think that whoever killed him wanted him to be found, but why?"

"Whoever has Debbie could have scratched out those letters with the intention of shifting the blame for her disappearance onto a dead youth."

Forbes turned to Alison but spoke so everyone around could hear. "I want soil and DNA samples taken from this whole sight as a matter of priority. There's a chance that whoever did this is still holding Debbie. As far as the public and everyone else here is concerned, until we know why this boy has been killed, or until we find Debbie Thomas, this is a probable case of suicide. The best chance we have of finding her alive may involve us playing along with whatever game the kidnapper thinks he's playing.

Allowing him to think that he's fooled us may relax him enough to make a mistake. Is that clear with all of you?"

13

"Three weeks, one day, and counting," Jane Goodwin scowled at the bathroom scales below her damp feet. At five a.m. she'd given up on the idea of any more quality sleep, crept out of her lonely bed and headed for the shower. The thrill of Adam's proposal and secretly arranged wedding had been replaced by an urgent need to tone her neglected body and shed the remaining three-quarters of a stone gained by comfort-eating since the death of her mother. A quarter of a stone had dropped off in the first three days of her slimming regime, but in her second three days she'd lost nothing. But then diets were like that – they aimed to fool you. There was only one thing left to do, and that was to cut out the wine completely. She needed to psych herself up, to stop worrying about her ex-husband finding out about the wedding, to increase her exercise, and to buy a snugly-fitting dress with matching shoes and bag.

Nothing too difficult about any of that!

The difficult part involved telling Lucy.

In her head she'd been rehearsing how to tell her eight year old daughter about the wedding without involving an actual date. It was likely to be an emotionally charged conversation about wedding dresses and bridesmaid's dresses which Lucy would be way too excited to keep to herself. The very last person who needed to know about the wedding was Lucy's father.

Her ex wouldn't be able to stop their wedding, even he wanted to, but she'd lay money on the man finding a way of spoiling at least some part of her special day. In both his business and his private life, the man's ego didn't allow for the remote possibility that others might see him as the loser.

The first time he'd seen her and Adam out together, at a newly-opened French restaurant, he hadn't been able to resist marching across to their table. *"The plain ones always make the best wives,"* he'd said to Adam while staring at her. *"I go more for sophisticated elegance nowadays, but good luck with her, I'm sure she'll make an adequate police officer's wife."*

Neither of them had given him the satisfaction of a response. His remarks had stung, but they'd been nothing less than she'd expected from him from the moment she'd seen him in the doorway. Three months after that he'd tried, but failed, to fit Adam up on an assault charge.

What worried her most about him was his money-laden influence on Lucy, but there wasn't an awful lot she could do about that. She could only hope that he wouldn't offer to buy his daughter the most expensive designer bridesmaid's dress that he could lay his hands on in an attempt to make her the star turn of the day. Of course Lucy would always be Jane's brightest star, but she couldn't have her little girl turning into a spoilt madam who thought that she only had to click her fingers to be given the best of everything.

Some kidology was called for. She would show Lucy some fashion catalogues to determine what styles of dresses her daughter favoured at the moment, and then choose something suitable for the type of day they had planned.

Her brain suddenly felt frothy with excitement. She could push the stuff she didn't like about herself – namely her inability to walk past a newly opened bottle of wine – to one side for the next three weeks.

No problem!

If her ex could be kept in the dark about the date of the wedding, and Lucy's dress and her own waistline were her biggest worries, then she was one lucky bride-to-be. She would celebrate that thought with one last glass of chilled wine before beginning her three weeks of abstinence.

*

Debbie opened her eyes. It was six a.m. according to the clock he'd left with her. She could expect him any time soon; he could be on his way right now. The fourth day of his warped idea of courtship, and so-called tasks, had been sickening and she'd barely got through it. She knew now that her self-control was going to be pushed to the limit. That was what she feared the most – that it would be her actions which would precipitate the violence and not his. If she lost it completely and panicked, or if she couldn't do as he asked, how would he respond? He appeared calm for the most part, but was he like an elegant swan and paddling away like fury below the surface? She smiled – he was hardly a swan – not even an ugly duckling – in fact a warty, floundering toad looked good in comparison.

But if he lost control there might be no reasoning with him. She could end up being raped or killed due to nothing more than a blip of hesitation from her and a temper-tantrum from him. A momentary loss of self-control on her part could snuff out her life. That realisation had shaken her. He'd been calm and gentle with her, at least since that first night, but only because she'd remained compliant. Could she control her own actions well enough to keep things that way, whatever he asked her to do?

She couldn't be sure.

She had to push for that letter.

Time was running out and the next episode of her nightmare was about to be played out.

He was on his way.

"Hello my beautiful Debbie," he sounded upbeat as he stepped off the gantry and onto the rope ladder. "I can't believe how fast this week has gone, or that when I leave you today we will be more than half way through our nine day courtship. Are you pleased to see me?"

"Yes… yes I am." On a scale of one to ten her fear level had dropped from a ten to a seven, despite his ridiculous time limit.

Loathing accounted for the missing three measurements of her feelings towards him. She loathed his stinking hands as they smoothed down what remained of his grey hair, and she loathed the grating sound of his voice. She even loathed the straw-covered soles of his work boots as they left the ladder and brought him towards her.

"There's a cool breeze out there today and storm clouds are gathering on the horizon. There's been a threat of thunder for days now. You're better off down here."

"Am I?"

Either he didn't recognise her sarcasm or he was ignoring it.

"I may be wrong, I may be very wrong, but from the way you've begun to look at me, I think you are actually starting to fall in love with me. No, don't answer – I don't want those words to roll off your tongue until you're absolutely certain, and until they come not just from your heart, but from your soul."

The words on the tip of her tongue couldn't be further from those he wanted to hear. *I want to see your head boiling in a vat of oil, but only after you've let me out, and only after I've wrapped those sodding lights around your scrawny neck and pulled on them until your eyes are bulging from your ugly head and you can no longer draw a single breath, you twisted, sick pervert.* Instead she opted for a short burst of flattery. "I'm realising that you're a good man at heart."

"That's good to hear, Debbie. This is your fifth day of tasks, and again I promise not to do anything to hurt you. But before that I'd like us to talk for a while. Do you have anything you've wanted to ask me?"

"Anything...?"

"Anything at all..."

Dare she ask about a letter? Maybe that would be too obvious. Better to ask about him – to show an interest in his life. "You hinted that you'd had a few girlfriends in the past, and I can understand that, but what made you choose me?"

"You're so sweet and pure, how could any man resist you? I fell in love with you weeks ago, and on that rowdy school bus you always looked so uncomfortable, as though you didn't fit in. You're so much like me. I've never felt comfortable in crowds. Does that answer your question?"

She nodded and gave him a genuine smile. So he was either using the service bus or had watched it go past on more than one occasion. Any creep looking at schoolgirls or staring through the windows of a school bus should have been noticed.

She pictured her friends how she last remembered seeing them. Were they getting on with their lives – would Jessica's wedding go ahead? She hoped so. She didn't want what had happened to her to ruin her cousin's big day.

"Now it's my turn to ask a question. But first, I want you to take off what you're wearing and put on this special dress. It belonged to my mother but she only wore it a few times, and I've washed it specially. There's no need to be shy with me, Debbie, you forget that I've already seen and handled your naked body."

Forget… never…!

The dress looked like a vintage one; floor-length with two layers of fabric and a frill around the bottom hem. If she was to hazard a guess, she'd say it was a maxi dress from the nineteen-seventies. At least it would completely cover her. His tongue flicked around his jelly-like lips as he gently smoothed out the dress on the bed. She turned away and began to undress.

It was tight – Debbie was a slim size ten but his mother must have been a size eight or less. And unless it was her strung-out nerves playing tricks, even the dress smelled slightly of fox spray. She'd no intentions of asking him about the odour. He'd be offended, certainly, but more importantly it was something he wouldn't have expected her to recognise. There was one fox lair in the woods half a mile from her home, and several more on the hillside, on the neighbouring properties.

If he didn't mention contacting the outside world before he left, she was going to have to be brave and suggest it. Now wasn't the time. He was standing in front of her and taking her hands into his serpent-grasp.

"My question, my beautiful Debbie, as if you haven't guessed," he dropped onto one knee and she heard what sounded like cartilage grinding against bone, "is will you do me the great honour of becoming my wife?"

I'd rather attend my own funeral; she was so close to blurting out. "I respect you. You see what you want and you go for it," to say yes straight away might make him suspicious of her motives. This could be one of his so-called tasks. "And I could love you, I know that. And you're right about me being uncomfortable around people. I guess that's why I've never had a proper boyfriend."

I'm still at school, for heaven's sake, she wanted to scream at him. *Why the hell would I even consider marrying a creep like you*? "Love and security are important in life, so yes; I'm thinking that maybe we could make a go of it."

He leaned back onto his heels and her stomach tightened. Had she said the wrong thing – failed the test? Had he seen that she'd say anything to get out of this hell hole?

"Help me up, will you?" He pulled down on her hands.

She almost laughed in his face, but at the same moment realised he was letting his guard down. If she'd had any kind of a weapon closer to hand she could maybe have pulled her hands clear and floored him. He was growing careless. Tomorrow she'd be better prepared.

"I can scarcely believe it. I know you're eighteen, and we won't need permission to marry from your parents, but I'm sure they'll give us their blessing when they see what a perfect couple we make." There was that idiotic grin again. "I'll propose again more romantically once we get out of here – I know how you young ladies like that sort of thing, but for now we have a binding contract, you and I, till death us do part."

Your death, and sooner rather than later if I have anything to do with it.

"We do...?"

She felt absurd. The fear level had plummeted to a number five on the emotion scale and she wanted to begin laughing at herself. Exactly one week ago she'd been in her sunlit bedroom, deciding which of her dresses to wear to the fitting and which perfume to use. Now she was stuck in a cave, in a forty year old dress, accepting a marriage proposal from a middle-aged creep with BO and halitosis, and cattle dung on the soles of his boots.

"And I can see no reason for us to wait. Tomorrow I'll begin looking at venues. There will be some who'll try to put obstacles in our way, but dealing with the difficulties ahead of us will only make us stronger. As long as we both want the same thing, and I sincerely believe that we do, no one and nothing will stand in our way."

And he hadn't finished yet.

"I have a gift for you." From his trouser pocket he produced a worn, velvet box. "This was my mother's engagement ring. You can wear it on whichever finger it fits until we can get it adjusted for you. May I try your left hand first?"

She lifted her hand. She felt light headed. She knew it was the adrenaline, the fear and the tension of not knowing what to expect next from the snake-creature.

"My darling, you're trembling; it's the excitement isn't it? I know just how you feel. My heart is pounding. This is such a magical moment for both of us. And look... look... the ring fits perfectly on your wedding finger. That has to be a good omen, surely. Our union is meant to be. Together we can overcome anything. We can build a life together. I can father your children."

In your dreams!

This was it. There were only four days left and this was the best chance she was likely to get today. It was time to ask – while he was full of himself and maybe not thinking clearly. She returned his gaze. "I'd love to be able to share our news with my family. They'll hardly believe it. Yesterday I think you suggested a letter to them?"

Tick, tick, tick, she concentrated on listening to the workings of the clock on the plastic table – unless it was his brain she was hearing, turning her suggestion over inside that age-spotted skull of his.

"Tomorrow my darling, I promise, now read something from yesterday's national newspaper for me and then I must go. Everyone I meet today will wonder why I'm smiling so much. It will be difficult to hide, but I can't help it. And I can see that underneath your nerves you're feeling just the same. That's good; that's excellent even."

She reached the end of a dull article about a new trade deal with China, while mentally preparing for what she knew was coming next.

He grabbed at her shoulders, pulled her to him, and gave her his usual, slobbery, goodbye kiss.

"You may keep the dress on. It suits you."

Then he arranged her food on the table, collected his empty bag, and for the first time walked away without peering over his shoulder.

"Well that wasn't too bad, Mr Constrictor." Talking to herself was something she hadn't done for years, something she'd left behind in her childhood, but she muttered upwards at his repulsive silhouette as it disappeared into the darkness. "If that was your idea of a task for day five, bring on day six. Just allow me get a letter out of here, and then you'll see how much I want to marry you, you disgusting creep."

*

Mary Stone listened to her two girls playing outside. Having already shelved the night-time fears which had again sent them scurrying across the landing to Mary's side of the bed, they were enjoying the freedom, the cool summer breeze, and the early morning sunshine. Zelda had slept at Mary's side of the bed since their second night in the house. She had flat-out refused to spend the night in any other part of the building. They'd bought a second dog bed and placed it in the bedroom, but even with that the dog's behaviour was becoming noticeably worse. During the day she was reluctant to leave Mary's side for longer than a minute or two and wasn't far away from being afraid of her own shadow. Besides feeling spooked by Zelda's behaviour, Mary hated seeing the little dog so permanently unhappy.

Peter remained unconcerned and his attitude was annoying her.

"It's just the creaks and groans of an old house airing out," he'd assured the girls in the early hours.

Now he was standing in the kitchen and telling her the exact same thing. "The old place has had no proper heating in it for years. Uncle lived in one room downstairs for as long as I can recall. I'd be more surprised if there weren't any old timbers drying out and creaking. And all the pipework needs renewing; pockets of accumulated air in those can make a hell of a racket. Zelda and the girls will settle in soon enough. They're used to having traffic rumbling on through the night, that's all. And yesterday morning, I forgot to tell you, through the kitchen window I saw a large dog fox, and we know what eerie sounds they can make."

When she'd tidied the girls' room and made the beds yesterday, she'd thought, just for a few seconds, that she'd heard the sounds the girls had described. She knew she'd never be able to completely settle into the property until she could make sense of what was going on. And something was going on, of that she was certain. She should have been talking it over with Peter, not dwelling on it – not too sure of his dismissive reaction to even mention it to him.

Peter ought to be more concerned – why was he not investigating further? Why was he not working to put all of their minds at rest? Why was he not as concerned as she was?

There was one uncomfortable answer to all those questions. She pushed it to the back of her mind.

That was the moment, she realised later, when her distrust of him had begun developing into a small seed of hatred.

Peter returned upstairs to prepare for an interview and Zelda shadowed her out into the garden. Swallows swooped and chattered, hunting at incredibly high speeds for insects disturbed from the long grass by the children, and somewhere in the hills a pair of lapwings were calling out to each other – those hours spent enduring Springwatch with the girls hadn't been wasted. Even the trees on the valley sides were more vibrant shades of green than those she remembered noticing in the London parks. To the majority of people this place would be heaven on earth.

So why couldn't she accept Peter's explanations and settle into the house?

Dark clouds were gathering this morning. It hadn't rained since they'd arrived and the soil on the steep slopes, and in the garden, was as hard as stone. Maybe Peter was right after all and the old house was simply warming up and drying out… maybe.

She watched the girls for a few more minutes, her heart bursting with love and pride, but at the same time tinged with fear. "Stay close to the house, both of you."

Peter had returned to the kitchen. Despite being almost a foot taller than her he looked vulnerable. And he sounded sincere when he told her that he loved her. The interview was a formality, he said, but it was clearly unsettling him. He pecked her on her head as he always did before leaving the house, and left her standing in the entrance hall, listening to his car accelerating away.

Something was preventing her from being hopeful of everything turning out right, and that something was becoming more difficult to live with by the hour. How was it possible for her to remain here with such lingering doubts about her husband and his family, and their possible involvement in some very heinous crimes? But if she walked out now, and she was wrong, she would be putting her marriage at risk and removing her girls from the safety and security that they took for granted.

But supposing she did nothing, and her worst fears were realised...?

The deeds to the property were beckoning from the upstairs drawer, but tempting as it was to get them out and take another look at them, for now she would leave them where they were. It was Friday morning, Ben Allsop's day to work in the kitchen garden, and he was later than normal. He'd offered to bring some of his surplus cabbage plants, and for once she was hoping he'd be in a talkative mood. The kettle was warm and the biscuits were plated up. It was an uncomfortable sensation, but she was beginning to feel more threatened by her husband's presence than by that of a part-time gardener who was twice her age and who seemed genuinely concerned for her and her daughters' safety.

At the first crunch of gravel on the driveway she flicked the switch on the kettle.

"Ben, would you like to come in and have a drink with me."

He didn't need asking twice.

"That's very good of you, ma'am."

"Biscuits...?"

"You're getting to know my ways, ma'am."

"Please, call me Mary. Take a seat. I've been thinking about our conversation on Wednesday and some of the things you hinted at."

"Oh aye, peeked your interest, have I?"

"Something like that, and I'm sorry if I was rude to you."

"I understand. Think nothing of it. You're in unfamiliar territory and there are police everywhere – you're bound to be a little tense."

"I've got two friends down in London who I'm sure would be interested in investigating your mother's notion of Derbyshire's own version of the Bermuda Triangle."

"It's not a notion – it's here all right, all around this place."

"Would you like them to dig into… whatever it is? They take on investigations for newspapers, solicitors, and even the police and private investigators. They're freelance researchers and if they uncover a meaty story they can make serious money. If there's a story there to be sold to a magazine or to the national newspapers, they'll reward you financially."

"I can't see the harm in them looking."

"Do you think you and your mother could compile a list of the missing women for me? You never know; my friends might even be able to locate one or two of them."

"I can give you a list right enough, but take my word for it; they won't find any of them. I can even name some of them now for you if you'd like?"

She nodded but was aware of the tremble in her hand as she poured out the tea, and the knot in her stomach as she picked up the pen and notepad that she'd put out ready.

"You know about Debbie Thomas, and you've seen the news that Faith Crispin's disappearance is now being linked to four others whose cases were believed to have been solved?"

She nodded again.

"And the two girls who went missing on the day of the mine explosion – I told you about those – Lilly Saunders and Betty Taylor? But you want to hear about the others, don't you?"

"I'm interested in anything you've got to tell me, either about the missing women or about Peter's family or this property."

"Then you might be better off with some sort of recording device than that notepad." He sounded serious. "I don't want to alarm you too much, so I'll tell you a bit about the missing women today, but then I must get these cabbage plants in before they start to wilt. Once they're in I'll cover them with fleece to protect them from the sun while they get established, and then all you'll have to do is keep them well watered."

He set down his half-empty mug and looked at it.

"Will you need another drink?"

"Yes please Mary; it's thirsty work out there this morning, and I must say that for a Londoner you make a fine cuppa."

What geography had to do with tea-making escaped her, but the man's odd ways were growing on her. She flicked the kettle back on.

"Now then," he began after noisily using his tongue to remove the remains of his third ginger biscuit from his back teeth, "I'll start with Dora Mathews because she's the one mother still occasionally talks about. She went missing sixty years ago this month. Mother was nineteen and recently married, and I was a baby, when Dora told my mother about some fantastic modelling job she'd been offered down in London. Dora's parents objected but were unable to stop her and so she packed a bag, called in to say cheerio to my mother, promising faithfully to let her know how she was getting along, and then caught the bus to Buxton to connect with a train to London. She was seen getting off the bus and walking across the car park, and that was the last anyone ever saw or heard of her. Her parents called for an investigation but because of her age and because she'd packed a bag, I don't think much was ever done. Mum still looks for the postman every morning, and still gets despondent when nothing arrives from her friend."

"Your mother sounds like a good woman."

"She is, and she helped in the searches back in the seventies, when two local girls went missing within a couple of months of each other. Margaret Williams was nineteen, and Tania Davies was eighteen. No trace was ever found of either of the girls. In the early eighties a sixteen year old went missing about ten miles from here and the police reopened all the old cases, but a month later her remains were found and a schoolteacher admitted to murdering her but not to knowing anything about the earlier abductions. People quickly forgot about all the others after that. Then in the early nineties a twenty year old from this side of Buxton packed her bags to go on holiday with a group of friends but never made it to the airport. Her name was Francis Pollock."

He reached for another biscuit and his second mug of tea and remained quiet for several minutes while Mary studied her list of names.

She broke the silence by reading out the names. "So let me check that I've got this right – Lilly and Betty went missing in the thirties, Dora in the fifties, Margaret and Tania in the seventies, Francis in the nineties, Zoe, Christine, Joanne and Lucy who've been in the news this week disappeared between 2002 and 2008, Faith less than two years ago, and now Debbie – a total of twelve women?"

"Those are the ones I know about. There could of course be others whose families thought they'd just left home and never bothered to get back in touch. Now don't you consider it strange that every single disappearance happened within a ten mile radius of this property?   You find me another similarly sized, sparsely populated area in Britain where so many young women have disappeared, without any trace of their remains ever being found, and I'll dig your garden from top to bottom for nothing."

"But they're decades apart. The same person can't be responsible for all the disappearances."

"I'm not suggesting that. In fact mother thinks young women were going missing from around here even before the day of the mine explosion. She just can't remember any names. You could try looking in the local newspaper archives; I believe they're available at the library. Now thanks for the tea but I really must be getting on with what you and your husband are paying me for."

"Thank you for talking so openly with me. I do have one more question, though.   When I was looking at the deeds for this property I noticed a familiar surname. The owner of the land to the north of us, the hillside behind this house, is a Mr Stephen Garratt. Is he any relation to the serial killer who's just died – Brian Garratt?"

"He's Brian's uncle, but he's a very nice chap. Brian's grandmother lived in Leaburn and had ten sons, so you'll find the name cropping up a lot. It goes without saying that he was the black sheep of the family. It's something the people around here don't want advertising. In fact you might find some of the locals turning against you if your London friends make a meal of it."

"I understand, and thanks for the warning, Ben."

She watched him slide his wellingtons on and then gently lift the box of plants. That had been one hell of a way to end a conversation – with yet another warning.

14

Debbie's fingernails were broken and torn, but she'd managed to loosen and then retighten every bolt and every wing-nut on the amateurishly-made bed. She picked up a rough stone and rubbed it across the worst of the jagged edges of each nail, one at a time. An image of Jessica's manicured fingers and beautifully understated engagement ring flashed into her mind. If her friends could see the state of her nails now they'd be appalled.

The hours were dragging, but at the same time she was running out of them. It was a terrifying feeling. To trust in his statements that he was intending to allow her to leave this place would be foolish. He was most likely going to do one of two things, and she had to be prepared for either eventuality. If he left her to rot she could, with difficulty, climb at least part of the way out, but if he intended to kill her she would need as many defensive weapons to hand as possible.

She now had two lengths of timber on the underside of the bed which could easily be removed, and with a wing-nut protruding from the business end of each one, they should, if needed, turn into effective weapons. And she would keep one torch on each of the tables.

It wouldn't be enough just to immobilise him. If she was lucky enough to get the upper hand she would be forced to kill him. She wouldn't normally harm a fly, but she'd spent so many hours imagining how good it would feel to be pummelling his face until it was nothing but a blood-soaked, spongy mess that she knew she wouldn't hesitate to use as much force as was necessary to finish him off.

She had to be a realist – it was more than likely that one of them was going to die down here.

If only she could persuade him to take a letter out...

...and here he comes again.

She kicked the stone under the bed and slipped the ring back onto her finger. How she'd love to ram his mother's ring past his flabby lips and down his throat before smashing those lips to oblivion.

"Good morning my beautiful fiancé," he beamed his sickly grin at her as he approached the bed.

She didn't move as he sat on the bed beside her and held out an already opened, family-sized bar of milk chocolate.

"I've brought this for us to share." He was looking at her ring finger.

"Thank you." Two of the chocolate squares were already missing. His grimy fingers had already touched something that she would normally have craved. The thought made her stomach heave.

"Have you missed me, my darling? I want you to be happy while we share this because I'm afraid that for our sixth day of courtship I have some distressing news. I've brought last night's local evening paper so you'll know I'm telling you the truth."

"It's not my parents...?"

"No sweetheart, it's not your parents. Now eat your chocolate and I want no more questions from you until it's gone."

Every piece stuck like glue to the roof of her mouth and then to her throat. But it was food – it was fuel for her body.

He took the final square for himself before unfurling the newspaper and handing it to her. For once she was finding it impossible to hold his gaze. The look of expectation in his eyes and the drugged, flabby-looking expression around his mouth was one that she hadn't seen before.

She checked the date because the headlines didn't make any sense. It was yesterday's – Friday's.

But there had to be a mistake – Wayne would never have killed himself. They hadn't been an item for long but she'd known him for years. She'd known his family for years; they were happy, outgoing, loving people.

"Wayne wouldn't..." Her breaths came in short gasps; there was a rushing noise in her ears.

"But you did say you two weren't serious, didn't you?" His voice filtered through to her.

"It's not..."

"It's a good thing really – for us. It means that you can forget about him and concentrate on our blossoming relationship."

She clenched her jaws and pushed the paper back at him. To lash out and sod the consequences was so, so tempting, and if he'd placed one stubby finger onto any part of her at that moment she probably would have done just that. But he didn't move and she concentrated on regaining control. The impulse moment passed.

"He must have been a weak young man, not the sort worthy of a girl like you."

"I can't believe he'd do that," she whispered. To raise her voice would mean losing her battle. "He loved his job. He wanted to find me. He wouldn't have done that."

"The newspaper says suicide. I knew you wouldn't believe me and that's why I brought it to show you. I wanted you to read the article for yourself. You mustn't get too upset, my darling.

How could that boy have made you happy when he couldn't cope with his own life? Surely you realise now that we're destined to be together. All his death means is that there is one more star in heaven, and when we're outside together at night we can look up into the clear sky and try to imagine which one is your friend."

His hand slid across her shoulder blades and cupped the top of her arm. She was being slowly pulled towards him. "Please... no... I've had a shock... I need a few moments... I still can't quite believe it... I can't believe that he'd..."

His eyes narrowed. She'd angered him, but in that moment of real physical pain she didn't care. Wayne was a lovely, gentle young man who she'd secretly hoped she might be spending the rest of her life with. She wished now that she'd expressed her feelings. But it was too late.

"You're a sensitive girl," he droned on into the side of her face, "and I like that about you. I can understand you need time to process this news, and to cheer you up I've decided to allow you to write to your parents." He reached into his bag and pulled out a pen and a notepad.

From desolation to elation; she didn't know whether to laugh or cry, and in the end did neither. She'd craved for this moment; she'd dreamed of it and she'd planned, but all the time without the luxury of any real hope.

Writing a letter wasn't the same as actually making contact with the outside world – there was no guarantee that anyone other than the two of them sitting on this rats-nest of a bed would ever see it and she had to remember that, and temper her hopes. But while there was the slightest chance of the letter getting out she had to at least be on her best behaviour and do nothing to make him change his mind. She needed to be able to anticipate anything which might create friction with the snake-man. She couldn't risk him changing his mind at the last moment.

The fact that it could just be another one of his sick games had to be pushed to the back of her mind.

Her hands shook as she took the pen and notepad from him. She rested them on the bedside table. "May I use my own words? Then my parents will know I'm not being forced to write this. They'll believe what they're reading – that I've met someone special."

"As long as I approve it, my darling, you may write whatever you wish, but you must make it a short letter. I can't stay with you for much longer."

There was a real chance that all he was doing was humouring her, but if there was the tiniest chance that the letter might reach her parents, or the police, then she had to make the most of it.

She'd planned so carefully for this moment.

For a few moments her brain refused to co-operate, but then the words flowed through her hands onto the paper.

To mater and pater,
Sorry for the untold bother I have caused but a whirlwind romance has swept me off my feet – all is well and we will see you both very soon – we are in a Very Unique and Lovely Place, made Extra Special by a wonderful person who will explain all when introductions are made. Please don't worry or search for us – love you both from the Bottom of my Heart – like dad would say – love is never in Vein,
your loving daughter, Debbie.

She watched him reading it, certain that if he looked up he would see her chest pounding from the inside.

"Mater and pater...?"

"Dad's father was a reverend and he used to tease me by speaking like that. Those are the pet names I have for my parents. No one else knows that, so they'll be sure the letter is from me."

"And you've misspelt the word vain. Are you trying to trick me?"

"No, of course not, let me correct it. Writing such a short note when I wanted to say so much to them was making me emotional. I just wrote what I felt. Please don't be angry."

"Why all the capital letters?"

"I've written that way for years. I like to emphasise the important words in a sentence. I read how an American songwriter always wrote that way and I copied his style."

"Yes, I like it. It tells me a little more about you. You care what people think of you and your ideas. You want your feelings to be fully understood. I don't like that you had to steal someone else's style, but I'll forgive you that one small indiscretion." He brushed her damp cheek with the back of his hand.

"Will you see that my parents get the letter… please?"

"I'm a man of my word, Debbie. You'll come to appreciate that fact during the many happy years we have ahead of us. By tomorrow you'll have recovered from the shock I was regrettably forced to give you. You'll be feeling better and I'll expect some proper physical contact from you in return for allowing this letter. That's how relationships are meant to work. Do you understand?"

"Yes." She was never going to have anything resembling a relationship with the man who she felt certain had killed her first boyfriend. She accepted his wet-fish kiss, watched him pick up the newspaper and walk away, and balled a tissue in the palm of her hand.

As Constrictor slithered away into the void she let her tears fall without bothering to wipe them away. He'd killed Wayne; young, vibrant, sensitive Wayne with his whole life to look forward to, and tomorrow, unless she'd been rescued by then, his visit to her was going to be even more depraved. She had approximately twenty-four hours to prepare.

She would do whatever was necessary for a chance to be in her parents' arms again – and for Wayne – for a chance to skin his killer or put him away for a very long time. What better reason could there ever be? She intended surviving long enough to make the bastard pay.

*

"This is the Saturday, six a.m. briefing of Operation Barley," Forbes began. "Two hours from now it will be exactly one week since Debbie Thomas was last seen." He was about to add the word *alive*, but the feeling, or maybe just the hope he was experiencing was that they weren't yet looking for a body. "The well-publicised reconstruction is due to begin at seven forty-five." He looked at the eager faces in the incident room. Off duty officers and specials swelled the usual numbers. "Tomorrow, in conjunction with Buxton station, a reconstruction of the time of Faith Crispin's disappearance is also due to take place. Alan has been liaising with officers from Buxton and both girls' disappearances are set to make front page news in the local papers and half-page articles in the nationals, with rewards being offered for any usable information. I expect you all to attend both reconstructions. Those of you who were meant to be off duty shouldn't find it too much of an inconvenience to spend a few hours in the areas where the girls were last seen. I want to hear of any local gossip surrounding either of the cases, and anything you might hear concerning the four newly reopened cases."

"Are we planning reconstructions for all of them?" DC Green asked.

"Possibly, but for now we concentrate on Debbie. She may still be out there, waiting to be found, and Faith's disappearance may hold vital clues to her abductor or her whereabouts. From today I'm linking the death of Wayne Soames to the on-going investigations of Operation Barley. Yesterday morning's post-mortem showed that Wayne had been struck on the head from behind by a piece of twenty-two millimetre copper piping, not hard enough to kill him, and possibly not even hard enough to knock him out, but probably hard enough to stun him. He had bruises consistent with a size ten boot being held against his shoulder blades, and bruises to his chest and his wrists where he'd struggled. In other words, he was stunned, tied up, and then held underwater until dead. We can ask the press to continue going along with the suicide theory for now but..."

"Sir, we've already lost that one." DC Jackson held up her phone. "I was checking Facebook for local gossip and found Wayne's friends posting comments about his death. They're connecting it with Debbie's disappearance, and they're no longer buying into the suicide story. They all believe he was murdered."

Forbes checked his watch and picked up his jacket. "Then we'd better all get moving."

*

The letter had been searing a hole in his pocket since he'd left his beautiful bride-to-be. If what she'd written was in fact the truth, then his life was about to change forever. He couldn't wait to get home to study it.

He wanted to believe every word she'd written but his many previous disappointments had trained him to be cautious. Had she put some sort of a clue in it? But then what did she actually know about where she was, or about who he really was? Was he was being over-cautious? She couldn't tell them anything because she didn't know anything. Even so, it would be good to put his mind at rest by studying it some more before posting it.

There was enough time. There was a collection from the village post box at eleven-thirty and he had a stamp ready.

Debbie would be so pleased with him when he told her that the letter was winging its way towards her home.

But first there was just enough time for a shower before strolling into the village for his Saturday morning's entertainment. He would be attending the reconstruction of the morning he and Debbie had begun their life together. Of course he couldn't go up onto the top road where he'd taken her from, and he couldn't show his face too early in case someone recalled seeing him up and about at that time of the morning last Saturday, but he could enter the paper shop at the same time as he had last week and soak up the atmosphere in the village.

He could privately revel in the sweet memory.

How incredible was that – how many people ever got to do anything even remotely like that? It was another omen that they were meant to be soul mates.

The police had been asking for everyone who'd been in or around the village last Saturday morning to return in similar clothing and in the same vehicles, and to retrace their steps as closely as they could. He'd gone to the village shop for his morning paper after he'd left Debbie asleep in the cave. His clothing wasn't a problem, nothing too distinctive; jeans with tee-shirt and a sweat shirt, but he couldn't risk arriving in the truck. A four mile, round-trip walk would be good exercise, and he needed to keep in shape now for his new fiancé.

He considered his options.

The police would be filming everything. They did that at reconstructions; he'd picked up that tip from watching the television. This morning wasn't really optional, his absence would be noticed, but tomorrow, if he went to Buxton at all, he'd wear something totally different and style his hair differently. And even then he'd do well to remain in the shadows. He also knew that the police used something called facial recognition software. They would be comparing faces from both events and looking for matches. Maybe he wouldn't go to Buxton after all. It was almost two years since he'd been there to collect Faith, so how likely was it that his absence would be noticed after that length of time?

He paused before unlocking his front door. No one was watching him – he wasn't being followed. Everything was going according to plan.

He flicked the kettle on and then sat at his kitchen table with a cold piece of toast and Debbie's letter in front of him.

The sequence of capital letters made no sense to him, no matter how long he'd stared at them. Maybe Debbie had been telling him the truth about her style of writing.

If he was to take part in the reconstruction and catch the post he couldn't spend too long studying her words. Satisfied that she wasn't tricking him after all, he picked up the envelope that he'd left on the table.

DNA was identifiable from saliva – everyone knew that. He wiped the envelope and letter to remove his finger prints, prepared it for posting using tap water, and then tucked it into his trouser pocket.

The main street looked exactly as it did most Saturdays; apart from the truck-sized Major Incident

Vehicle parked beside the old market house. The village wasn't packed with people as he'd expected. Even so, he hesitated before brushing the letter against his shirt to remove his prints once more, and allowing the precious letter to drop into the mail box. That there was no one near enough to him to see the envelope he was gripping with the cuff of his sleeve was an unexpected relief. But even if there had been – why would anyone take notice of an ordinary letter being posted in an ordinary post box?

It clattered to the bottom of the metal box with more noise than he'd thought possible from the small enclosed space. Horrified, he looked around, expecting to see net curtains twitching and of hordes of grey-haired old ladies peering out from behind them to see what all the noise was about. No curtains moved.

He casually walked into the village shop, just as he had done on the previous Saturday, in fact just as he had done once or twice every day of the week, every week of the year for as long as he could remember. The fridges and freezers buzzed. Other than that, and the young, fresh-faced girl cheerfully greeting him from behind the counter, the cluttered space was ominously silent. For once he didn't answer her straight away. The atmosphere seemed to be underlining how awkward he felt and he almost turned to leave, when a uniformed policeman suddenly stepped from behind the tinned goods shelving.

He had to push through these next few moments.

He had too much at stake to mess up.

15

He held out the correct money for his ordered newspaper and took the folded tabloid from the girl's hand with one fluid movement. He spoke one word, "Thank you," exactly as he'd done the previous week. That was part of his plan. He couldn't risk attracting attention by sending the shop worker scurrying off for change or entering into a conversation.

The officer was watching him.

A couple with a small child entered the shop and he focused on their meaningless chatter. *"Are you sure that we came here at exactly this time last week, honey?" "Yes, I'm sure. I remember seeing that man over there." "Oh yes, I think you're right."*

They smiled and nodded at him – the morons. He remembered exactly where everyone had been walking or standing that morning – that wonderfully exhilarating morning which would be burned into his brain with more permanence and more security than any computer could ever have hoped to achieve on any modern disc or memory stick.

Who would have played the part of Debbie this morning? All the policewomen he'd seen were too old to carry off an effective impersonation of a teenager. Maybe one of Debbie's friends, or maybe a policewoman's daughter would be playing the part. Whoever it was, they would never be able to match his Debbie for beauty and innocence.

Some of the holidaymakers had travelled hundreds of miles to take part, so he'd heard, so he'd been right to come. He would have been missed, and his uncollected newspaper would have drawn attention to him.

He couldn't help hesitating in the doorway, closing his eyes for a second, and picturing Debbie in her summer dress.

"Excuse me, sir..."

The policeman was blocking his exit from the shop.

He'd expected to be interviewed. Everything was cool. He was ready.

He took a deep breath and smiled at the young, serious face.

"Step to the side of the doorway a moment, please. Your name is...?"

"Richard... Richard Meadows... how can I help, officer?"

"Would you confirm how you arrived here today?"

"I arrived on foot, the same as I did last Saturday. I enjoy a walk on a summer's morning." He looked down at his knuckles – they were white. He needed to slacken his grip on the newspaper while the constable was writing.

"Were you here at the same time last Saturday?"

"I believe so, yes," he was back in control. "Give or take a minute or two."

"And last week did you go anywhere else in the village?"

More questions; he should have been better prepared. His plan had simply been to listen to the questions being put to the other customers. Then when the police got to him he would have been ready with his answers. He tried to filter out the distraction of the family at the counter. "No, when I left I walked back home."

"Do you know the missing girl?"

"No… that is… I've seen her around… I know of her… I didn't see her last Saturday."

"Do you own a vehicle, sir?"

"Err… no… and my walk home takes me in the opposite direction from where she lives."

"Thank you, sir…"

"I'm sorry I can't be of more help."

Just piss off you stupid copper… go and bother those other people.

The corner of the newspaper came away in his hand and he quickly stuffed the stray piece into his pocket.

"… and your address is, sir?"

"Edgefold Cottage; it's a tied cottage belonging to the farmer I work for." Two men walked past him, out of the shop. He hadn't seen them come in. The older one was tall, middle-aged and with an air of self-confidence about him. The other was younger, smartly dressed, and with more of a natural suntan than his older companion. Why wasn't this bloody copper talking to them?

"Does anyone live with you?"

"No, I've lived alone since my mother died." They would be checking up on him, but let them. He could fool them easily enough until his relationship with Debbie was rock solid – or at least solid enough to withstand the attention they could expect to receive when they finally came out of hiding together.

"Just one more line of questioning, sir, and then I'll let you finish your morning in peace." The young, uniformed policeman was looking right through him, into his soul and beyond.

He returned the steady gaze but felt beads of perspiration forming on his brow. Would it draw attention to them if he wiped them off? Yes, it probably would.

Stand still you fool.

"Anything I can do to help, officer."

"A local youth named Wayne Soames has been coming into this village several times a week for the last few years. Would you be familiar with him?"

A picture of a smiling Wayne appeared in front of him, inches from his face. "Err... I may have seen him on occasions. I didn't know him. Is this the youth who killed himself?"

"Can you recall when and where you last saw him, sir?"

"Err... I'm not sure. Weeks ago probably... I don't know."

His own sweat was betraying him – big-time. Those tiny beads were amalgamating into larger globules, one of which was slowly tracking its way down past his left eye. He blinked but the tell-tale droplet continued its steady, downward path. "Why are you asking me about him?"

He shouldn't have added that last question.

"You hadn't noticed him with Debbie on any previous occasions then; only the two of them had apparently been dating for a couple of weeks?"

"A couple of weeks...?"

"That's what we've been told, sir."

"Err... I don't know what you're asking. The boy's dead, isn't he. He killed himself... he killed Debbie and then killed himself. Isn't that what this reconstruction is about – to find out exactly what he did, and when?"

"What makes you say that, sir?"

"That's what the folks in the village shop were saying yesterday morning."

"Do you come into the village often? Can you recall anything else you've heard said about the couple?"

"Err… about… I don't go… well I do… most days… no, I don't know anything. I don't listen to gossip. I came here today to help, but I can't."

"Thank you, that's all for now. We'll be in touch if we need to speak to you again." The officer began scribbling something down in his notepad and then sauntered towards to the counter.

The noisy family had left the shop without him noticing. They were on the pavement. Someone else was questioning them.

He turned back to the counter – his officer was talking to the girl. Was he asking about him?

Two women walked through the shop doorway.

They were looking at him. Why would they be looking at him, and not at the policeman?

He leaned on the doorframe.

Now the stupid constable was moving, heading for the door, going outside, straight past him – why would he be doing that? Why not just move on to the next person?

He stepped outside. The sunlight was dazzling him, making him lean on the external doorframe before permitting him to focus on anything that was happening on the pavement.

Keep calm.

The mist cleared.

His constable was talking to the two men who'd left the shop a minute earlier. That was it... the officer just wanted to interview the two that he'd missed. Everything was all right.

He hugged the paper to his chest.

"Wayne Soames was murdered, didn't you know?" The woman suddenly standing beside of him was leaning conspiratorially towards him. "That's what everyone's saying now. He was murdered by whoever took Debbie. Wayne must have found her and been killed for his trouble. That's what the police are thinking. Dead or alive, Debbie's somewhere close by." She nodded as though she'd imparted a state secret and then straightened up and took a large bite of what looked like a slice of chewy flapjack.

He needed a drink. He stumbled back into the shop, picked up the nearest can without reading the label and fumbled for change while he waited to pay.

Back on the pavement he drank half the contents in a series of long, deep gulps, pausing only once to belch. Only after another belch did he began to feel slightly better.

They were never going to find her.

*

At three-thirty the sky to the east was glowing in anticipation of another hot day and DCI Forbes was arriving home. Alison wasn't exactly waiting up for him with open arms, but she had left the hallway light and the landing light on, and had fallen asleep with an open book on the duvet, and with her bedside lamp casting a soft glow over the room.

"There's a sandwich in the fridge if you want it," she mumbled without opening her eyes. "Oh, and did you manage to jog anyone's memory?"

It was approaching twenty-four hours since he'd left the house and her response to his late arrival was better than he'd expected. He observed a moment of silence before closing her book and placing it on the bedside table. After spending a large part of his day in the company of the public, most of whom had been eager to help, the sound of Alison's soft breathing was bliss.

He'd asked the people taking part in the reconstruction to come dressed as they had been last Saturday and everyone had responded incredibly well, although he suspected that some of the women had applied an extra layer of make-up for the cameras.

He looked at Alison and remembered that he'd never, ever seen her in make-up, not even when they'd attended formal gatherings together. Her face looked almost the same when she was half-asleep as it did when she was preparing for a press conference or any other important event. Only the occasional jar of face cream and tube of tinted lip balm had ever sat alongside his aftershave in the bathroom cabinet. For a few seconds he studied her relaxed features and wondered whether she would even wear any make-up on the day of her wedding. Probably not, in fact he doubted that she had ever even owned any.

She would choose her outfit for that day with great care, she'd always been a smart dresser, and she would select one of her many friends to help with her long, thick, dark hair, but that was as far as her vanity would permit her to go. "You romantic old fool," he muttered, "but we've been living this way for far too long now. She's never going to agree."

"Hmm… what's that… who's agreed to what? Has there been some progress in the case?"

"Nothing concrete," he slid his shoes under the bed and placed the bed cover over her bare arm, "but we may have a new line of enquiry. I'll tell you all about it in the morning."

She pushed the cover away, pulled herself into a sitting position and scanned the crumpled duvet.

"I've put your book over there. And I suppose that now you're awake you won't allow me to sleep until I've explained."

Smiling mischievously and nodding, she patted his pillow. "I can watch you undress as you tell me."

He knelt on the bed and reached across her to adjust the touch-lamp to an even lower setting. His face was inches from hers and their eyes met.

"You romantic old fool," she laughed.

Her remark caught him off guard. "Would you believe me if I told you that those were exact words I was muttering to myself a minute ago, just as you were waking?"

"Not for one second." She was laughing again. "Now get undressed and give me the low-down on your day."

"The reconstruction went well enough. It helped that it was a fine and sunny morning, just like last Saturday. We think that everyone turned up who was in and around the village that morning, and there were several more onlookers milling around on the road."

"I suppose that's only to be expected. People are curious, or they want to help if they can. Have you got them all on film?"

"Of course, and we've been comparing the footage to the statements taken throughout the week."

"So what's the new angle?"

"Throughout the morning uniformed officers were having informal chats with people out and about in the village. PC Windsor noted an exaggerated and agitated reaction from a middle-aged man who entered the shop for his morning newspaper."

"Shy people often act nervously around authority figures. We all know that."

"Yes but it was some of the things he said, as well as his mannerisms, which alerted the constable. After the conversation, PC Windsor asked the girl behind the counter if she could confirm the man's name and address. She could, but she also remarked that last Saturday and this Saturday were the latest she could recall the man ever having arrived for his paper. He was normally one of her first few customers of the day, a routine that he'd followed for years, apparently. She'd thought it was odd."

"Did PC Windsor question the man about why he was later than normal collecting his paper? There might have been a perfectly simple explanation."

"No he didn't. He's an experienced, fast-thinking officer who knows better than to put pressure on a potential suspect while there's still a chance that Debbie is alive."

"So what happens now?"

"We have him under surveillance. The suspect lives alone at the top of quite a long dead-end track and we've got someone watching his house from a distance overnight. We need to find out as much as we can, as fast as we can, about this man, but we want to do it without alerting or panicking him. If he is holding Debbie we don't want him to run. Also, if he's responsible for the death of Wayne Soames, then killing in cold blood isn't alien to him. But right now, sweetheart, I need to grab three or four hours of sleep." He slid into the bed and felt Alison's body move towards him. His eyes automatically closed as his head hit the soft pillow.

"All right, hint taken, I guess the romance will have to go on hold for now. But before you fall asleep, what was it you were saying when you first came into the bedroom? Who was never going to agree to what?"

"Oh it was only something to do with a questioning technique. Don't worry; it will sort itself out. Goodnight and sweet dreams."

16

What Forbes hadn't told Alison, in the early hours of the morning, was that he had authorised Adam and two other plain-clothed officers to take a cursory look over the cottage occupied by Richard Meadows while the man was being kept under surveillance at the farm he apparently worked at. They'd returned after an hour to tell him they'd found nothing to suggest that Debbie might be being held there. Now he was eager to hear their full reports.

"We gained access through the kitchen window," Adam switched on his mobile phone and glanced at it. "A sash window was propped open with a small block of wood, and you'd said that if we could gain entry without damaging anything then we were to do so."

"With a young life possibly at stake, we're justified in breaking a few rules."

"The cottage is a typical two-up and two-down farm labourer's residence. It's sparsely furnished but quite tidy. He sleeps in a double bed, but then a lot of single people do. The attic was empty, we found no indication of a cellar and we didn't disturb anything. It helped us that it was so isolated, but if he is the kidnapper then that will also work in his favour. We checked the garden shed and the garage and we shouted Debbie's name, but we didn't find anything to suggest that she, or any other woman, had been there lately."

"And you left everything as you found it?"

"Yes sir and the only things we took were our own photographs." Adam was sounding cautiously optimistic. He held out his phone. "I've not uploaded them yet. After going in without a warrant I wasn't sure you'd want them as part of the official records."

"That will depend on whether or not Richard Meadows is our kidnapper."

"If you look at the bedroom photos, I think you'll agree that Meadows has an odd taste in reading matter."

"Mills and Boon novels... how many are there... six?" Adam was right, that was odd for a farmhand.

"Yes sir, romance novels usually aimed at the ladies, and not the sort of thing a middle-aged man would want to be seen reading."

"Did they appear to be well-read copies?"

"They were all purchased from a charity shop in Matlock for the princely sum of twenty pence each. The stickers were still on the backs of them, and were dated within the last four months. I believe the shops date them when they go out on sale so they can rotate their stock."

"Were there any other books or electronic reading devices in the house?"

"I noticed a bible and a dictionary in a cupboard, and a microwave cookbook in a kitchen drawer. We know that he took a national daily paper each day, but there were only three in his living room. He walked to work carrying yesterday's edition. He also took the local evening paper every night because his name was written on the top of the six copies in the living room. I did notice that Monday's, Wednesday's and Friday's editions of this week's evening papers were missing. I've just checked with the publisher and Monday's was the one covering the interview with Wayne, Wednesday's had a picture of Debbie's parents on the front page, and Friday's edition featured the discovery of Wayne's body. The village newsagent has confirmed that all ordered copies were collected on those afternoons. Sunday's Monday's and Thursday's editions of the national newspapers were missing but I haven't found anything of relevance in any of those."

He felt the same surge of optimism that Adam had obviously experienced. "I wonder... did he take it to Debbie to torment her, or to threaten her, or punish her? If that is the case it means that she's still alive."

"Yes but where is he keeping her, sir? She can't be too far from here."

"Who's watching him this morning?"

"PC Rawlings is there now. The suspect owns about eighty acres of rough grazing land, extending up into the hillside, with large areas of it covered by rocks and gorse bushes, and one large cattle shed with about thirty calves in it. We searched the area when Debbie went missing, but DI Lang is over there now waiting to go over the grounds with a cadaver dog and its handler, just as soon as Meadows leaves. He goes there every morning to feed the calves, apparently. We're hoping that she's still alive but we have to accept that we might be looking for a body by now."

"He hasn't got a car, has he?"

"No sir, but it's only a short walk across two fields to the farm he's employed at. I don't suppose he needs one."

"Check whether he's got a driving license. He might be borrowing a vehicle or have an unregistered one stashed away somewhere."

"Yes sir. We've already run his name through the police national computer but nothing was flagged up."

"Didn't it strike you as odd, just how easily you gained access into his home yesterday?"

"Yes sir, we all felt that. It was almost as if he was inviting us in."

"Let's pay his employer a visit. We'll say that we're rechecking every outlying property in the area, and while we're there we'll find out as much as we can about Mr Meadows."

*

Of all of the picnics she'd prepared, on bright sunny mornings, Mary Stone was finding this one the most difficult. If she'd had her way she would have been taking her girls to a safe, public, well-maintained local park somewhere in London, but that wasn't her real problem. Her new-found ambition of settling into country life was disintegrating almost before she'd had time to act on it, and she was struggling to keep her emotions under control, especially in front of the children. The girls were excited and Zelda was infected with their enthusiasm, alternately dashing off to play with them and returning to the safety of the kitchen, and Mary's legs. All three of them trusted her to keep them safe.

Trust was an emotion she was feeling less and less familiar with. Peter had gone out for a drink last night, as had been his habit one night a week since they'd been together, but last night he'd been unusually late home – it had been almost midnight.

When he did arrive home she'd pretended to be asleep. And when she did eventually nod off she'd fallen into a series of disturbing dreams involving waves of young women wandering around the garden, all in their night cloths, and all looking for an entry key to Dale End Farmhouse. Alone in the house, she'd rushed to the doors only to find the bolts crumbling in her hands. She'd cried out and woken with a start.

It had been barely light but Peter had been dressed and about to leave the bedroom.

"I've got an appointment with a potential private client who wants to see me before he sets off on holiday later today," he'd told her. "It's with someone I met last night. You were asleep when I came in so I was going to write a note this morning and try to leave without disturbing you. I'll only be a couple of hours."

He'd spent more hours away from the house than in it during the past few days. His 'couple of hours' would no doubt become four or five and he would arrive home with another plausible excuse.

But that was it — they were plausible excuses, so why was she getting so hung up about it?

The answer was simple. Debbie had vanished the morning they'd arrived in the area, and there was one far more distressing question that she couldn't get out of her mind.

Were young women being abducted to order?

She'd listened to him creeping down the stairs and then filling the kettle.

He'd taken his phone downstairs with him, and his laptop and jacket would be where he always left them at night, in the hallway. For the first time since they'd been together she wanted to check through his pockets and take a look at his phone, but then realised he might have both his phone and laptop password protected. Then again he might not – never having even considered checking up on him before she'd no idea.

Two minutes after the kettle clicked off he'd returned to the bedroom with her mug of tea. "The girls are both still asleep and Zelda looks reluctant to move from her bed. Don't get up. I'll be home as soon as I can."

Two more minutes had passed before the front door had clicked shut and she'd jumped out of bed and padded across to the window, being careful to remain hidden by the curtain. The need to see him driving up the steep slope towards the road had been too strong to ignore.

She blinked; jolted back to the present. Hannah was walking through the kitchen doorway.

"Mummy, mummy, are we going yet." The cheese crumbled, her knife slipped, and blood spurted onto the chopping board.

"Mum, put your hand under the cold tap, quick… quick." Amy pushed past her sister and tugged at her mother's arm.

"Sorry mummy," Hannah's red face crinkled.

"It wasn't your fault, sweetheart, mummy was daydreaming." It took a supreme effort not to flinch as the cold water bounced off her injured finger and swirled blood around the white, enamelled sink. "I wasn't being careful enough."

"But it's bleeding so much..."

"It's good for a cut to bleed. It's just my body washing out any germs before it heals itself back up. Look, it's almost stopped now. I'll put a plaster on it and then we'll finish off the picnic together."

"I don't want any cheese," Hannah pouted.

It took the three of them almost half an hour to reach the top of the lane, mainly due to Hannah's need to examine every insect and every bug which had the misfortune to cross her path. "Who's going to be the first to spot the footpath sign and the stile?" Mary tried to encourage them along. For the first time in her life she'd bought an Ordinance Survey map and was hoping to follow a footpath. She'd planned quite a long hike, but they'd got all day and the weather was in their favour – not quite as hot as the previous few days, but fine and dry.

"There it is look, mum," Amy yelled. "There's the sign, and the path goes straight through that field full of sheep."

"Mum, look," Hannah added as she peered through the narrow gap in the granite stile, her eyes still glued to the ground, "it's just like the poop from Katie's rabbit, only it's absolutely everywhere."

Two sheep-filled fields later the girls had developed several games, all based around missing the sheep droppings, and the further they walked from the farmhouse the more relaxed she was feeling. The suspicion and subsequent guilt had been pushed to the back of her mind, but only temporarily. Until she could be certain that Peter was in no way involved in Debbie's abduction, those emotions would only ever be at the end of a short fuse on a slow burn.

Peter's life revolved around technology and she couldn't risk him stumbling on her suspicions. She'd bought a new phone and set up a new e-mail account, consciously acknowledging when she'd paid for the phone that her marriage would be in tatters if he discovered it.

After e-mailing Dorothy and Claire with everything she knew about Derbyshire's own 'Bermuda Triangle', her nerve had held and she'd sent a second message asking them to check on Ben Allsop and her husband, as well as on her husband's family.

The girls were ahead of her and Zelda was pulling on the lead. She wasn't too tempted to check her in-box every few minutes.

They had been uncomfortable minutes when she'd been putting her fears into written words, but her options were limited. Arming herself with information was the only way she could see of being able to move forward and seriously consider settling with her girls at Dale End – and asking for outside help seemed her best way of getting it.

She dragged her thoughts back to her little family.

"When we get into the next field," she told Amy, "we should meet a well-known track known as the Limestone Way. Can you see it yet?"

Amy ran to the next stile and helped Hannah to clamber through it. "No sheep in this field, mum, but no track either. There's a path where lots of people have walked. Our path meets it so I think that could be what we're looking for. I think I've found it."

"Found what?" Hannah puffed.

"The Limestone Way," Amy lectured her sister. "That's the famous path we need to follow. Come on slowcoach; this way."

"Wait a minute girls; let's stand here a while and take in the view. Can you see that grand property down there, right in the centre of the valley?"

After a few minutes of concentrated peering and pointing, both girls nodded. "That's Chatsworth House where a Duke and a Duchess live, and it's surrounded by parkland where sheep graze alongside herds of deer. There's an enormous fountain worked only by gravity, and a river for children to paddle in. One day when Peter's not too busy we'll all go there for a nice walk," she almost added – *just as long as I'm wrong and we're still living here when that day comes,* but instead she looked into four sparkling eyes and silently prayed that she wasn't offering false dreams.

"Come on mum," Hannah tugged at her hand and Zelda whined with excitement. "Look at that funny gate. Only one person can get through it; why?"

"It's made that way so that people can get from one field to the next, but the sheep can't."

"That's daft." Hannah stood like a tiny, angry old woman, with her fists wedged firmly into her sides. "The walls on both sides of the gate have fallen down. The sheep can just walk over them."

Her youngest daughter was right. The walls had fallen into disrepair many years earlier. "I expect the gate's been here an awful long time, and now the farmer allows his animals to graze both fields at the same time."

The next obstacle the girls reached fitted her mental picture of what a stile should look like – two granite posts with the gap between them not even wide enough to allow a lamb to clamber through. Zelda and Hannah would both have to be lifted over. Amy just managed to lever herself through and was pretending to pull her sister through the impossible gap.

"Your tummy's too big, Hannah," Amy giggled.

Mary joined in the game, pretending to pull her youngest daughter back through the stile while Amy tugged from the opposite side, thankful that no one was around to see them as Hannah pretended to scream for mercy. At her side, Zelda whined in excitement and just for a minute her stomach felt less knotted. The three who depended on her the most were her buffer between what was going on inside her head, and reality. For the first time since leaving London she laughed until her sides hurt.

Hannah finally accepted the inevitable and agreed to be lifted over. Then Mary scooped Zelda into her arms and followed her girls into the next field. It was strewn with rocks and gorse bushes, but devoid of farm livestock and so she decided to take a chance. "I think this field is safe enough to let Zelda have a few minutes of freedom." She bent down and unclipped the lead.

She was following the girls along the winding, rocky path, fighting the urge to check her new phone, when Amy shouted.

"Mummy, mum, yuck... Zelda's found something really stinky over there, near those bushes. She's digging in something and we can smell it from here."

*

It was Sunday morning – his turn to do the shift that no one ever wanted to do, but at this time of the year as long as he showed his face for an hour or two to check on the cattle, it didn't matter what time he clocked on. There were no more calves due to be born until the autumn and the cows were all healthy. He deserved a lie-in. Debbie would understand why he was late once he'd explained to her how hard he'd had to work yesterday to keep their relationship a secret.

His own sweat had been the only thing to let him down, but he was confident that he was one step ahead of the police. From the thin layer of dust he'd deliberately left on the kitchen windowsill, he now knew that he was a suspect. Forewarned is forearmed, as his father used to say.

He knew that two people, possibly even three, had been inside his home while he'd been at work yesterday afternoon, but there was nothing to be concerned about. There was nothing even remotely incriminating in his house. Debbie's handbag and clothes were all in the caves, and a few days from now, with her at his side as his willing partner, there wouldn't be anything that they could charge him with.

Not that he had lied to Debbie – he had written a letter explaining where she could be found; he just hadn't told her that yesterday he'd burnt it, along with every newspaper that she'd touched, just in case his things should be fingerprinted. In a few days from now it wouldn't matter anyway. She would either be in his home, which the police had already checked, or she would be another failure. He'd been praylng for the former, rather than the latter.

He really felt that she was coming round to his way of thinking. Yesterday, after he'd allowed her to write that letter, she'd smiled at him, and she no longer looked close to tears and fearful when he approached her.

They absolutely could be soul mates.

Once she'd passed all his tests and they'd announced their love to the world, the police would look like fools.

The time was fast approaching for the final test, and after that there would be no going back for either of them.

17

The painted, cow-shaped sign, where the gravelled road met the tarmac, read Edgefold Farm, Proctor and sons. Forbes eased his Mercedes onto the rougher surface. The hedges were neatly trimmed and the grass down the centre of the lane had been cut very recently.

He couldn't remember ever seeing such a tidy-looking farmyard.

Richard Meadows hadn't left his cottage yet, but both Forbes and Adam checked that their phones were in their pockets before stepping from the car. The surveillance team were to warn them if Meadows was heading towards his place of work. Suckler cows and their respective calves were contentedly grazing in the surrounding fields, and there was a smell of newly-made silage in the air. No dogs came rushing out to greet them; instead a tall, middle-aged man poked his head out of one of the sheds and then strode out towards them with long, bounding strides.

"Mr Thomas Proctor?" Forbes held out his ID, "DCI Forbes and DS Ross; could we have an informal chat with you?"

"Come on up to the house," Mr Proctor's booming voice matched his enormous frame and his loping stride. "I was about to go in for a coffee. What's this about? You've searched my land already – not that I mind, of course. I know Debbie and her family and it's terrifying to think of what might have happened to her." He was ducking through the doorway into his kitchen before he'd finished speaking.

"We're double-checking a few localities." Forbes glanced around the typical farmhouse kitchen. At the heart of the room was a large range, and on one of the worktops, leaflets and papers were piled high. "How many people do you employ here, Mr Proctor, and what can you tell us about them?"

"Take a seat both of you. You'll stay for a drink, won't you?"

"Thank you, but we haven't time."

"No, of course not, I'll get straight to the point for you. I've one part-timer, Ben Allsop, who only comes when I need an extra pair of hands; with the silage or the shed cleaning, or the TB testing. He's doing some gap work for me at the moment as it happens – he's handy with the dry stone walls. Then I've two full-time employees: Richard Meadows and

Anthony Carter.   Richard's worked for me since leaving school, and his cottage up there on the hillside comes with the job. His father worked for my father and Richard was born up there, quite literally, his mother never attended a hospital, so I was told. Richard's a bit of a loner, a bit odd, always skulking around as though he's angry at the world, but he's a good all round worker and he's especially good with the livestock. He'll turn up at all hours of the night when we're in the middle of the calving. Anthony's worked for me for about twelve years now. He lives in the village with his wife and two young daughters. He's very anxious that you find whoever has taken Debbie, even more so since you've linked her abduction to those historic cases. Anthony's more of a mechanic, anything that breaks down, he can fix. He's a first class welder and he can turn his hand to a bit of basic plumbing. He's a good man to have around and I'd trust him with my life."

"Richard was in the village on the morning that Debbie went missing, and he attended the reconstruction yesterday. What can you tell us about him?"

"He had a difficult childhood. His mother suffered terribly with her health. She had bad nerves, and some sort of muscle-wasting disease, I believe. Very few people ever saw her and she eventually went into a home somewhere and passed away soon after. His father was a surly bugger, and my father only kept him on because of his sick wife.

Maybe that's where Richard gets his odd behaviour from."

"Can you be more specific?"

"I just meant that he doesn't mix with people. I don't think anyone ever had much time for Richard when he was growing up so nowadays he prefers his own company. He goes to the Nag's Head occasionally, and he goes to the village shop once or twice every day, but he rarely ventures much further than that. He inherited some fields and a reasonably-sized barn up on the edge of the moor, so he has some calves of his own and spends an hour or so up there every day. I saw your people searching there the day after Debbie went missing. It's his half day today, so he'll be here in an hour or two just to check on the cows. Right now he'll either be at home or with his own livestock, but you're welcome to go up to his cottage to talk to him if you need to."

Forbes didn't say that he'd known the exactly location of the man since midday yesterday. "No, that won't be necessary thanks; it's just a routine enquiry at the moment so there's no need to tell him we've been asking about him."

"I understand."

"We saw that he has a licence but doesn't own a vehicle. Does he ever borrow any of yours?"

"He sometimes uses that navy pick-up over there. I allow him the use of it as a perk of the job. My wife and I each have our own car. And of course he's got his own tractor and loader for feeding his cattle."

"Have you ever owned a white van of any description?" Adam asked.

"Until about eighteen months ago, yes we did, and Richard often borrowed that one too." The farmer's brow furrowed slightly. The penny was beginning to drop.

"Do you remember the morning that Debbie was taken – did Richard have the pick-up that day?"

"Yes, he had it for a couple of days at the end of that week, including Saturday."

"When did he return it, can you remember?"

"He came to work in it on the Saturday morning, but he was later than normal. And he's used it since then. I think it was Wednesday last week when he borrowed it, and Friday morning when he returned it. Can you tell me what this is about? Why do you want to know about our vehicles?" Forbes could see the unease increasing in the farmer's eyes. Wayne's body had been discovered on Thursday and Mr Proctor was remembering that.

"Just one more thing – do you know whether Richard has ever had a partner, of either sex?"

"Not that I'm aware of, no."

"Mr Proctor, we're going to have to seize that pick-up, but while there's a slim chance that Debbie is still alive I don't want anyone other than you to realise that. If we arrange for a recovery vehicle to collect it and deliver it to our forensics team, could you tell anyone who asks that it developed a fuel leak, or something else equally believable, and that it had to be towed to the garage?"

"I can do that. I'll phone Richard and tell him he isn't needed today. I don't think I could look him in the eyes if I saw him."

"No, we'd rather you didn't do anything out of the ordinary. We'll organise a vehicle to be standing by if you'll phone us when Meadows leaves your property after doing what he's paid to do."

"I understand." The man's face was grey.

"Hopefully this will be settled one way or the other before much longer. And thank you for your co-operation, and your discretion."

*

With Zelda back on her lead, at arm's length to avoid getting the stench of what she thought must be foxes onto her trousers, Mary pasted a smile onto her face and continued on with the walk. She didn't know an awful lot about the countryside, but a stinking mound of earth at the entrance to a hole in the ground, surrounded by gnawed bones and various animal limbs suggested foxes to her.

Thank goodness she'd brought wet wipes and sanitizing gel.

Since that unwelcome discovery, half of the sandwiches and all of the cakes and drinks had been devoured and the three of them had re-joined the road back down into the village.

They fell into line on the narrow pavement and as they did so a vehicle pulled up alongside them. The smart move would have been to keep on walking, but Hannah stopped, looked into the vehicle, and smiled at the occupants.

"Do you want a lift, Mrs Stone?" Ben Allsop was shouting from the passenger seat. "There's room for you all in the back."

Both girls' eyes were pleading with her to accept. "Thank you, we would if Zelda didn't absolutely reek. We think she found a fox's lair in the gorse bushes on the hillside. I'm surprised you can't smell her from there."

"Aye, now you come to mention it, we can." Ben said. "Even the rural foxes are moving closer to the villages and farmhouses now in search of an easy meal. That's because there aren't enough rabbits around these days. Too many folks with no idea of how to manage the countryside have been shooting and gassing them. And because of that the foxes are decimating our ground nesting bird populations. It's all right giving protection to the creatures at the top of the food chain, but when there are too many predators and not enough prey, everything suffers…"

"All right Ben," the driver of the Subaru butted in. "The lady doesn't need one of your lectures. I'm sure she'll settle in to our country ways soon enough without any help from your soapbox. I'm Tom Proctor, by the way, and I live at Edgefold Farm, about three miles from your property. Ben's been doing a spot of dry stone walling for me and I'm just taking him home. I'll no doubt see you around."

Mary nodded and then watched the truck drive away.

Peter would probably be at home waiting for them by now. She was feeling less calm by the second. Mr Proctor was obviously an affluent local farmer who trusted Ben Allsop. Their obvious, easy relationship had been as good as sign lighting up saying – *Mary you can trust this white-haired man.*

*

Debbie Thomas had finally given in to boredom and begun reading the books Mr Constrictor had left. But Black Beauty reminded her of the open fields and hills around her home, and Little Women reminded her of her own bedroom and the hours she'd spent trying out combinations of outfits and hairstyles. As a means of taking her mind off the mess she was in, the books were worse than useless. She'd decided that the noises she kept hearing must be from the local foxes in their lairs, despite sometimes sounding spookily like the cries of a woman, and that being so far underground was distorting the sounds.

This was his day seven, and three days from now she was likely to be either a free woman, or a dead woman. This was her personal, alternative version of the run-up to Christmas, just like when the shops displayed posters telling harassed shoppers of how many sleeps remained until the big day. She had two sleeps left.

The odds were stacked against there being more than two sleeps left for one of them.

Mr Boa Constrictor was slithering down the ladder. He was late.

"Debbie, my beautiful fiancée, I'm so sorry to have kept you waiting. I couldn't get to see you quite so early this morning, and I can't stay for long. I hope you won't mind too much." His shoulders slumped as he walked towards her. "I mind – I hadn't intended it to be like this. I'd wanted us to spend more time together this weekend, to get to know each other properly, but so many people are still out there looking for you. We have to be careful a little while longer, my darling."

"My parents won't stop looking for me. Did you post my letter?"

"My, my, we are inquisitive today, aren't we? Yes, my angel, I posted it on Saturday. It should arrive with your loving parents on Tuesday morning. That's significant, don't you think?"

"I don't…"

"Tuesday – day nine, the ultimate day of our courtship, when you'll be taking my final test and be one day away from the moment of us entering into the world together as a couple. Your letter will act as an introduction. That's what's significant about it, my darling. Don't you want to know why I'm so late today?"

"I thought you said it was because of people searching."

"Yes, yes, that as well, but mainly it was because I had such a late night last night. I was celebrating at home, you see, because I was too excited to sleep. The police had organised a reconstruction of the morning we met, so of course I had to go. But I was good. I fooled them all. They asked questions, but I fooled them. Aren't you pleased that I fooled them, my Debbie, my angel?"

"Yes..." *His angel* – that would be funny if it wasn't so sick. If she did ever manage to overpower him he'd discover that she was his nemesis, his hell on earth, his worst nightmare come true, in fact anything but his angel.

"I knew you would be." He either didn't notice or was ignoring her silence. "Now read from the front page of today's newspaper for me."

She did as he asked. It was a national newspaper, thankfully without any mention of her or Wayne on the front page. Maybe they were mentioned inside – she didn't wish to know.

"That was good, Debbie; now, for the seventh day of our courtship I want you to remove all but your bra and panties, and then lie on the bed with me. I'm burning with desire to caress your body. I want to feel the softness of your throat, the firmness of your breasts, and then the moisture of that special spot between your legs. I want to savour the taste of you, and the feel of your body yielding itself to me, and I want to see that soft smile forming on your lips, just for me. I want to believe that, like me, you can hardly wait for our full bodily union when it finally happens next week."

She felt repulsed, but at the same time pathetic. Turning her back to him and undressing quickly was the only form of protest open to her. At least he wasn't talking as though he was about to rape her.

She imagined being with her friends, laughing and chatting, walking through the streets of Chesterfield and looking into shop windows for new dresses to try on before heading towards a favourite coffee shop for a drink and a cream bun.

For once her imagination had blocked him out too well. As her dress fell to the dusty floor a rough hand landed on the back of her neck. Her body was pulled backwards, off balance, and his cool flesh pressed against hers.

Behind her he'd removed his trousers, sweatshirt and a grey tee-shirt.

Falling onto the bed with him felt like the start of the nightmare she'd only imagined until now. His lips were greedy, lustful, and pressing onto her face so desperately that they hurt. One of his hands entwined a thick clump of her hair. There was nothing she could do to lessen the assault. She was powerless.

Rough fingers went inside her knickers and hot breath forced its way up her nose and into her mouth. She tried not to breathe. All the blood seemed to be rushing into her ears; there was so much noise inside her head that she could barely hear him.

He bucked against her leg and grunted.

She felt the hardness of his body pressing into her thigh.

Fear and humiliation battled for supremacy. She felt more isolated and helpless than she'd done at any time since he'd abducted her.

Suddenly he stopped and she saw that flabby, repulsive look on his flushed face.

He could have raped her, but if that had been his intention he would be doing it by now. He wanted her to submit to him, like a whipped puppy, and he still expected her to actually desire him.

Still panting, he rolled away, stood up from the bed and stared at her. "I want you in every way possible, my darling, but not until we're married. I'll try and restrain myself, but I'm not sure that I'll be able to. You are so, so beautiful, and such a tease to a man like me. But you can get dressed now. Regrettably, I really must go."

18

Forbes faced the packed Monday morning incident room with Ms Victoria Stenson at his side. "This is the seven a.m. briefing of Operation Barley. Firstly I'd like to thank you all for coming in yesterday. I know some of you had other plans."

"We all feel we're getting closer to finding Debbie," DC Emily Jackson spoke from the side of the room.

"The reconstruction of Faith's disappearance has produced a few possible leads and Buxton officers are following up on those and will keep us updated. Wayne Soames was last seen leaving college at about four-thirty on Wednesday afternoon. He caught his usual bus and was later seen walking less than a quarter of a mile from his home. From there he was killed and his body dumped in the river. Two witnesses reported seeing a dark pick-up with a single occupant driving slowly along the route Wayne took, between the five and five-thirty that day. I believe it could have been our suspect, Richard Meadows, in the vehicle we know he had the use of on that day. That vehicle has been with the forensic team since late yesterday afternoon. We think the same vehicle could have been used in the abduction of Debbie Thomas."

"It's nine days since she was taken. Are we still working on the principle that she could be alive?" DC Green sounded sceptical.

"After forty-eight hours, in most cases like this we turn our thoughts to looking for a body. Cadaver dogs have already covered a wide area around Edgefold Farm but found nothing. I'm trusting in what the forensic profiler, Ms Stenson, tells us – that this case is not typical of most sexually motivated abductions. If we assume that Meadows is responsible for five other abductions in this area over the last sixteen years, then we begin to see a pattern. The women are all of a similar appearance and age, were taken at between two and four year intervals, and Debbie's phone was the only object found near any of the abduction sites but was well hidden in the undergrowth. I'll hand over now to Victoria."

"It's almost unheard of for a psychopath, or a sociopath, to be able to limit their actions, especially over so many years. I believe that these women are possibly being kept alive for a long time – two years or longer. There have been a handful of cases worldwide recently where women have been found after many years of captivity. I think there is some evidence to hope that this could be another of those cases."

"What evidence?" DC Green shouted up.

"The regular time lapses, for one. He takes these women for a purpose. Your suspect is a loner, and while that in itself doesn't signify anything dangerous, it is a marker we use when profiling killers. As far as you're aware this man has never had a partner and lives in an isolated cottage, hidden from the road by a long driveway and by bushes and trees. Also he doesn't have a pet of any kind."

"He has cattle of his own, and apparently he's good with his employer's livestock." Adam said.

"Those are a source of income, and he's following in his father's footsteps. He won't have formed an emotional attachment to them. I understand someone gained entrance to his home. I know I can't put this in my report, but his choice of reading matter could be significant. I think your lonely man may be living in a fantasy world of love and romance, and happy ever afters." She paused to look at her notes. "As for his mother, from what we know she was a sickly woman who was dependant on Richard and his father for all her needs. It's feasible that your suspect is looking for a woman who he thinks will mirror the only female in his life who meant anything to him, and who will be dependent on him – in other words, a prisoner."

"But that doesn't help us find Debbie," DI Lang added. "We've had Meadows under surveillance since midday Saturday and he's only been to his calf sheds once, the farm he's employed on twice, and the village shop three times. He's only been out of our sight when he's been inside his home or his sheds, both of which we've searched."

"Did he carry anything into the calf sheds?" Forbes asked.

"Was he carrying Debbie, do you mean?" Lang sounded slightly sarcastic. "No, he had a half-full sack of what appeared to be calf pellets. He left after about an hour with the empty sack."

The profiler looked up from her notes. "Do you know what he purchased from the village shop?"

"We watched him entering and leaving the shop, but we couldn't then go in and start asking questions without arousing suspicion."

"It might be an idea for a plain clothed female officer with a shopping basket to follow him into the shop."

"I'll organise that," DI Lang responded.

"Also it might be worth sweeping the area again with heat-seeking equipment. It's just possible that he took her some distance away initially, but has now brought her back closer to his home."

"I still think we ought to just bring him in." An unidentified voice came from the back of the room and several of his officers appeared to be in agreement.

"It's your decision of course, DCI Forbes," Ms Stenson added. "I can only advise, but I believe he's probably killed before, and therefore if cornered, has no reason not to do so again. Or once he's in custody he could simply refuse to co-operate and allow her to die where she is."

"I'll request a heat-seeking hellcopter over the area again as soon as possible, and if that comes up with nothing, and if no new information comes in, we'll make a final decision about bringing him in for questioning tomorrow. We should have some results back from the pick-up by then." A part of him hoped that something would happen to take that decision out of his hands.

*

Mary Stone watched Peter and the girls leaving the house for their morning walk with Zelda. She'd feigned a headache when really she'd been desperate for a few minutes alone to make a phone call. She switched on the new phone – there were no missed calls. Was that good or bad news? She dialled the London area code.

"Dorothy, Claire, how's it going? I haven't heard from you for a while." She hoped she didn't sound too clingy.

"Hello there country girl, you sound stressed – chill out." Claire's calm manner fooled many of her acquaintances. Her brain was sharper than most people gave her credit for. "We're both here and you're on loudspeaker." The two women shared a flat to keep down expenses and pool resources. At least that's what they told anyone who asked.

Dorothy joined in. "The Derbyshire Triangle theory is certainly interesting, going as far back as it does. We've even found accounts of women going missing from that area before the 1932 mine explosion. We're researching as far back as the eighteen-nineties. But while the police have a live case and a young woman's life could be on the line, we don't want to go poking around too much. We're recording what we find for a possible story at some future date. Sorry if that's not what you wanted to hear."

"I understand, but what about Ben Allsop?"

"We've found nothing to worry us. He's on record for a couple of drunk and disorderly convictions, but those were thirty years ago, and neither him nor his family show up on the police national computer. Your Peter's name, however, comes up in some very high places – did you know that?"

"What do you mean?"

"Dorothy, stop teasing the poor woman," Claire interjected. "Your Peter's work revolves around computers, doesn't it?"

"Yes, he writes software programs for government institutions and for all kinds of industries. He's even done work for nuclear fuels, and he was out in Iraq for a while before we got together. It isn't all as exciting as it sounds. He also works in schools, which he hates, and a lot of his time is spent undoing the damage caused by hackers and viruses. He's not a fan of the internet."

"Now that is odd." Claire said. "At the very least – it's at odds with what we've found. He seems to spend a considerable part of his day on the web. Does he always take his laptop and tablet with him when he leaves the house?"

"Unless he's walking the dog, yes, and then he has his phone with him."

"Have you checked his laptop or his e-mails?"

"No, I've considered it, but I'm afraid of him realising it's been used while he's out. I want to trust him, but more than that, I want him to believe that I trust him. I could be overreacting to some perfectly innocent coincidences."

"Don't read too much into this, Mary, but you know that we have occasional contact with the FBI and the CIA?"

"Yes...?"

"The thing with the FBI is that they never interfere with the investigation of another agency in any official or non-official capacity without being asked. And even if asked, an agent would have to ask permission from his agency to become involved. In other words, we can ask them for help but we don't always get it. If we uncover anything of interest to them we pass it on, and in return, while they won't often give us actual information, they will confirm or deny most things that we ask them. Have you heard of the dark web, or the deep web?"

"I've heard of the dark web."

"Your Peter brushes against that side of the internet, so to speak, and the FBI have confirmed that they have Peter's name on one of their many, exceedingly long lists of individuals who regularly do that."

Mary almost laughed out loud. "He tackles cyber-crime. He works to eliminate computer viruses. Of course he's going to come into contact with the illegal side of the internet."

"That's what we told the FBI agent in London last night – nothing to worry about then. And the rest of his family appears to be as clean as a whistle, so if I was you, I'd stop worrying and get on with enjoying life in the Derbyshire hills."

"But we will continue digging," Dorothy assured her. "You know us – no stone will be left unturned." She laughed. "No pun intended. Take care of yourself, country girl."

*

The vibrations from the overhead helicopter made the sack on his shoulder seem more of a burden than usual. Since realising he was a suspect he'd abandoned the rucksack as a means of transporting Debbie's food and put everything he needed for her and the calves into one sack. The trudge across the upward sloping field with the calf pellets that his boss allowed him to take seemed longer and more tiring than usual. The continual hot weather was sapping his energy and he was looking forward to descending into the cool atmosphere of Debbie's cave.

He had made a mistake; how big a mistake only time would tell. Instead of spending a day considering whether or not to allow Debbie to write that letter, he should have accepted her offer for what it was and made sure that it caught Friday's post, complete with a first class stamp instead of a second class. Then her parents would have received it on Saturday, or today at the latest, and the search would have been called off by now. When he'd posted the letter on Saturday he'd been so afraid of being seen that he hadn't checked whether he'd been early enough to catch that day's collection.

He'd been careless. Her parents might not be getting the letter of introduction until the day after tomorrow.

The shed door rattled shut behind him, blocking out the noise of the blades; the bone-rattling sound being instantly replaced by the cries of hungry young bovines.

This wasn't going as he'd intended; he was feeling pressurised when he ought to be feeling excitement and optimism for his future. He was hungry for details about his fiancé's life and personality, and what better way was there of spending time than with a beautiful woman. But he'd only been able to spare her an hour out of each of his days today was no different. This was their eighth day of courtship and he'd hoped to make it more special and more sensual for Debbie than anything he'd accomplished so far. But he was being watched, and to spend longer with her than normal wasn't a risk worth taking. Today she would have to be satisfied with his amended version; a shorter version of what he'd had planned, but tomorrow would still be the climax for her. No part of that was going to change.

*

It was nine a.m. and Mr Boa Constrictor was descending the rope ladder with a carrier bag hooked onto his arm, just as he had done yesterday. It looked awkward for him. Something must have happened to his rucksack.

"Debbie, my Debbie; I'm so sorry that I couldn't come to you any earlier. But I'm here now – so stand up and let me look at you."

Again, something had changed. She could tell by looking at his drooping shoulders. It was safest to do as he asked.

He reached the bed, bringing with him a stronger than usual wave of body odour. His face was almost plum-coloured and his breath was coming in wheezing gasps as he pulled a DVD player from the bag. "Do you... do you remember this?"

"Yes."

The machine clonked onto the table and Constrictor flopped onto the plastic chair beside it. He recovered quickly – too quickly. His lips curled and he leered up at her. "Today I want to watch you slowly and seductively undressing in front of me. I want you to remove every single item of your clothing. I don't want you to dance with me; I want you to dance for me. You can dance seductively – I know that. In the days before you were aware of my love for you I frequently admired your silhouette against your bedroom curtains. You weren't shy then, so don't be modest now. Don't hold back. I want you to put on a private, erotic showing just for me."

So he lived close enough to walk the fields behind the farmhouse – the fields her bedroom window looked out onto. He had to be on at least one policeman's radar of suspicion by now, surely? What could be taking them so long to find her?

"When you've teased and titillated me to my satisfaction I want you to lie on the bed again. I want to caress your curves and taste your skin again. I can't get enough of you. I want us to be as close as we can be without actually making passionate love. I want you to beg me to take you and to come inside you, with your young arms squeezing me to you. I understand that as a virgin you will be hesitant, but believe me, when it finally happens everything will feel so natural because we have fallen in love so deeply and so desperately. Now begin."

The movements of her legs felt alien. She had no option but to act out the next hour with as much courage as she could find.

*

Forbes addressed all the officers in the incident room. "The air support unit returned to base this morning with nothing new to report from anywhere on the moors. The helicopter tracked our suspect to his calf sheds, but with the heat from so many moving animals found it impossible to tell exactly what he did after entering the building. Meadows remained there for his usual hour and then walked to work where he's remained all day. I want two volunteers to accompany myself and DS Ross to those sheds later this evening, about an hour before darkness falls so that we don't have to use any lights. We'll take a closer look at the structure of the building.   Who is due to be watching Meadows tonight?"

"I am sir." DC Harry Green raised his arm.

"You'll alert me if he leaves his house."

"Yes sir."

"If I didn't have such a strong gut-feeling that Debbie was still alive, the man would be in our cells by now. As it is, he isn't going anywhere without us knowing about it. And if I'm wrong, and Debbie is already dead, then another twelve hours or so aren't going to make any difference."

19

"Good morning my beautiful Debbie." Constrictor's throaty voice echoed down from the top of the metal ladder. That hadn't happened before.

He sounded even more breathless than yesterday.

As usual she couldn't help but look upwards, but this time his normal silhouette wasn't there. In a primal response she pressed her thighs together. She'd almost wet herself. Gooseflesh prickled her whole body. Something else was filling the void – something dark and solid, and it was very rapidly descending the long access shaft towards her.

She pictured it filling her prison and squeezing the breath from her lungs.

Then she recognised sacking; the same sort her mother threw over the engine of the tractor in the barn on frosty nights – old, dirty-brown sackcloth.

With a dull thud and a ping of metal it landed on the metal gantry. Then the familiar, grotesque shape of Constrictor emerged above it.

She pressed her legs together and wanted to cry. Whatever it was, it had to be something to do with her final test. She shrunk into the bed and groped below the frame for the wing nuts of the two loose timbers. For once, touching them didn't make her feel even remotely safer.

His heavy work boots clonked along the gantry. He picked up a coil of rope, looped it once around the metal framework, and then heaved the package over the side. About one third of the way down the rope acted as a brake and the package jerked. Then it descended more sedately to the floor. It brought with it a different, even more putrid smell than the one Constrictor always left behind.

He was stepping off the rope ladder and over the package. She realised she hadn't looked at him as he'd climbed down.

"This is day nine." He smiled as he approached her but she couldn't respond. "This is the day that I give you the opportunity to prove your love for me. Now please do be quiet."

Her face felt wet. She'd been sobbing. She was shivering, near delirious, and on a scale of one to ten her fear level was already exceeding twenty.

"I've told you before that I won't hurt you. All I want to do is love you. Now stop that infuriating noise."

"I know… I'm sorry." She swallowed down a mouthful of bile. "What is that?"

"That, my darling, is your ultimate test. You'll never guess what it is but I won't keep it a secret from you for much longer. First I want to sit beside you and listen to you reading from last night's evening paper. This will be your last time of reading for me down here – tomorrow we'll be reading the paper together, entwined in each other's arms on our own sofa in our own love-nest."

The back of her throat burned and she tasted stomach acid again. She battled an impulse to pummel him with her bare fists as the bed sank under his weight.

This was it – there was no going back from today. He'd told her that.

This really was it – whatever it was.

She read from the front page, as usual. A lady in her nineties had been beaten up in her own home for a measly twenty pounds. The woman's carer had told the police that was all the money she ever kept in the house and the victim was in hospital and likely to remain there. It was a tragic story but she clung onto every word. While she was reading, nothing else was happening. She reached the end of the article and released the sob she'd been able to contain until that moment.

"It's a sad world we live in, Debbie, but I'll shelter you from all of that." His voice was slurred, as if he was drunk on his own self-importance. "You read the story well, considering how excited you must be to be starting your final day in this place. I know that tomorrow we'll be leaving together because I feel so sure that you'll pass the test. I love you, Debbie. You know that I love you, and this time tomorrow we'll be lovers in the normal world, and bound together forever by our secret. Will you tell me, today, for the very first time, that you really do love me?"

She could have spit in his face, but this wasn't the time to make him angry. This was the time to fold the newspaper, place it carefully on the bed in the narrow space between them, look into his watery eyes and tell him what he wanted to hear. "I do love you. I love you as much as I believe you love me." Nothing less than abject fear had dragged those words from her lips, and even then they'd almost choked her.

She tried to imagine the stinking bundle wasn't still at the foot of the rope ladder. She couldn't look towards whatever it was, nor could she hold his gaze any longer. She stared down at the floor.

"Oh my Debbie, I do believe that you're bashful. You are so sweet and innocent. You can't imagine how I've longed for this moment. Say it again, just once more."

"I love you, Craig, I love you." She felt wretched but managed a smile. Her life could depend on how she behaved during the next hour.

He stood up.

"I'll make you a good husband. I have my own place, and a steady job." He was walking towards the bundle with the supermarket shopping bag still slung over his arm.

After ten long strides he stopped. The bag landed on the floor with a thud and he bent down to reach inside it. "And you won't have to worry about me ever being unfaithful to you."

As if...!

"There will only ever be you, Debbie."

Her right hand grasped one of the two lengths of wood under her bed. Both were loose but wedged into other struts of timber, so that sword-like, they could be drawn out either for defence or attack. He wouldn't be expecting her to turn on him, and it would only take a second to retrieve them.

Paper rustled, he straightened up, and the overhead lights glinted on a metal blade.

Her fingers uncurled.

She'd been kidding herself – two lengths of timber were no match for a six-inch blade.

But at least they weren't needed for defence – not yet. The knife was being used to release whatever stinking mess he'd lowered down to her.

She heard involuntary sounds coming from her own throat.

"Oh no… please no…"

Constrictor was actually crazy… crazier and far more dangerous than she'd imagined him to be.

He was talking to the bundle – to something alive and moving.

She watched him peel back the sacking, but with the knife maintained in his sweaty grip, and she watched him flash his toothy grin at something tangled and matted.

The woman – it looked vaguely like a woman – blinked. She must have been awake all this time, awake and listening, too frightened, or too injured, to move.

Debbie focused on the knife – if only – if only she was superwoman, she'd kick it from his grasp and then happily fling him against the wall and watch him come crashing back down to the floor. And then she'd do it again, and again.

The whimpering sound as he was cutting the ropes from the woman's legs could have been from either of them – from her own throat or from the poor sod on the ground. She wanted to block out everything – the image – the sound – the smell – the fear – the sheer horror of the situation the two women were now in.

"Debbie Thomas, meet Faith Crispin," he stood up and looked from one woman to the other. He was smiling as he drawled out the words. To him it seemed to be a normal, everyday introduction. "A while ago I wanted Faith to be my wife, but it didn't work out. We weren't right for each other, were we sweetheart? The trouble was that while I was courting her I became quite fond of her, so I kept her down here, in a similar cave to yours, Debbie. Those noises you told me about the other day – they must have been coming from Faith. The caves and tunnels in this hillside below my land are like giant rabbit warrens. Some are natural openings and others were dug out in the search for minerals, and some, like this cave, are a combination of the two."

Debbie watched the woman's ribcage. There appeared to be barely any flesh there and it was rising and falling very irregularly. She realised hers was doing the same. She felt light-headed.

"I came to think of her as my pet." He unfolded the remainder of the sacking to reveal a woman who was little more than a skeleton. "She became my little pet rabbit in my own giant warren. You wouldn't believe how many sacks of carrots she's eaten while she's been down here. No really – I've fed her carrots, and cabbages, and calf pellets, and she's had rainwater to drink as it's filtered through the rocks, just as I explained to you on that second day. It's staggering how the human body can survive on so little."

"Let her go…" Debbie could only whisper. If she failed his test today, she was not only looking at her own future, but at the prospect of letting this girl die. Faith didn't look as though she could survive for very much longer, not on what he was feeding her.

"Oh no, I can't do that. I've held her here for far too long. People would never believe that I only wanted someone to love, not after all this time. But like I said, I'm quite fond of her. I know that's hard to understand looking at her now, but I can't bring myself to put her out of her misery. At the same time I can't stomach the idea of just abandoning her to starve to death down here. That's where you come in, Debbie."

"Please... let her go." She forced back a sob and tried not to sound desperate. "I'll vouch for you. I'll tell them that you didn't mean to harm her. I'll tell them you've treated me well; treated me with respect and looked after me. It's not too late to put this right. I'll stand by you, I promise."

"You will... you'll stand by me...? Oh sweetheart, you've no idea how much joy those words bring to my heart. But to prove your love for me, and to tie us together forever, you must do this one thing for me. Before I return to you tomorrow morning, to begin our life of love together, you must kill her."

"No...," she couldn't get any more words out. This must have been his plan all along. What was he trying to do to her – drive her insane with one sick task after another? Had he never had any intentions of letting either of them out; had he just toying been with them?

"Only last week Faith begged me to finish her off. You'll be doing her a real favour."

"I can't…"

"Oh but I think you can. Don't you see how everything has fallen into place for us? Your parents should have your letter today, telling them how you've fallen in love. And if after killing Faith, you tell anyone about her, I'll simply tell them that you saw Faith as your rival for my affections, and that you killed her in a fit of jealousy. Her death will be recorded as a crime of passion, my darling – quite apt, don't you think?"

"If I refuse…?"

"Then I guess we'll find out how long you can both survive on carrots and calf pellets, won't we? But I hope it won't come to that, I really do. If you love me as you say you do, you won't have to think twice about completing this final task because it will signal the beginning – the real beginning, of our unbreakable bond."

"How am I supposed to…?"

"That's more like it." His face lit up like a child's on Christmas morning. "I knew you'd come around to my idea once you'd got over the shock of seeing poor Faith. Just remember you'll be doing it for us. I'll leave these ropes I've just cut. You can use them. I suggest you strangle her from behind, and that way you won't have to look into her eyes as you're doing it. It's a shame; she used to have such beautiful eyes."

Debbie waited for the footsteps to cease and the door to clang shut and then grabbed a carton of juice.

She cradled the woman's head in her lap. "I'm not going to hurt you. Can you manage to drink some of this?"

"Finish me off... I don't care..."

"Don't say that. Can you walk? Can you get to my bed if I help you? I've got some food."

"We're both going to die down here."

"No we're not. I've got a..."

Faith grabbed her arm with a surprising strength.

"Shush, don't say any more." She covered Debbie's mouth with her other hand.

Her impulse was to push it away, but she didn't. She stopped breathing in until the ice-cold hand dropped back down.

Then she listened as Faith whispered. "Don't you realise we're being filmed?"

20

The helicopter's failure to find any traces of Debbie's whereabouts had left Forbes feeling physically sick. And he'd felt even worse when forensics had reported back to him late in the afternoon that they'd found fibres matching Wayne's jacket on the back seat of the pick-up and two hairs of the same length and colour as Debbie's on the floor of the vehicle behind the driving seat. Those samples, along with hundreds of others, had gone for analysis, but short of using that fact to delay the arrest of Richard Meadows any further, he was going to have to do what he'd resisted until now, and bring the man in. Many of his officers believed Meadows should already have been brought in for questioning, but he was the SIO on the case, and his gut feeling of Debbie's life being in his hands had prevented him from doing just that. As he considered delaying for another few hours, his phone sprung into life.

It was PC Katie Brown. "Sir, I've just handed the surveillance of Richard Meadows over to PC Coates. Before that I watched Meadows walking up to his calf sheds as usual, arriving there at six a.m., and he stayed there for seventy minutes, about ten minutes longer than the previous two mornings. From there he walked down to the village shop and I followed him inside. He bought his usual copy of the Sun newspaper, two strawberry yogurts, and a box of out-of-date cakes. An odd thing happened when the woman serving him made a comment about him buying a lot of cakes and yogurts lately. His face turned almost purple. He stammered something about developing a sweet tooth and then almost ran from the shop. PC Coates took up the surveillance from there."

"Thank you Katie, and well done. You can go off duty as soon as you've logged your report."

So where the hell was Debbie? They'd found no trace of her in the calf sheds in last night's search, but Meadows only went there, his place of work where he was in open view all the time, and his home which they'd also searched. Wherever she was the bastard was feeding her on old cakes and yogurts.

His phone chimed again.

This time it was PC Tracy Wilson, the family liaison officer. "Sir, I'm with Mr and Mrs Thomas now, at their house, and they've just this minute received a letter from Debbie. It's postmarked locally. I've secured the letter and the envelope in evidence bags, and Mr Thomas is copying out its contents. It states that Debbie is well and has left of her own free will to be with someone, but her father is convinced that isn't the case. He believes Debbie has placed clues in the letter. I need some assistance here, sir. I'm out of my depth with this. He keeps babbling on about Latin."

"Who speaks Latin these days?"

"His father was apparently a reverend, sir. And Latin is still the language of science, so I believe, and natural science was Debbie's passion."

"I'm on my way." He grabbed his jacket and car keys. "Adam, you're coming with me."

*

"Where is Meadows now?" He shouted into his phone as he sped towards the Thomas's home.

"From the shop he went home," PC Coates's voice crackled over the speaker, "but only for five minutes, then he walked to work. His employer sent him to mow a field, ready for making silage apparently. I spoke to Mr Proctor ten minutes ago and he's sending Meadows to work well away from the farmyard. He doesn't think that he's noticed the absence of the pick-up yet. I'm watching through the binoculars and I'd say it's going to take him at least another couple of hours to complete the field."

"Don't lose sight of him and let me know immediately if he goes anywhere."

Tyres skidded on gravel and he ran to the open front door where PC Wilson was looking relieved to see him.

"Mr Thomas isn't making much sense, sir, at least not to me. He's convinced there are several clues in the letter and he's distraught because he can only solve one of them. He's in the living room. He's confirmed the letter is in Debbie's handwriting."

"Inspector Forbes," Mr Thomas jumped up and grabbed both visitors by their jacket sleeves. He half-dragged them towards a dark oak, polished dining table, on which were the original, secured letter and envelope, and a writing pad and pen. "Look at this... look... mater and pater... Latin for mother and father... Debbie went through a phase when she was at school of calling us by those names, but she hasn't done it for years. My father taught Latin for a number of years until the local school phased it out.

He used to tease Debbie by speaking in Latin when she was a child and she picked it up remarkably quickly. She finds her old memories useful now that she's studying the sciences at school. She wants us to read Latin into her letter – I know she does."

"We'll work it out together, Mr Thomas. Adam, take a photo and send it off to the incident room. Tracy, would you make us all a cup of tea, and we'll put our heads together to see what we can make of this letter."

Debbie's mother was speechless, whether from shock or the tranquilisers she'd been prescribed he'd wasn't sure yet. She was perched on the front edge of a leather armchair with a laptop on the coffee table in front of her. Her eyes looked wider than Forbes remembered them being the last time he'd seen her, and her face was flushed, as though she wasn't sure whether to laugh with relief at seeing her daughter's handwriting or break down with frustration and grief.

"Mrs Thomas, try to relax a little. That laptop won't thank you for gripping it like that. Everyone is doing their best to find your Debbie. Now which clue do you think you've solved, Mr Thomas?"

"Look at these capital letters, Inspector. Debbie would never write like that – not without good reason. I've listed all the capitals, but I've only got one word."

"Let's see what you've got down."

"These are the capitals: T S I V U L P E S P B H V D and one word jumps out – vulpes is Latin for fox – the red fox. We have one foxhole on the edge of our land, and I know of two other lairs, up on the hillside. But I just can't make any sense of the other letters."

Adam leaned forward. "Maybe the first T and S are irrelevant. Every sentence begins with a capital, whatever it is."

"SI is Latin for if," Mrs Thomas sounded hoarse and her eyes were watering as she looked up from the Latin to English dictionary she'd opened on her laptop.

Forbes scribbled down three short phrases. "So we have: if there is a fox, where there is a fox, or maybe when you've seen a fox, but what about the next letters?"

"That's what's frustrating me. Debbie's relying on me to understand her, but I can't."

Adam pointed to the first line again. "Would Debbie normally speak that way, Mrs Thomas? *Untold bother* seems an old-fashioned term for an eighteen year old to be using."

"Not my Debbie…," she croaked.

"The main words in that first sentence are *sorry, untold,* and *bother,*" Adam continued. "Their first letters, SUB, prefix many words. Submarine, subterranean, submerge… Could she have chosen those words in the hope that we'd pick out the first letters?"

"Under something," Mr Thomas grasped Adam's arm again. "Our Debbie is underneath something."

Adam was on a roll. "That makes sense. That could explain why we haven't found any trace of her yet. The mountain rescue teams explained that there are probably numerous old mines and tunnels around here not on any maps. The thermal cameras on the helicopter didn't find her because our man has her hidden well below ground."

Mr Thomas seized on Adam's meaning. "You think she's somewhere close by, don't you? You said our man... Have you got a suspect? Is it someone we know? Is there something you're not telling us? You promised you'd keep us informed."

Forbes shot Adam a scathing look and then took over, lowering his voice to calm the situation. "We think we may have a lead, that's all, and although we don't have anything concrete yet, we do have a possible person of interest, Mr Thomas."

Mrs Thomas let out an indistinct squeak and PC Wilson placed an arm around the woman's shoulders.

"We're still working on the assumption that your Debbie is alive," Forbes knew the hope he was offering might be a false one, but after seeing the letter he'd gone from thinking she was possibly still alive to being pretty damn certain, "and for that reason I don't want to say any more. Please try to remain positive, and I promise you that the moment we know anything definite, good or bad, you will be told."

"But the clues... we haven't solved them all..." Mr Thomas placed both hands flat on the table and stared at the letter.

"DS Ross has already e-mailed a picture of the letter to the station. As we speak, there are more than a dozen officers taxing their brains over those clues."

"We'll pray for you all, won't we love?" Mrs Thomas whispered. Then she looked down at the laptop and let out a deep, guttural sob.

"We'll have to take the original letter for analysis." Forbes explained. "It may hold vital forensic clues. Meanwhile keep thinking about what your daughter might be trying to communicate to you, but without getting yourselves into any more of a state. I'll keep my full team working on those clues until we've cracked them. Between us we'll work it out. My sergeant will fetch a map from the car and you can show him where you think the foxes are living. But please leave the searching to us. If Debbie is alive and close by, we can't risk putting her in any more jeopardy."

*

The incident room was almost too quiet. Just the odd flurry of clicks broke the silence until PC Gary Rawlings leapt from his chair.

"I think I've got it, sir. For the last sentence she wants us to do the opposite of what we did in the first sentence and concentrate on the words beginning with capitals, not just the letters themselves. If I do that it reads: *Please, Bottom, Heart,* and *Vein.* And in the same sentence as *please* we have the word *search.* If we treat the words *please search,* and *bottom,* as self-explanatory, and then put the words *heart* and *vein* into a Google search, I think we might have solved her clue."

"Well don't stop there..."

The flurry of clicks had ceased and all eyes in the room were on PC Rawlings.

"Vein, apart from the obvious in all of us, comes up as a fracture in rock containing minerals or ore. When I put *heart* into a Google search, followed by the word *vein*, the Latin definitions read as *superior vena cava* and *inferior vena cava.* I think she's trying to tell us that she's at the bottom of a cave – possible one dug out in the search for minerals, and that would tally with the prefix, sub, for subterranean. I know we were in contact with the Peak District Mines Historical Society, and that we searched every known mine in a ten mile radius of Debbie's home and Edge Fold Farm and cottage, but there must be at least one that we've missed."

"We called on the local caving society," DC Green added, "and we had tracker dogs out there. Surely one of them would have found her."

James Haig, the crime scene manager, stood up from his desk. "I happened to be with those tracker dogs and their handlers when they were close to the shed that Meadows uses for his calves. I recall the dogs showing great interest in a fox hole up there. The handlers pulled the dogs away thinking they'd been distracted by a fox recently going to ground."

Forbes walked to the decorated Ordinance Survey map on the wall – yellow pins for the lead and spar mines, and pink pins for the three fox lairs Mr Thomas had identified. He studied it for a few seconds. "How close to the sheds was that? There are no mines or fox holes marked on here for that immediate area."

"A hundred yards maybe, to the north of the calf sheds. It was a large hole, surrounded by fairly dense gorse bushes, but if that was the kidnapper's access point then your surveillance team would have spotted him. There's an open field between the sheds and the hole."

"It's got to be worth a closer look, sir." PC Rawlings seemed to be speaking for everyone in the room.

"Adam, check that Meadows is still at work," Forbes picked up his jacket, "and then phone his employer and ask him to make sure our suspect doesn't leave. We need a probe of some sort. DC Green, phone the council and ask whether they've got anything they use to look inside drains that we can have the immediate use of, along with someone to operate it. Phone the dyno rod company as well, and as many of the local plumbers as you can find. Ask them all same thing and we'll see who gets to the

site first.   We need to get back up there straight
away, and no one is to use a siren."

21

"This is not a fox hole." The painfully thin, fair-haired
young man from the council stated with a confident
smile and an equally confident air of authority. "It's
lined with nicely dressed stone and it drops away
steeply. What you've got here is a fairly wide, well-
preserved breather shaft for a mine – and a very
deep one at that. It's a real beauty."

For a second Forbes got the impression that the
man was about to offer to squeeze his wiry frame
down into the hole.

"It looks clean and dry," he continued, "and
there's a good up-draught."

"Keep the probe going," Forbes looked over the
man's shoulder at the screen on the piece of kit that
the electronic eye was attached to.

"We're down almost fifty feet and the hole's
opening out even more. There... see... it's a cave. It's
not a large cave, but it's a cave. Let me see if I can
jiggle the probe about a bit – that's a technical term I
like to use. Oh yes, there she is, and she's a real
beauty.   Those rock formations don't happen
overnight. I'd say that was a natural cave." The man

beamed up at the surrounding faces as though he'd struck gold. For the hopeful officers, he very nearly had.

"What's that?" Forbes pointed to the screen.

"A bit more jiggling… yes… that's it… it looks like cushions, or even a very small, very dirty mattress. There's some fabric at the side of it as well, oh and a metal bucket. I've found some odd stuff down drains and under low bridges, but a mattress in a cave? Now that is a new one on me. It's one for the memoirs if I get around to writing them. But looking at the size of those things, there must be another entrance somewhere. You're the detectives, but that's the only way I can explain it."

"No sign of Debbie…?" Forbes looked up from the screen and saw the man's smile slipping away.

"I'm very sorry, but I'm afraid there's no one down there now."

Forbes blinked back a tear and Adam looked in a similar emotional state. They stared at each other, mutually horrified. "I think we've found where he's been keeping her. Where's that bloody entrance."

"It has to be somewhere very close, sir."

He raised his frame to its full six foot ten inches. Suddenly it seemed impossible to get to the calf sheds quickly enough. "Everyone – across to those sheds. Contact the Derbyshire cave rescue, the fire brigade, and the hospital. I want a paramedic and an ambulance on standby. I want every bale of straw moved, and every nut and bolt in that shed unscrewed as quickly as possible. And DI Lang…"

"Yes sir."

"Get yourself and another officer down to Edgefold Farm and bring that bastard back up to here – after you've arrested him."

"On what charge, sir…?"

"Arrest him for the murder of Wayne Soames – for starters."

Six of the calves, Simmental dairy crosses according to farmer's daughter DC Sharp, were about to be moved into an adjacent pen as the team painstakingly worked its way through the shed.

"Sir, under this straw, there are clean, freshly greased bolts on the base of this metal feed barrier."

"There's a spanner hanging on the wall here too, sir," another voice added.

Forbes stood shoulder to shoulder with the chief fire officer, each man shining a torch down into a four foot wide circular tunnel with a metal ladder running down one side of it. A pinprick of light shone back up at them.

"There are two women down here." The first of the two fire officers to descend the ladder shouted back up to the entrance that it had taken a dozen determined men and women almost an hour to find. "One's in a bad way. We need a paramedic down here." After a few seconds he continued shouting upwards. "The other is confirmed as Deborah Thomas and she says she is well enough to climb out."

"Has anyone phoned Debbie's parents?" A voice came from somewhere in the shed.

"A few minutes ago... they're on their way," another answered.

"Debbie is coming up now," the voice of the fire officer bounced off the walls of the cave and up into the shed. "I'm accompanying her."

"Ambulance arriving now, sir," PC Katie Brown hadn't gone home at the end of her night shift. She was shouting from the doorway.

As Forbes saw the top of Debbie's head appearing he was reminded of a new life being delivered into the world. He'd never wanted to be a father, but for a brief moment he thought he had a glimpse of how an expectant father might feel at that critical moment. "Someone phone them again..."

He pulled Debbie clear, watched the top of the fire officer's helmet retreating, and then directed the paramedic into the deep tunnel.

"Thank you... thank you," tears rolled down her cheeks. "I'm all right... I'm all right. The girl down there, she's... she's Faith Crispin. I remember her going missing. She's been down there almost two years. He's had her down there for almost two years." She'd needed to get that information out before she could give way to full-blooded, heart-wrenching sobbing in his arms.

He scooped her up, PC Brown gently took hold of one her hands, and the three of them headed out towards the ambulance.

"Your parents are on their way," Forbes finally said. "They're on their way here now." He could have told her that while she'd been sobbing into his jacket, but her words had stunned him. And judging by the faces of his team every single one of them was suffering the same mixed emotions.

Suddenly he could only manage a whisper again. "Will someone please bring me the phone number of Faith Crispin's parents?"

22

"Richard Meadows," Forbes was staring directly into the man's eyes for the first time. They were nothing like the cold eyes of the serial killer, Brian Garratt. They were watery, tearful, more like the eyes of someone newly bereaved – someone lost in despair. "We have some questions for you and the duty solicitor is here to help you. Do you understand the charges against you?"

Meadows nodded, sniffled, and then reached for a tissue.

"Can you tell us how many women you've abducted and whether you've held all of them in those caves and mines on your property?"

"How many...? I'm not sure... I've lost count... four I think, on my own, but before that there were a few with my dad – before he died. And yes, they all went into the caves."

"When did your father die, Richard?"

"About ten years ago, I think." He sounded as sorrowful as he looked.

"Can you recall any of the women's names?"

"Of course, I'm not stupid."

"Can you tell us?"

"Debbie – my Debbie – she'll tell you I never hurt her. We're engaged to be married, did she tell you that? Is she waiting for me? When can I see her?"

"Yes, she's told us. What about the other girl down there? Did you hurt her?"

"She's called Faith Crispin. That's a silly name, don't you think? I was in love with her but she spurned me. I couldn't allow her to have her freedom back, you must see that, but I could never have hurt her."

"What were the others called?"

"There was a Lucy, a Joanne, and a Christine."

"That makes five."

"Yes, four plus my Debbie, but I don't count her because we're going to be married."

"Can you remember if there was ever a girl in your caves called Zoe Stirling?"

"Yes, but she was one of dad's. You can't expect me to remember all the names of his, but I can remember one other. That was Dora Mathews, and she was my mother. He moved her from the caves and kept her in our house for years so I guess that she was the only one he was ever really fond of. None of the others ever made it into the house. He wasn't very kind to her though. I think that he kept her quiet with drugs and she kept on getting pregnant. Apart from when she had me, she always miscarried. That's why I wanted my own relationship with a woman to be different. I wanted to experience what my father never did – I wanted to feel true love. You can understand that, can't you?"

Adam leaned forward. "How long has your family owned that piece of land?"

"Since sometime in the eighteen hundreds; and granddad and great-granddad had women in those caves, if that's what you're getting at. There was a while when they were unoccupied because the family was extracting spar. There are tunnels leading out in all directions. It's like a maze down there. It's amazing." He sniggered. "But when the veins of minerals ended, so did the money. Of course the caves have been made much larger and much safer by the mining. That was when the air vents were installed, for one thing."

Forbes took over again. "Did you know Brian Garratt?"

"Oh yes, good old Brian, he covered brilliantly for dad and me, don't you think? He was dad's cousin. But he was much more like dad than like me. He was one mean son of a bitch. Now he was what you would call a proper serial killer. He killed purely for the thrill of it. He didn't take care of his women at all."

"In your own words and in as much detail as you can, I want you to describe to us how and why you and your family have imprisoned so many women in the caves underneath your land."

"It might take a while. Can I have a cup of tea – milk and one sugar?"

"Why not," Forbes sighed. "We've got all afternoon. We'll take a ten minute break and we'll all have one." His throat was dry and he wanted a few minutes away from the man. It was hard not to feel anger for so many tortured and wasted lives, yet if he'd allowed it to show, Meadows would probably have taken his anger as a compliment – his brain seemed to be wired in such an obscure manner. Possibly the drugs fed to his mother had affected the development of his reasoning, and for all they knew, the same thing might have happened with his father. All the same, it was hard to understand how generations of his family had escaped justice, and never even been suspected of any crimes against women. How many others were there out there in society, just like him, living in plain sight of their friends, their employers, and their neighbours?

*

Mary Stone was sitting on the sofa in the living room, half-listening to the sounds drifting through the open window of Peter and the girls as they raced around the garden, and half-watching the evening news.

Her attention suddenly focused on the television and her breath caught in her throat. She picked up the remote, turned up the volume, and then let out a massive sigh of relief.

A local man had been arrested. A complete stranger was responsible for the abductions, and his family had literally been getting away with murder for decades. All this time the disappearances had been down to depraved degenerates who just happened to live nearby, and had been nothing to do with her Peter, or his family, or this house. Her waking nightmare was over. The poor women had been held in the mines and the noises responsible for spooking so many people for so many decades could finally be explained away.

Her girls were squealing with excitement at something in the garden and for the first time since her arrival she felt a warm glow of happiness.

It was going to take Amy and Hannah a while to calm down enough for her to put them to bed, but for once it didn't matter.

Her greatest challenge tonight was going to be concealing the sudden change in her mood from

Peter, but suppressing her emotions was a miniscule price to pay to avoid having to explain away her suspicions of his involvement in some horrific crimes.

She went up to her bedroom, checked that her new phone was switched off properly, and secreted it into the pocket of her raincoat. The heat wave had been forecasted to continue for another week, at least.

*

"Faith Crispin is very weak, sir, but expected to make a good recovery," PC Katie Brown looked shattered, but had returned from the hospital to personally share the news with those still in the incident room before finally going home for some much needed sleep. "She's too weak to be interviewed yet, but before I left she wanted me to know that when she first went into the caves there was another girl there who subsequently died from malnutrition. Her name was Lucy Spencer. Faith wanted her family to be informed."

"I'll call on them before I go home. It's been a long day of highs and lows," his phone rang and he lifted it from his pocket, "and I suspect it isn't over yet." His screen showed the name James Haig, the crime scene manager.

"Michael, I don't mean right now because we're packing up for the day, and the overnight scene guard has just arrived, but we've found something that you need to see. Could you swing by the caves about seven in the morning? We've found something that might shed new light on your case."

23

Mary Stone breathed an even larger sigh of relief than many in the district as she watched the breakfast edition of the local news on Wednesday. Watching the television wasn't normally the first thing she did, but she'd woken in the early hours and not been able to get back to sleep, worrying that the police might have made a mistake and that this morning they'd be letting Richard Meadows walk out of the station as a free man.

The news was more detailed than it had been last night. Pictures of the calf shed and the hillside which had concealed the girls filled the television screen. She recognised the shed, and the granite stile, and the area of gorse bushes – the crime scene had been far closer than she'd realised. She'd actually been out walking in that area only a few days earlier. Debbie and Faith had been directly under her feet. How scary was that?

Then the familiar clench of fear spread through her as she recalled the aftermath of that walk – could that have been why Peter had been disproportionately angry when she'd told him about

Zelda digging in the entrance to the fox's lair? Had he actually known that the women were there? Was he as guilty as that Meadows chap, or was she becoming paranoid again? Ought she to check her hidden phone?

Immediately after her last conversation with Dorothy and Claire she'd checked out the deep web and the dark web. She'd read that an estimated ninety-nine per cent of internet activity was conducted on those two mediums. The deep web, just one layer removed from the World Wide Web, accounted for most of it – being full of scientific, academic, medical and financial data, and conducting perfectly legitimate activity. But the dark web, which was what the FBI and the CIA had identified Peter as accessing, was reported as having some horrifying content. To log onto it required specific software, configurations, or authorisations, and Peter obviously had some or all of those things.

Her body was on auto-pilot as she prepared breakfast; even Peter noticed. *'Time of the month',* she'd told him. That always worked. Her mind was back in the same state of turmoil as it had been less than twenty-four hours ago. She wouldn't be able to settle to any household jobs until she'd spoken to either Dorothy or Claire.

The dishes were cleared away, Peter had made an excuse about needing to go out to buy some hardware for his computer, and from the bedroom window she was watching Zelda and the girls playing together in the garden.

She retrieved her phone and waited while it powered up.

"Hi there, country girl, we've seen the news." Dorothy sounded reassuring. "We had a bet on how long it would take for you to call us and I won. I'm ten pounds better off now, so thank you. We still can't do anything which might impact on the police investigation, even though the girls have been found, but we have a head start on a damn good story. How can we help you today?"

She described the foxhole incident. "You probably think I'm being paranoid, but will you continue investigating Peter for me?"

"We've never stopped, but the FBI is notoriously slow in getting back to us when we want a favour. Unless we have information to trade they'll usually only give us a yes or no answer, which means we have to know the right questions to ask. They're never keen on sharing information. But we'll give their London agent another prod, so to speak. Leave it with us; we won't forget about you and we won't let you down."

*

James Haig had the dusty appearance of a man who'd already been at the crime scene for several hours, despite it being only six in the morning, and an hour before Forbes had said that he'd be with him. The forty-eight year old crime scene manager was known for arriving on scene dressed in jeans and sweat shirt and being mistaken for a member of the public, his clothes un-ironed and his dark hair streaked with silver at the temples, but this morning he was even more dusty and dishevelled than normal. And as he approached, Forbes saw wet straw and animal manure clinging to his wellingtons.

He greeted Forbes with his usual wide smile. "The yard's a mess, I'm afraid. We turned out all the calves last night and drove them down across the fields to Edgefold Farm. The farmer there will obligingly house them until they've all been matched up to their cattle passports and can be sent to the Bakewell livestock market. Preserving the crime scene below ground isn't a problem, Michael, but animal disturbance above ground is another matter." He looked at his wellington boots and screwed up his face. "Health and safety are our greatest concerns below ground, but I wanted you to see something up top as soon as possible. Let's get suited up and I'll show you something curious."

Forbes followed him into the calf shed. Without so many furry bodies milling around the shed it seemed considerably larger and more peaceful than when he'd left it the previous afternoon.

"He had mains electricity connected to this shed, but no meter as far as we can tell. Most of the cabling is pretty old, but do you see that newer-looking wire?" Haig pointed out a double row of cables running from the roof to the floor.

Forbes traced the cabling upwards. One wire was obviously for the lighting, but the other went to a small grey box. "What's the purpose of that box?"

"That, according to my digital forensics analyst friend who kindly responded to my shout for help late yesterday afternoon, is a transmitter. Everything is being examined in situ first, but without taking it down and examining it our best guess last night was that it was sending out a signal of some sort over the internet. I'm told that it's most probably a video surveillance system, but that someone has shut it down. The thing's as dead as a dodo now, and you'll need to get your technical team onto it, but where do you think the other end of the cable leads?"

"To one of the two caves...?"

"To both actually, and someone's gone to a lot of trouble rigging it up and disguising it behind the feed barriers and the ladder. The cable divides into two and is connected to two micro-cameras, one in each cave. Both Debbie and Faith have been kept under surveillance. I've been inside the Meadows property this morning and not found any internet devices of any sort. His mobile is very basic – texts and calls only, his television is the old-fashioned tube type, and up to now we've found nothing in his home to suggest that he's remotely interested in modern technology."

"You think someone else rigged this up, but what for? Neither of those girls was going anywhere. It wasn't as if they needed watching."

"That's your puzzle, Michael. My job is to secure all available evidence – and that is unexpected and substantial evidence."

"Just what time did you start work this morning, James?"

"Oh you know me. I don't go by a clock in the summer. If a job needs doing and I'm awake, then I get up and get on with it."

"Good man, but what does your wife think about you leaving her at the crack of dawn?"

"She doesn't complain. I think she rather enjoys having the bed to herself for a few hours, and I always take her a cup of tea upstairs before I leave. As wives go, she's a good one. She hates ironing but loves cooking, and to me that's the right way round." He gave his stomach a hard slap. "You ought to try it for yourself, Michael. Make an honest woman of your Alison, why don't you?"

"I might just do that," he laughed more at the thought of how often the subject of marriage had cropped up over the last few days than at James's comments, "if she'll have me."

*

Richard Meadows had been waiting in the interview room with his solicitor for half an hour before Forbes felt ready to pick up the questioning where he'd left off the previous evening.

"Brian Garratt was a blood relative of yours, you told us yesterday, and he knew about you and your father and grandfather, and the caves, and for six years he covered for you all. What you need to tell us now, Richard, is who else was ever involved in the abductions?"

Meadows smiled. For a minute he said nothing and Forbes was wondering whether he'd understood the question, but he had.

"Debbie is mine. Why would I share?"

"Who did the electrical wiring in the sheds?"

"I can't remember – someone my dad found. I was never fond of Uncle Brian. He gave me the creeps if you want the truth. I know that you looked into the soul of that loveless creature, Inspector, so what did you see, other than his black heart?"

"Did Brian ever use the caves?"

"Of course not; he was family but we all did our own thing. He covered for us and we'd have done the same for him. It's just a shame he chose to let us down at the end with those letters. Dad would have been absolutely furious; he'd have torn his head off if he'd got a hold of him. I mean, you don't do something like that do you, not to family?"

"Are you any good with electrical devices, Mr Meadows, are you interested in today's technology?" Forbes steered the questioning back.

"You mean the electricity supply to the shed. Dad and the electrician rigged that up so it would by-pass the meter in the house. You can't pin that one on me. I can replace a fuse or a plug, but that's about my limit."

"What can you tell us about the micro-cameras in the two caves – the ones wired up to the remote internet video surveillance system in the roof of your calf shed? That's pretty high-tech stuff for someone who can barely change a plug."

"I don't know what you're talking about."

"If you didn't install them, then who did?"

"I don't know."

"It isn't a difficult question, Richard, who else knows about, and has had access to, your labyrinth of tunnels and caves?"

Meadows looked at his duty solicitor, who was making no attempt at justifying his salary.

"I don't know," he turned back towards the table and mumbled downwards.

"Richard you're going to prison for a very long time," Forbes doubted that the man even cared but he had to try. "If you're moulding yourself on Brian Garratt and covering for someone, you're overlooking one huge difference. Other than you, no one knew about Garratt's deceptions until after his death. He fooled us and he fooled the courts. By boasting about his crimes he made everyone believe that he was mentally ill. Whereas you on the other hand, are looking at the real possibility of being placed into a maximum security prison if you continue to withhold information which we know you possess."

"I didn't do that technical stuff."

"To accept that statement from you we need to know who did."

"I can't tell you. You're going to lock me up anyway, so I'm never going to say who it was. Debbie will be waiting for me in the cottage when I do get out – she's promised to stand by me. She's told me she loves me, did I say that? And we're engaged. I gave her my mother's ring. Is she still wearing it? Have you seen her today? Is she outside waiting for me?"

Forbes sighed inwardly, and sensed Adam and the solicitor doing the same. If the man was acting, he was damn good. It was looking more and more likely that Meadows was one of the few people who managed to reach middle-age outside of a prison or a secure hospital unit without being able to tell right from wrong. There was a technical name for the condition, and no doubt Victoria Stenson would be able to remind him of it, but right now he had no idea of what it was, and he didn't care.

"Richard, listen to me. Brian and your father are gone, and you are looking at spending your remaining years in prison. We know that you come from a large family, and that most of your relatives are decent, law-abiding members of society. If you are protecting just one bad apple in your family, now is the time to tell us. Are you protecting a family member, just as Brian did?"

"No comment – that's what they say on the television isn't it, no comment? How is Faith, by the way, no one will tell me anything? She used to be such a pretty girl."

Forbes left the question unanswered and walked out of the interview room.

*

Mary Stone opened the packet of chocolate biscuits she'd been saving for the girls and set them down on her kitchen table in front of Ben. She'd never seen him looking so down.

"I can't keep mother from watching the news for much longer," he studied the biscuit packet but didn't take one, "and she always scours the local weekly newspaper for anything concerning anyone she might know. These days it's the obituaries she usually turns to first, but this week's edition will have that killer's arrest splashed all over the front page."

"You should be the one to tell her about Dora Mathews, and about how close-by her best friend was for all those years and how she was held prisoner and drugged. Her only full term pregnancy resulted in a killer, but that wasn't her fault, and hopefully she never knew what her son had been drawn into. It won't be an easy conversation to have, but from what you've told me about your mother she doesn't deserve to hear all of that from the media."

"Would you come back home with me today and sit with her while I tell her? You can bring the girls, and Zelda; they'll help take her mind off things.

Only she's been asking when she's likely to meet you and the little ones, and if I ask one of her old friends to sit with her they'll be clucking around her like an old hen. I know my mother. She'll look on you as the breath of fresh air that you undoubtedly are to this valley, and you haven't met many people from the district yet. Look on it as your good deed for the day. What do you say?" His eyes were pleading with her and looked about to spill tears down his face.

"When you put it like that, how can I refuse?" She watched his face light up and his hand reach out towards the biscuits. "We'll follow you back to your cottage in about an hour."

Ben's mother was at least twelve inches shorter than Mary, and probably weighed twice as much. The smiling, silver-haired woman herded them all into her living room. Her round face was lined, but looking at the framed, faded wedding photograph on the shelf in the alcove beside the fireplace, she'd obviously been an attractive, but dark-haired girl at the time of her best friend's disappearance.

Had the natural colour of her hair possibly saved her? It wasn't something she would ever feel able to ask.

"Sit down mother while I put the kettle on. While it boils Mary and I have got something serious to tell you."

Ben wasn't hanging around now. Perhaps he was afraid Mary might change her mind and run out on him, leaving him to break the news alone and then pick up the pieces as best he could.

Zelda and the girls were all sitting quietly, as though sensing Mary's discomfort, but like Ben had said, supporting and comforting someone elderly and fragile would be her good deed for the day.

Together they broke the news and dried the tears. And Ben had been right about the girls; their presence did revive the old lady. Within thirty minutes the tea had been drunk, a sponge cake had been finished off, and Mrs Allsop was chatting with the girls and admiring the colouring books they'd brought along.

Ben's mother had worn Dora Matthews like a millstone around neck for sixty years, all the while knowing she would never see her best friend again, but never knowing what had happened to her or what suffering she might have endured. Finally learning the truth of what had happened had seemed to cut that millstone loose.

"So tell me, Mary," she leaned forward in her armchair, "now that the kidnapper's been apprehended, do you think you'll be able to wash the big city out of your hair and settle at Dale End?"

"I'm seriously considering it," she shot a look across at Ben and then realised there was nothing wrong with this old lady's eyesight.

"Is there something I'm missing, my dear? Is there something else you two need to tell me?"

"It's nothing for you to worry about, mum. Mary wanted to know more about Dale End, that's all, and maybe some of the history of her husband's family, before she made her final decision."

"It's a big step," Mary added. "But while I'm here I feel I ought to tell you about some friends of mine back in London who are looking into your theory of Derbyshire's own version of the Bermuda Triangle, with a view to selling the story. Although after what we've seen on the news this morning, the mystery seems to have been solved. But if there is a story there that they can sell, you and Ben will be in line for some commission as it was Ben who first mentioned it."

"I don't need the money, my dear, but I suppose it could go towards my funeral pot."

"Don't say that, mum."

"Don't fret, lad – you could use it to give me a good send off. I didn't want to go to my grave never knowing what had happened to Dora, but now I don't mind quite so much. But I still sense some reticence on your part, my dear. Are you sure there isn't anything at all I can help you with?"

"Just knowing I've made my first female friend in the village is enough for today, thank you. When I start researching into the history of Dale End I might like to pop along and ask you a few questions, if that would be all right?"

"You can call round any time, for any reason, with those lovely girls of yours and that happy little dog. I'm so pleased to have finally met you, my dear."

24

Zelda and the girls were sleeping. Mary picked her new phone out of her raincoat pocket and stared at it. Peter had texted her to say that a new private client needed his help and that he wouldn't be home for another hour. Was she being disloyal to him by asking Dorothy and Claire to continue checking on his background?

She'd married him just two weeks after her decree absolute had come through and it had always sat uncomfortably at the back of her mind that she hadn't really known very much about him, or about his past. She'd asked, but he hadn't been very forthcoming. With two small children and a broken heart, had she been too naïve and too desperate for her own good? Had she allowed her need for security to cloud her judgement? He'd seemed to be everything she'd wanted in a husband – after two difficult pregnancies and births, her friends and colleagues had all told her how lucky she was to find a man who loved her and her girls, but who didn't want children of his own.

Had it all been too good to be true? The need to know was still gnawing away at her.

"Hullo there, country girl," the familiar voice instantly lifted her spirits.

"Dorothy — I was just wondering whether you had anything on Peter yet."

"I wish we had good news for you. Peter was active around the dark web until Tuesday afternoon, but before agents could lock onto his signal it ceased, and he hasn't been active since. The FBI agent in London has promised to e-mail us the moment Peter activates that signal again, but it's a live output of some sort and nothing is saved. It's transmitted somewhere else in the world — it could be anywhere, and then lost into the ether. It could be nothing for you to worry about; he could be working undercover, trying to trap scammers or hackers, or something else equally plausible. Have you considered coming straight out and asking him about his work? Maybe he'd put your mind at rest."

"No, I don't want to do that. Knowing you're checking on him is enough. You will let me know the moment you know anything definite, won't you — good or bad?"

"Stop stressing, we promise to e-mail you on this address the moment we have anything."

"I'm keeping the phone switched off, but I'll check it two or three times each day. Don't forget me. I'm relying on you to put my mind at rest."

*

Warm, but heavy summer rain rattled down from the Wednesday afternoon sky onto the muddy farmyard where a dozen vehicles were parked. The weather couldn't have broken at a worse time. Forbes squeezed his Mercedes onto the grass verge and hurried past the bullet-pocked sign which read Edgefold Cottage Farm. His scene manager was waiting for him in the entrance of the shed, well out of the rain, and this time already wearing a white protective oversuit.

"You'll need to suit up." James Haig handed him a flat package. "You haven't been down into the caves yet, have you?"

"I've been content with your videos," he'd been avoiding descending into the depths of the caves, and so far he hadn't needed to see the underground crime scenes for himself, but an hour ago he'd had a direct request to attend.

This time the entrance looked anything but dark. The entire tunnel and cave system was lit up like a fairy grotto and he could hear voices and people moving about below him. He hesitated and wrinkled his nose.

"Bit whiffy, isn't it?" Haig twitched his nose, "but it's quite safe. We're pumping fresh air into all the caves and the air quality's being constantly monitored – after you, Michael."

From the metal gantry the space looked a hive of activity, swarming with white-suited, elf-like creatures in hard hats, some on their hands and knees and others bagging and tagging anything which might be needed as evidence, should the Richard Meadows case ever reach the courts.

"There's a tunnel leading off this gantry. We didn't find it until just over an hour ago. We'd assumed it to be just another fissure in the rock face, but once you've squeezed through you'll see that it opens out into another large space. In you go, Michael."

He recognised Alison's silhouette. She was the closest the Leaburn station had at short notice to a forensic archaeologist, and as so often happened, she'd beaten him to the crime scene.

The smell was stronger in the more confined space. It was a mixture of putrefying animal remains and human excrement, but with a distinct minty smell.

He realised everyone below ground, except him, was sucking on an extra strong mint, or something very similar. Alison offered him her packet and he gratefully accepted.

"This way, Michael; I've not been here long, just long enough to establish that what the search-trained officers found an hour ago were human remains. The ones I've looked at so far are all female. Some have been here for decades, but the worst of the smell is from the group of five over there which includes the most recent cadaver. That was what the officers uncovered first."

"Five sets of remains...?"

"There are definitely five in that heap, and probably another six which could have been here for anything up to a century, over there in the far corner."

The heap of dust and dirt Alison pointed to had grey bones and clumps of hair protruding from it. He'd never seen so many bodies in one place. In the unnatural light the scene reminded him of images he'd seen that had come out of the extermination camps of Nazi Germany. A scenes of crimes officer was rigging up more lighting to further expose the end result of decades of human suffering.

"At least Faith and Debbie seemed to have been unaware of the proximity of this crypt," he muttered to no one in particular.

"These caves have provided a dry environment," Alison continued as though she hadn't heard him, "so decay has been slow. And there are no immediate signs of rodent activity down here. Maybe we're too deep for them, or perhaps Meadows had a good supply of poison at ground level. Either way the remains are very intact. If some of these are the women on your list they should be easy to identify."

"So this was why the four women Garratt falsely claimed to have killed were never found. They were entombed in here, and I suppose the fifth one in that group will pre-date Garratt's killing spree."

"It could be Richard's mother, Dora Mathews," James Haig offered.

25

TWO WEEKS LATER

"This will do me just fine." In the centre of Leaburn, Adam Ross was placing two foaming pints of Burton's bitter onto a table in the corner of the White Lion public house. Then he plonked himself down next to his boss. "Two years from now I'll be forty, and while that hardly makes me over the hill, it makes this my first choice for the perfect stag night." He took several gulps of his beer. "I'm more than happy spending a pleasant, uneventful, Thursday evening in the company of close friends."

"And we've all got to work tomorrow," Forbes reminded the small group as he lifted his glass to eye level and checked that his pint was as crystal clear as he liked it to be.

"You're too fussy about the clarity, if you don't mind me saying, sir," DC Green straddled the small wooden stool and looked across the table at Forbes. "As long as real ale smells and tastes good, it'll do you good. Any bits floating around in there can only be clumps of yeast, and they'll do you no harm. Look on them as your daily ration of vitamin B."

Adam lifted his glass again. "Well here's to a quiet day at the office tomorrow." The other two took the top couple of inches off their ale by way of an acknowledgement, just as DI Lang and PC Rawlings joined them at the table.

Forbes set his glass back down, still not sure that the liquid it contained shouldn't be a fraction clearer. "It will be four weeks on Saturday since Debbie Thomas was getting all dolled-up to go to her dress fitting. I had an e-mail from her parents today to let me know that she was recovering well, and that she'd begun to walk the dogs again without being accompanied. That's one plucky young lady."

"Faith still needs counselling," Adam was recalling his own mandatory couch sessions with the police psychiatrist after the sudden death of his wife, "and her family has been offered money for her story, but I think it will be a while before they're ready to face the media again. I'd feel better if we knew who'd been transmitting images of the girls from those caves."

"As would we all," Forbes looked around the half-full room of early-evening drinkers, most of them on their way home after a full day's work. "Unfortunately, without an IP address there's no trail to follow. It could be someone in this bar right now, and we'd have no way of knowing. That's the attraction of the dark web for the criminals and perverts. It's virtually impossible to trace the source of the material being transmitted, and while there are sick people out there willing to pay for the privilege of watching it, it will continue."

DC Green followed his boss's line of sight to the three youths at the adjacent table who were all staring down at their mobile phones. "I still find it hard to believe that men would pay to sit and watch women who'd been imprisoned like that. I mean, it wasn't as though they were doing anything. I've seen clips of *Big Brother,* and *Celebrity Get Me Out Of Here,* and they're bad enough, but at least the people in those programs were doing and saying things. Did Meadows ever satisfactorily explain his obsession with the newspapers?"

"He refused to confirm our theory, but the general assumption is that if people were subscribing to watch live transmissions they would want some assurances that they weren't watching old, rehashed footage. I suppose the climax to the coverage would have been if the women had died of starvation, or if one had killed the other, as Debbie has said Meadows instructed her to do. Snuff videos have been around for decades and there seem to be no shortage of people wishing to watch them. We can only guess that what was showing, to those people who'd subscribed, was somewhere between a big brother show and a snuff video."

"The father and grandfather abducted girls for the more usual, sexually motivated reasons," Adam said, "and Meadows only had his wages going into his bank account. He lived very simply with no gadgets and no cash lying about anywhere on his property. He's just a damaged little man with a twisted outlook on love. There has to be someone else out there, a name that we haven't come across yet, and for all we know someone who's planning a repeat performance somewhere. The trouble is that we have no ideas on how to find him or stop him. We rescued two young women, and that gave everyone involved in the investigation a buzz, but I can't shake the feeling that we got something terribly wrong."

"It is possible to get everything right, or to do everything right, but still fail," DC Green shrugged.

The conversation was spiralling the wrong way.

"This is meant to be a celebration," Forbes raised his glass again, "of Adam's last days of freedom and impending nuptials. We're here to forget work for a few hours." He'd recognised the pained expression on Adam's face. His friend's mind wasn't solely on work – it was on his late wife, Erin. It was time to bring her out of the shadows and into the open. "Before we go any further with this evening, and I hope that Adam won't mind me saying this, but I remember Erin as being a warm and selfless young woman who I'm sure would be pleased with the direction that Adam's life is taking, and be comforted to know that her son, Ryan, has a woman like Jane to mother him. I'd like to propose a toast... to Erin..."

"To Erin..." Five glasses clinked together but only one person in the bar turned his head to look at the source of the celebrations.

Peter Stone stood alone at the end of the bar. He needed another drink, not as the result of a hard day's graft, because he'd spent the day alone in the house, but as the result of several unpleasant phone calls. He was up to his eyes in debt. He'd made a series of bad investments over the last few years and the people he'd persuaded to part with their money were demanding the return of their capital.

The London property was in shared ownership with Mary and the building society, and anyway it was going to take time to liquidate it. Dale End Farmhouse, however, was in his sole name. There were companies out there who bought properties for cash in a matter of days. They paid below the market value, but once things had settled down again that would be a route that he could take. His plan then would be to grab the money from the sale of the farmhouse and start a new life somewhere. He'd no idea where, but it would be a legitimate new beginning that people would understand he needed to make.

But that was no use to him now. Before he could do any of that he had to raise enough money quickly to pay off his immediate debts. And that was what he'd been working on for much of the day.

The only other alternative he had was to get into his car tonight, drive away, and forge a new identity. The trouble with that idea was that he didn't want to run. He'd had more than enough of flitting from one country to another, from one continent to another, and remembering different aliases. That was a young man's game. The authorities everywhere were tightening up on people opening new bank accounts, and even with a new identity you needed a legitimate account in order to exist in most civilised countries. Without one it threw up too many problems and raised too many questions. He knew how to make money – shedloads of it – he'd just been unlucky for a while. But like he'd told his creditors today, he had a plan, and things were about to change.

At some indefinable point during the four weeks since they'd moved to Derbyshire, Mary and the girls had begun to bore him. He was the kind of man who, when he looked over the other side of the fence, always saw greener, lusher grass. Two years ago he'd fancied being part of a family with sex on tap and cooked meals on request, but he was ready for the taste of freedom again.

While in the Middle East he'd learned how to manipulate the hidden depths of the internet – the dark web, as it was called. And his luck hadn't all been bad since he'd returned to Britain. His first stroke of good fortune had come when he'd realised just how poor his uncle's hearing had actually become. The noises from the breather shafts at the edge of the property couldn't have been from anything other than a female in distress, and with equipment borrowed from work he'd quickly located the source.

The irony of the women's predicaments was that if the locals hadn't been so backwardly superstitious for so many years, they would have been found much sooner. But then he wouldn't have had the opportunity of perfecting his latest money-making scheme.

During his nine day, *'will she or won't she'* transmission, the numbers of new subscribers to his site had gone from one a week to one a minute. He'd been amazed at the numbers of sad perverts willing to pod out good money to watch very little. But it had come to an abrupt end, and he'd even lost some of his equipment. It was a good thing he had plenty of back-up, more up-to-date stock. The trouble was that these types of schemes took time to set up – time that his creditors weren't allowing him.

He couldn't prevent himself from glancing over at the five men in the corner of the bar. He'd recognised them from the television; they were the main reason his income stream had folded so abruptly a fortnight ago. They looked happy enough with life, and hardly overworked, but he was about to change that for them.

His contacts were ready, his hired goons had been paid in advance, and his subscribers were slobbering over their screens. If everything went according to plan he would begin live-streaming thirty-six hours from now – at ten o'clock on Saturday morning to be precise, and then the money would begin flooding in again. It would be different from his last broadcast – more of a slow build-up leading to a promising cliff-hanger. He was even taking bets on the outcome of the sixteen hour program.

This time tomorrow he would be in the Highlands of Scotland, where he'd remain until Sunday morning. He had a conveniently-timed, legitimate reason for being four hundred miles away from his home over the weekend. A family-run hotel needed an up-to-date security system installing, and that little job would pay reasonably well, but the husband of the hotel's owner had requested something extra. He wanted micro-cameras fitting into some of the guest rooms, and spyware software installing in his wife's computer and laptop without her knowledge. What he wanted those things for didn't concern Peter, he guessed it was why no one more local had been offered the job, and as long as he was paid in cash for the extra work he would be happy.

After a long and tiring journey home on Sunday he would then remove all signs of the micro-cameras from his own property before making a distraught emergency call to the police.

His creditors would be paid off, his accounts topped up, his freedom gained, and he would have two properties to sell and shed-loads of subscribers waiting for another transmission.

Life was looking very promising.

26

Mary had three days – Friday, Saturday, and most of Sunday ahead of her to dedicate to Zelda and the girls. She fully intended to spoil them. Her only niggling thought was that she hadn't heard from the London girls for a few days, so while Amy and Hannah were occupied with their bowls of cereals she went back upstairs. The phone was exactly how she'd left it in her raincoat pocket.

"Of course the FBI is still monitoring him," Claire reassured her, "but we still both think you're worrying unnecessarily."

She told them how distant Peter had become, and how he'd needed to work in peace and quiet on Thursday and suggested that she and the girls go out for the day, which they'd done. And then she told them the main reason for her call – his supposedly work-related trip to Scotland. "…but I can't shift this gut feeling that he's lying to me."

"We don't have the resources to find out what he's up to up there, I'm afraid. We're good, but not that good."

"I don't think he's being unfaithful. In a way that would be a relief, it would be something I would know how to deal with. I'd pack my bags and leave him. But I just can't shift this awful, sick feeling that it's something much worse."

"You're getting yourself into a state again. What time did he leave?"

"Two o'clock this morning; he wanted to beat the traffic on the M6."

"That's seven hours ago. He should be well over the border by now and his car should have been logged on the overhead motorway cameras. We'll check for you that he's actually gone if you like? It won't take many minutes."

"Can you do that from your home?"

"Have technology, will travel…" Claire laughed. "You'd be surprised at what we can access with our computers these days. It's all a matter of having the right contacts."

"If you could do that at least I'll be able to relax for the weekend. Shall I phone back?"

"No need country girl – it's coming up now – yes, Peter's car has been logged heading north this morning. If he is transmitting anything from up there, and if he's changed his settings, it may take a few hours for the agents to lock onto him. We'll let our FBI man in London know what's happening. But please stop worrying over something that's probably perfectly innocent. Enjoy your weekend and make the most of the great outdoors."

"I'll leave this phone on and keep it with me. You will call me on it if anything happens, won't you?"

27

Mary sighed, feeling more irritated than worried. Peter had obviously taken the vacuum cleaner out of the cupboard while she'd been out of the house on Thursday. The cord was tangled and the attachments weren't how she always left them. She hadn't realised that he even knew how to use it. Still, whatever he'd been doing, at least she hadn't returned home to a mess.

She wanted to give the house its customary Saturday morning once-over before the girls came downstairs. They'd begun sleeping better, Zelda seemed more settled, and this morning the sun was shining and she had a picnic planned. It was going to be a good day.

The small patches of white dust along some of the skirting boards didn't worry her. The girls must have got hold of some chalk and made up a game. They were always doing things like that and she liked to encourage their imaginations. That tiny bit of mess was easily sorted.

*

Forbes sensed his detective sergeant's emotional fragility as the group of eight waited in the large, ornate entrance hall. It was the third time that he'd adjusted his buttonhole. DC Green, DI Lang, PC

Rawlings, and their respective wives, along with Adam's parents, all looked relaxed once introductions had been completed. He checked his watch for the tenth time that morning. The wedding was booked for eleven o'clock, twenty minutes from now. Jane would be here any minute with Lucy and Ryan, and Alison was with them to help things along. If anything had looked likely to delay the little group she would have phoned him.

A craft fair was being held in the same building, and people were brushing past them to reach the event. All of them smiled the moment they noticed the buttonholes. It seemed everyone's spirits were cheered at the prospect of a wedding – even if they didn't know the families involved.

There were no major crimes on his desk, the forecast for the weekend was for a fine, warm and sunny couple of days, and he'd fitted comfortably into a lightweight suit that he hadn't worn for at least five years. Everything was set for an excellent day.

The pavement was busy, and suddenly three generations of one family filled the wide doorway, seemingly undecided whether or not this was the correct entrance for the craft fair despite the posters announcing that it was. Above their chatter he heard Alison's voice.

"Excuse us," she was saying, "blushing bride coming through."

Just like the others they all beamed as they realised a wedding was about to take place, and then they traipsed past, following the notices, towards the stalls of jewellery and paintings and whatever else might be on offer to them.

Adam was the only one in the foyer without a smile. His face was white and his eyes filled with tears.

Forbes placed an arm around his sergeant's shoulders and leaned towards him. "Erin will always be with you," he whispered. "Today is for Jane."

28

At just before eleven p.m., a phone in London sprang into life and two girls put the books they were reading down onto their silk bedcover. One of them picked up the phone and frowned as she recognised the number. Then she began frantically signalling to the other to start up their computer.

"We may have had a stroke of luck," the agent's voice sounded urgent. "We're not certain but we think we may have found what Peter Stone has been transmitting onto the dark web for most of the day. Someone's been transmitting using similar codes to those found within the equipment recovered by the police in Derbyshire a fortnight ago, and the signals are coming from the exact same area.

There's a chance it could be the same person who filmed those girls in the caves."

"But Peter's in Scotland…"

"Such systems can be remotely activated, or he may have someone close by who's operating it."

"How sure are you that it's Peter?"

"We're not, not yet, but it seems too much of a co-incidence, given your concerns and what we already know about him, for it to be anyone else."

"Can you see it?"

"Yes, and I've sent a link to your computer. An image is going out now on to the dark web to thousands of creeps worldwide. It's being transmitted to those who already subscribe to paedophile and snuff sites, and that's how we found him. One of our agents in New York has been infiltrating the sites linked to child pornography and snuff videos. He's been subscribing to several sites for months now and this morning he was invited to pay extra to watch a new action site. The money paid out gets whisked into accounts in the Middle East within seconds. From there it could be going anywhere. Have you got the link yet?"

"It's opening up now," Dorothy replied. "If you're right, that means that Mary married a pervert. It could mean she and the girls are in danger."

"We're not sure yet that it's her husband. These people are clever. They hide behind firewall after firewall. Can you see the images yet?"

"We've got them. We have six separate pictures of six different rooms. It looks like a nice family house, but it's in darkness. We're zooming in. There's a night light in one of the rooms. I'll enlarge that image."

"Oh my God… oh please no…" Claire leaned towards the screen, "that looks like my jacket. That's my old jacket on that chair. I gave it Mary because it was too tight on me. Oh please no… look… look at those sleeping children… they're in the shadows, but don't they look the spitting image of Mary?"

"He wouldn't, would he…?"

"Go to the shot of other bedroom… someone's asleep under the covers… no, no, that room's too dark to see anything. Oh, please let us be wrong."

"No… we need to be right." Dorothy clasped Claire's hand. "If it is Mary we can warn her. If it's a stranger all we can do from here is watch."

"Where's the other phone?"

Dorothy pointed to her handbag.

"I'll call her mobile."

"Are you getting this?" Dorothy had almost forgotten the phone in her hand, still connected to the FBI agent. "Did you hear us? We think he's transmitting from his own bloody house."

"I'll contact the Leaburn police. I have the direct number of the SIO there. I'll try him first. You contact Mary and tell her to get herself and her girls out of that house as fast as she possibly can. Tell her not to even stop to get them dressed."

*

"Lucy and Ryan are fast asleep," Jane flopped down on the sofa beside Adam. "They've both been amazingly well-behaved today. I'm so proud of them."

"Nothing about this day could have been any more perfect." Adam placed his arm around the new Mrs Ross and kissed her cheek.

"Where is everyone?"

"My parents have retired to the spare bedroom, you must have just missed them on the landing, and there are four women settling down in the garage on the put-me-up beds, and four men in the tent in the garden. It's a warm night so don't worry about them – they've all survived much worse while on surveillance duties. We'll leave the back door unlocked in case any of them need anything. There are seven police officers dotted around this property tonight so we should all be safe in our beds. Everyone's slightly over the legal limit for driving and to call taxis would have brought an end to this wonderful, amazing, incredible day. It was a good idea of yours to arrange for them all to stay over. While you were upstairs they decided to give us some privacy, but before they jumped ship we all thought that as the children had been so good, they might like to continue the party tomorrow."

"Doing what – most of the food's been eaten?"

"We've enough food in the house to give everyone some sort of breakfast. As fast as people get showered and dressed, we can feed them – even if it's only with beans on toast. It'll be a case of first-come-first-served."

"And then what…?"

"The weather forecast is good so we thought we might all go back to Chatsworth, buy a hamper and whatever else we need from the farm shop, and then devour it by the river bank. What do you think, Mrs Ross, about an impromptu, shared, mini-honeymoon before the real one begins on Monday?"

"I think it sounds perfect. This day keeps on getting better and better. Taking it into tomorrow is a brilliant idea."

"Eleven-fifteen, Mrs Ross, and if we don't go to our bed soon we won't have time to consummate our marriage on the day of our wedding."

"Well that would never do, would it? Lead on, Mr Ross," she grabbed the hand he held out to her and giggled like a bashful schoolgirl.

*

Forbes folded his suit and placed it at the foot of his sleeping bag, thinking he really ought to have brought a hanger outside with him. He removed his tie and unbuttoned the top of his shirt. There was a clean shirt in his car which meant he could keep this one on. He'd slept in far worse places and it had been a pleasant, but tiring day. PC Rawlings had brought the remaining cheese and crackers out to the tent and the others were making short work of them before they settled down for the night. It was the earliest he'd ever known a wedding reception to end, but he didn't mind. Then he remembered his phone and reached into his jacket pocket. He almost dropped it as it sprung into life in his fingers.

"DCI Forbes," the unknown male announced in what sounded like a New York accent, "I'm sorry to disturb you at this time of night, sir, but I'm afraid we may have a situation developing."

"Who is this...?"

"Agent Martin Gregory from the London branch of the Federal Bureau of Investigation, sir..."

He phoned the station for back-up while the other tent occupants were pulling their best suits back on, scribbled a brief note for anyone who might wander outside and wonder why the tent in the back garden was empty, and then went in search of his car keys.

After giving it momentary consideration, he dismissed DI Lang's suggestion that they might be the subject of a wedding night practical joke. The agent's name had triggered a memory somewhere deep in his brain, and while there were some on his team who had an unusual sense of humour, it was bizarre even for them, and besides, what he'd heard on the phone wasn't even remotely funny.

They fastened their seatbelts, the speaker phone in Forbes's car lit up, and Agent Gregory began relaying everything he was seeing, which actually wasn't much. DI Lang was in the passenger seat and DC Green and PC Rawlings were in the back. In their sharp suits the four of them more closely resembled an undercover vice squad than off-duty country coppers.

But if the agent was right three lives could be in danger and everyone in his car had joined the force to serve and protect. Not one of them could have crawled into a sleeping bag and settled down for the night after the call he'd taken.

According to the sat-nav, under normal driving conditions they were nine minutes away from their destination, and unless there were other police cars already in the area, they were likely to be the first on the scene. It was almost half-past midnight and there were more rabbits than cars on the quiet, rural back road. By some miracle he avoided them all without needing to relax his pressure on the accelerator. One corner after another raced towards him until picked out in the beam of his headlights was the sign which meant he'd reached the edge of the village. He eased off the accelerator slightly along the half mile village street until he saw the sign *'Dale End Farmhouse'*. Then he hit the brakes.

"Two masked intruders have forced open the front door." Agent Gregory finally had something to sound excited about. "They both have knives and ropes. How far away are you? That family needs you right now."

"We have it in sight. We're about one thousand metres from the property. The house lights are on."

It was beyond stressful listening to the running commentary on the speakerphone, but it was marginally better than watching and commentating on such a scene while helpless to do anything to stop it.

He swung his Mercedes off the tarmacked road and DI Lang cracked open his window and let out a puff of relief – they could hear distant sirens – not that they would be close enough to assist for several minutes yet, but back-up was on its way.

The car nosedived onto the rutted, private lane. He'd never had sirens fitted to his own car, and for the first time he regretted the decision. He slammed his hand into the centre of his steering wheel and squeezed down on the accelerator again. DI Lang placed his hands against the dashboard and the Mercedes bounced down the track.

Agent Gregory was sounding frantic. "The woman's out of her bedroom. One of the men has just grabbed her. The other's trying another bedroom door. He's gone into the children's room. The girls are screaming."

He had to use whatever means he could to stop the assault, even if that meant the men had a head start in getting away. He held his palm flat against the centre of the steering wheel and pressed as hard as he could, as though by doing so he could make the pathetic noise sound louder. His greatest fear with alerting them was that the assault might escalate into a hostage situation.

"They've both stopped... one's shouting something... they've heard you... they're leaving. They're both running to the front door. You should see them any second now."

Two motorbikes, trials bikes judging from the way they roared away from the house and over the rough grassland, zigzagged their way up the narrow field beside the lane. Neither of them used a headlight and neither of them faltered. At times they were barely ten metres from the track, and under almost any other circumstances the four reasonably fit offices would have apprehended at least one of them. Tonight they would make no attempt. A police officer's priority was always his duty of care to the victim, and according to the frantic agent still shouting through the phone, the three victims in the house they were fast approaching were all in a state of shock, and the woman was on the floor and bleeding.

Agent Gregory had only seen two men. Across country, and without lights, unless the helicopter Forbes had asked to be scrambled was already in the vicinity, it meant that for tonight at least, the two would get away.

It also meant that the property should be safe for his officers to enter.

He pressed down on the brake pedal, and as he pulled on the handbrake exchanged momentary eye-contact with DI Lang. They were all trained in first aid, but it wasn't a skill any of them were well-practiced in. The doors of his car all flew open and the sound of approaching sirens cut through the still night air. For that he was thankful as he led his men through an open doorway into a silent house.

29

"You can't go down there, sir," the scene guard at the head of the lane stepped in front of the white-haired man who had parked his car on the grass verge and begun walking towards the tape. "Can I have your name?"

"Ben Allsop. Mother and I heard sirens a while ago and we both thought they were coming from Dale End. We couldn't get back to sleep and I just had to come and check that everyone here was all right. I had an awful feeling that something had happened to Mary and the girls. I did try to warn her when she first arrived. I should have tried harder. What's happened down there?"

"Are you a relative, sir?"

"No, Mary has no relatives, other than her husband, Peter, and her two daughters. Peter told me that, and she confirmed it to me the other day. She's not been living here long and mother and I are about the only people she's spoken to. Is she all right?"

"Do you know where her husband is now?"

"He's supposed to have gone to Scotland for a few days – something to do with his work. His skills with IT mean that he gets work all over the country."

"So you knew Mary was alone last night?"

"She was with her daughters, and Zelda."

"Zelda...?"

"Their little dog – look what's gone on? Maybe I can be of some help. I've worked there part-time for the last forty or more years. I know that place better than anyone."

"If you'll just wait here a minute, sir, I'll see if the Inspector would like a word with you?"

Sixty minutes later the night sky was beginning to brighten and Ben Allsop found himself being escorted back to his car, clutching the trembling whippet to his chest as though the animal was the most precious thing he'd ever handled.

He gently placed her down onto the grass verge. "Don't worry Zelda; I'll get you down to the vet's as soon as I can." Then he turned back to the officer. "Thank you again for allowing me to take her. She'll need some stitches in her shoulder but I can't see anything seriously wrong with her. She's in shock more than anything. I'll just walk her a little way along the grass verge, just in case she needs the toilet before I put her in the car."

"Let us know how she gets on," the officer appeared to be a dog lover.

"I will do." Ben had an inkling of how the dog was feeling. They were both in shock. He hadn't been allowed within fifty metres of the property; Zelda had been brought out to him by a plain clothed officer, but he'd seen enough to know that someone had been seriously hurt in the house. One ambulance was still parked in front of the door. It looked empty and Ben recalled how when a farmer had been killed in the neighbouring fields the previous year the ambulance had been parked there for several hours.

Whatever had happened was almost certainly something to do with Peter. But almost wasn't good enough, he could be mistaken, so he hadn't told the police anything they didn't already know. "Come on Zelda, just a little further for your Uncle Ben – just another few yards – just as far as that funny little box on the other side of the wall."

He looked behind but the policeman had lost interest. Reaching over the wall and brushing aside a clump of dried grass and mosses, he looked around again. All clear – he opened the lid of the box and unclipped a smaller, grey box. Then he stood up and pocketed the item, picked up the dog and returned to his car.

He soothed Zelda as he eased her onto his passenger seat. His hand trembled as he turned the ignition key. Next he had to break the news to his mother that last night's emergency vehicles had indeed been attending Dale End Farmhouse, and she would be distraught. She'd been looking forward to her Sunday outing, and to showing Mary and the girls around the grounds of Chatsworth House, followed by a picnic somewhere close to the river. He'd even oiled her wheelchair specially.

*

From his room in the hotel, Peter had watched the transmission as Mary had rolled out of their bed, as she'd fumbled for her slippers, and as she'd reached for her dressing gown. He'd watched her creeping down the stairs, and even noticed her hesitate as a phone began ringing in the house somewhere. Who the hell could have been phoning at that unearthly time? Had Mary got a lover – now wouldn't that be a sweet irony?

He'd watched the door being smashed in and Mary being rugby tackled as she'd tried to run back upstairs. At that point he'd switched off his computer, filled his glass with malt whisky, and retired to bed. It was one thing to watch people you didn't know being tortured and killed, but he was quite fond of Mary and even of the girls when they weren't making too much of a racket.

He'd had a good night's sleep and now his pay-as-you-go phone was the object making the racket from the inside of his glove box. It was early on Sunday morning and the southbound stretch of the M6 was quiet. He frowned, but reached across to check who was calling. Only a handful of people had this number. He clicked on the accept icon and then the speaker. "Ben... what is it?"

There was absolute silence for a few moments. He was starting to think he'd lost the signal when Ben Allsop's voice sounded out loud and clear. "You're a bastard, Peter Stone; did anyone ever tell you that, a complete and utter bastard?"

Then silence again.

He eased his foot off the accelerator. His head had too many scenarios racing around inside it. He'd accepted that he might not be the first person at Dale End this morning – that he might not be the one to find them, but he hadn't actually planned for that to be the case. He'd fully expected to have time to retrieve the transmitter from the wall at the top of the hill, to enter a silent house, to take the small cameras from the holes he'd made in the ornate plaster coving around the ceilings, to fill the holes with caulk from the tube that he'd left under the kitchen sink, and then to make the distress call to the authorities.

Ben must have been the one to find them. He must have been the one to make that call. That wasn't too much of a disaster. The cameras were incredibly well hidden and the police wouldn't be looking for forensic evidence on the ceiling – that was after all why he'd placed them there.

Ben was loyal but the call might still be a trick. "What's wrong, Ben? Spit it out, man."

"All hell has broken out at your house, and don't insult me by asking. The emergency services have been there since the early hours – since just after midnight."

"Who called them?" Damn, he shouldn't have been so squeamish. He should have continued watching last night. He'd made a massive mistake.

"Does it matter? Aren't you going to ask how they all are?"

"OK, how are they?"

"I don't sodding know. They won't tell me anything because I'm not a relative. They've been trying to contact you for the last three hours."

"I've had my main phone switched off for the journey."

"Oh how very bloody law-abiding of you, I'm sure. You bloody hypocrite! I called because I wanted you to know that I have the transmitter, or whatever it is, from the box under the wall at the roadside. Without that, even if they find cameras, there's nothing to say that you were doing anything other than installing a security system. I'm right aren't I?"

"How did you know?"

"Everyone knows about the cameras in the caves, and you're one of the few people around here with the knowledge to pull off something like that. And I was in your garden on Thursday. You didn't see me but I was watching you. I saw you doing something with a drill near the ceilings, and then I watched you hiding a box at the top of the hill, out of sight under the wall. Before it was light this morning I retrieved the contents of that box."

"Where is it now?"

"It's safe with me. I just can't decide what to do with it. How far away are you?"

"I'm about three hours away. Will you hold on to it until I get to you?"

"I was going to suggest that you kept your main phone switched off and that you came to see me first. Out of respect for your late grandfather I'll give you one chance to explain yourself."

The line went dead.

His brain was swirling so much that he almost missed the exit signs – three, two, one, he flicked on his left indicator. For what he had in mind a service station wouldn't do. They recorded everyone entering and leaving. He needed a quiet stretch of road.

A couple of miles on, he found one with an empty lay-by and no overlooking properties. He jumped out and walked to the rear of the car. In the boot he'd stashed everything he might need for a disguise and a getaway. He just hadn't expected to need the things quite so soon.

He changed the number plates, changed the items on the front dash, and his own clothes. He put new car seat covers on the front, and put the child seats into the boot and a rug over the back seat. Then he put on a dark, curly-haired wig, coloured his face with face paint from the girls' toy box, and sat back for thirty minutes before re-joining the motorway.

30

"The woman's condition is stable now. She suffered a vicious assault. Your prompt response probably saved the lives of three people, Michael. You'll have to take comfort in that," the police surgeon's voice crackled from Forbes's radio. A scenes of crimes officer who'd been dragged out of bed was walking past him and couldn't help but overhear the call. He reached out and patted Forbes on the shoulder. It wasn't something that happened too often, but it felt right. Perhaps everyone working away in Dale End Farmhouse needed to reach out to a friendly face at that precise moment. He returned the brief touch of comfort.

His radio crackled again, this time with an incoming call from the station. It was PC Philip Coates. "Peter Stone has been clocked on the M6 overhead cameras, travelling southwards, as far as junction thirty-two. He exited there over an hour ago and hasn't been picked up again. We've no idea where he is now, but the motorway traffic police know that we're looking for him."

"Thank you, Philip, keep me updated."

Something was chewing away at his brain. Something hadn't felt right about his earlier brief chat with Ben Allsop. The man knew more than he was prepared to say this morning, he felt certain. For the last hour he'd been puzzling over where he'd heard the name before. Suddenly it came to him. Allsop was employed as the odd job man on Edgefold Farm. He'd been raised in this area, so presumably knew everyone locally, but more than that – he had actually worked alongside Richard Meadows. He must have been well acquainted with the man. At the first opportunity he would have to go to Allsop's house and question him further.

After fifteen minutes of updating the ACC and organising the necessary teams over the phone, he walked outside for some fresher air.

"Morning Michael, this sounds as though it could have been a nasty one." James Haig, the crime scene manager was pulling his oversuit over his customary blue jeans and sweatshirt. His top looked even more creased than normal, as though he'd just grabbed it from the laundry basket. "Mother with serious stab wounds and her two daughters taken to hospital with her, I've been told, is that right?"

"Yes, and it isn't a straightforward mugging, or a robbery gone wrong. We've found cameras similar to those used in the caves. The FBI has already crossed paths with our chief suspect, the husband, and he was under investigation last night. His transmissions were being recorded and we're lucky enough to have a copy. From the angles of the footage we've located four micro-cameras in the plasterwork. They've not been touched yet."

"The FBI...? The big guns...?"

"None other – it seems that we're looking at something similar to the filming of Deborah and Faith, and not too far away either."

"It would be too much of a coincidence for them not to be linked, Michael."

"I agree, except that this time, fortunately, we don't have any bodies for you... just one suspect... as yet still missing."

"The same person for both cases?"

"We believe so."

"Then we'll get cracking and see what evidence we can come up with for you. You said cameras – have you located a transmitter, or anything similar to the technology found at the caves?"

"Not yet, no, and the cameras are even smaller this time. He's had to use new stock."

"If there's a transmitter anywhere on these premises, Michael, we'll find it."

With David Haig on the scene he felt confident enough to go in search of Ben Allsop. His instincts told him not to go alone. "DI Lang, DC Green, PC Rawlings... are you three feeling alert enough to accompany me to interview someone in their own home?"

"Have you got plenty of chocolate in that glove box of yours?" DC Green looked hopefully at him.

"I certainly have."

"Then we're with you, sir."

*

Adam Ross stood in the kitchen, in his dressing gown and slippers, reading a scribbled note on the granite worktop. Until that moment he'd thought he was the first one up and about. He went into the back garden to check that the tent was empty, and to make sure the note wasn't a practical joke, and then he phoned his boss. "Do you need me there, sir?" He felt awkward asking, with Jane upstairs looking after the children and telling them all about the new plans for the day. He was in a difficult position.

"No, you carry on with the day as we discussed it and when we get a chance to join you, we will. There are plenty of officers on the lookout for Peter Stone, but I wanted another word with someone before I called it a day."

"We'll see you later then, sir."

*

"He's taken Zelda to the vet's," the round-faced, white-haired lady in the doorway told them. "They only see emergencies on a Sunday morning, but when Ben phoned them and explained they told him to bring her straight down to the surgery. It's only a flesh wound that she's got but we didn't want to risk it getting infected. He left an hour ago so he shouldn't be much longer; you can all come in and wait if you like. I'll put the kettle on."

A hot, reviving drink was exactly what the four of them needed.

"Can you tell me what's happened at Dale End? Ben said he didn't think it looked good." As she talked she switched on the kettle and then led the way into a spacious but untidy living room. "Please make yourselves comfortable."

She moved bundles of clothes and newspapers; just enough for them to sit down on the matching pair of large floral sofas, and then sat in the single armchair beside the fireplace.

"A serious assault has taken place, and I'm afraid that's all I can tell you until we can contact a relative." Forbes was doing his best to be charming. He really needed that cup of tea or coffee. "Do you know the family well?"

"I've met Peter many times over the years, but Mary and the girls just once. My Ben's getting to know them all quite well. He was in a state of shock when he returned home this morning clutching that little dog."

"Anything you can tell us about the family might be helpful at this stage."

After several minutes of telling them all she knew of the Stone's family history, she then regaled them with stories of how she'd tried to locate her friend, Dora Mathews, and how upset she'd been to discover that for years her friend had been held captive so close by.

The kettle had clicked off without her seeming to notice.

"My own mother used to call this whole area *'the valley of doom'*. I knew no good would come of a young family moving in down there... I just knew it."

"Are we stopping you from getting your breakfast, Mrs Allsop?" Forbes hinted.

"Gracious, no, I've been up for hours. But I was getting you all a drink, wasn't I? Now would you like tea or coffee?"

Ten minutes later, with empty mugs beside them, his three officers looked relaxed and Mrs Allsop was still chattering away. One tiny dose of caffeine wasn't enough to combat their need for sleep. He felt his own eyelids drooping just as the door of the cottage burst open.

"Ben dear, in the living room, these gentlemen would like a quick word with you. How is Zelda? Is she going to be all right?" She stood up and took hold of the dog's lead. "I'll take the poor little thing into the kitchen for some food. Come along, Zelda, now what would you like? I've got a tin of tuna. Do you like tuna?"

The room fell quiet for a minute. Ben Allsop looked almost as stunned and exhausted as his own officers and Forbes waited while the man sunk into the chair his mother had just vacated. "We'd just like to know how familiar you are with miniature cameras, Mr Allsop, and whether you've had any more thoughts about where we might find Peter Stone?"

"Absolutely nothing, and absolutely none, but what have cameras got to do with me?"

"Possibly nothing, but we have to ask. Do you own a mobile phone?"

"Doesn't everyone, these days?"

Forbes held out his hand. "May I take a look at yours please?"

"Sure; I don't use it much. I take it with me when I go out in case mother needs me. I've used it once today; the first time for almost a week, to call the vets. You can ring that number if you need to check it."

Forbes noticed the colour change in the man's face as he handed over the phone. Most people had more than one phone in their house these days. "Is this your only phone?"

"Yes, like I said, I don't use it much, but if anyone needs a job doing they can get hold of me without bothering mother on the landline. I only need to top it up once or twice a year."

"Can you think of anything at all that might help us find Peter Stone?"

"No I don't... he should be home sometime today... that's all I know. Don't you have his mobile number?"

"His phone seems to be permanently switched off. Now why do you think he might have done that?"

"Maybe he's flattened his battery... how would I know? Are you suggesting he already knows what's happened to his family... that he's somehow involved... that's crazy?"

"No, those suggestions have just come from you. We merely want to find him as quickly as possible to let him know what's happened to his next of kin." Forbes watched Ben's face turn a darker shade of red.

"It was the way you were asking me that made me think that way. If I do hear from him I'll tell him to contact you, but I'm not expecting to."

"Thank you. We'll leave you in peace for now. Will you be at home all day?"

"I'm taking mother to her friend's house in the village for a few hours, but apart from that I'll be here."

"You are...?" Mrs Allsop poked her head around the open doorway. She sounded confused.

"I was going to surprise you, mum, seeing as we won't now be going to Chatsworth with Mary and the girls. Fetch your coat and we'll leave right away. You can take Zelda with you. She's obviously taken a liking to you and the vet said to keep an eye on her."

Ben's glance at the clock on the mantelpiece didn't go unnoticed.

Forbes fastened his seatbelt and watched Ben and his mother, with Zelda peering through the gap between them, driving away from their house towards the centre of the village. His visit hadn't really been necessary; he'd been hoping for, rather than expecting it to throw up any useable information. He checked the time on the dashboard. Nine o'clock; it was still early enough to rescue Sunday's plans. "I suggest we return to Jane's house to get a bite to eat and an hour or two of sleep. If the team needs us we can be back here in a matter of minutes." There were no words of argument from any of his three passengers.

31

Peter cleaned off his face and left the soiled tissues in the roadside dustbin, but for now thought it best to retain the wig and dark glasses. There was no point in taking unnecessary risks. He drove past the new cemetery and the old churchyard, and then the church. Ben Allsop's cottage was the first building along the main street, handily placed for his needs this morning, on the edge of the village. And with almost half the properties being holiday cottages, fully-booked at this time of the year, he would be able to park his car anywhere along the traffic-littered main street without anyone giving it a second look.

Uniformed police were once again spoiling the tranquillity of the village, but by using the footpath running alongside Ben's hidden vegetable garden he could easily be at Ben's back door without being noticed.

He needed to know what was happening at Dale End before making any decisions, but his main priority was to get that transmitter out of Ben Allsop's hands. So the nosy old sod had seen him installing it in the wall – that didn't explain why he'd thought fit to remove it from there. Maybe he was covering for him, maybe he wanted a cut of the profits, maybe he was intent on blackmail, or maybe he just wanted to lord it over him. Whatever the reason, without that bit of kit, unless he'd been unlucky enough for his work to have been seen by the authorities, even if the cameras were found there would be no proof of anything ever having being transmitted from the property. He could return home and play the shocked relative, but with his debts paid off and a sizable sum in his offshore accounts.

Of course if it had been seen by the authorities it would be a whole other story. He would have to abandon his inheritance and run, change his identity and set up more subscription only films until he got back on his feet.

He found a space and reversed into it – just in time. As the handbrake clicked on, Ben's car appeared. He was driving his mother along the village street, straight towards him. He turned to face and pavement. Through his wing mirror he watched brake lights gleaming – red for danger.

He watched Ben opening the passenger door and escorting his mother, and a dog which looked remarkably like Zelda, to the front door of a cottage where she was welcomed inside.

Ben remained outside, had a good look up and down the village street, and then climbed back into his car. That was amusing – was the old sod looking for him, as if he'd be walking along the street for everyone to see?

He turned away again as Ben drove past and parked up beside the pavement fronting his little cottage. After a quick check that the short section of street he needed to cover was empty, he jumped from his car and headed towards the wooden *footpath* sign.

*

Suddenly Ben was no longer tired. He was congratulating himself for reading Peter accurately. Through the wing mirror of his car he'd only needed a fleeting glance to recognise the furtive figure in the parked car. The wig and dark glasses looked ridiculous against Peter's pale complexion – the complexion of a geek who was never far from a computer screen of some sort. They'd be hard pushed to fool a blind man.

He let himself in through his front door, locked it behind him and went to the dresser in the hallway. His father's old pistol had been sitting there, beside a box of live ammunition, for years, but he'd kept it well-oiled and fired it once a year. He loaded it before unlocking the back door. Peter wouldn't be long, and he wouldn't want to be seen. The back way was the only way he would dare to approach the house – disguise or no disguise.

He only had to sit and wait, sipping at a small measure of his favourite scotch in the comfort of his living room with the pistol tucked out of sight on the sofa beside him. He was perfectly safe. Whatever happened in the next half an hour or so, he would have the upper hand.

He was right. After a long two minutes and four sips of the whisky, the back door clicked. "Come in, Peter. I'm in the living room. You've been a naughty boy. Come and explain yourself."

Peter's face as he walked through the doorway to the living room looked a mixture of shock and anger. His fists were balled. "Why did you have to take it, Ben? How much do you think you know?"

"That's no way to greet a lifelong family friend, Peter. Sit down, you look tired." He tried to sound relaxed but saw something in Peter's eyes that sent a shiver through him. It made his voice sound nervy. "To answer your first question, assuming you're talking about the transmitter, I don't really know why I took it. I saw you placing something there on Thursday and the next day my curiosity got the better of me, although if I'd had any idea then of what you were planning I'd have taken it straight to the police. This morning I was in shock and not thinking clearly. I took it on the spur of the moment. My dilemma now is what to do with it."

"That's easy – just give it to me. Where is it? I need to have it." Peter was the intruder, but was the one who sounded trapped.

"Patience, Peter, patience; I want you to explain to me why you would do such a thing. Why would you want to hurt such a beautiful, defenceless young family, especially one that adored you?"

"Are they all dead?"

"I don't know because the police won't tell me anything. They're looking for you in order to tell you first. How ironic is that?"

"Who found them so early – was it you?" His eyes were bulging.

"No Peter, it wasn't. Again, I don't know anything except what you tell me. So... why did you do it?"

"Money, pure and simple – you have to understand, Ben, I owed serious money to some dangerous individuals, far more than Dale End was worth, and if I'd had to wait for the farmhouse to sell, the debt would have trebled at least. I'd made bad investments and gambled with other people's money on projects which failed. After experimenting with the filming of the women in the caves, and realising the appetites of the crazies all over the world for something slightly different, I knew I'd stumbled on an easy way of raising huge sums of money."

"Were you involved in imprisoning those women in the caves?"

"No, I'm not a complete monster. I only use violence towards women and children when all other avenues have been closed off. My uncle was almost stone deaf in both ears but he hadn't always been that way. On one of my dutiful visits I quizzed him about the noises I'd heard and eventually he told me he'd turned his one deaf ear to the antics of the Meadows family for decades. Once I'd found the women all I had to do was threaten to shop Richard if he didn't allow me access to the shed and the caves. With my expertise in IT, and the research I'd done on money laundering and the dark web, it was a simple job for me to infiltrate the world of those who enjoyed watching other people suffering."

"You're as bad as any of them."

"I don't see it that way. If I wasn't draining money out of the pockets of the perverts, someone else would be. Is that why you took the transmitter, Ben, are you after a cut? If that's what it takes for you to keep what I've just told you to yourself then I'm sure we can come to some arrangement. After all, your mother might need extra care in the near future, and proper care is expensive. You could really help her. Family is everything, so I'm told, but I'd grown seriously tired of my family life. I saw last night's performance as a win-win situation – for me at least."

"And if I don't want to keep quiet... what happens then?"

"Well... like I just said... your mother's knocking on a bit... she might have an unfortunate accident."

Ben moved his right hand closer to the edge of the cushion. "You'd be locked away – you wouldn't be able to touch her."

"You forget that I was in Scotland last night, Ben. There are always people prepared to do nasty things for the right money. It's just a case of having the contacts. I could make you a rich man. Take a minute to think about it."

He didn't need to think. What he needed was to see Peter squirm. "My mother fretted for years about her friend, Dora. Your actions affect more than just the victims. Do you never feel any guilt... any empathy?"

"You're losing the plot here. Dora was the mother of Richard Meadows and that was way before my time. It was Richard's father who abducted her and he's long gone."

"I'm losing nothing, Peter. Dora, her family, my mother; none of them have witnessed justice being done. And what about all the other girls who've died in this area over the decades, and whose families and friends have suffered? Richard will be the only one ever to be punished. It isn't enough. It never will be enough. Mother always said this valley was cursed, but with Garratt dead and Meadows locked away, if there ever was such a thing as a curse we could be almost free of it."

"You're talking rubbish. I could change your life – yours and your mothers. Work with me on this."

"That would make me a part of the last remaining fragment of that curse. And that fragment, Peter, is you. Now stand up, I want you to take a good look at this because it's the last thing you're going to see."

His hand had been itching to slip onto the cold steel and finally he allowed it to pull the gun clear of the cushions.

"Think about the money... it's all about the money." He stammered but stood up anyway.

Both hands wrapped around the handle as he stood up with the barrel pointed towards the centre of Peter's chest. There was less than ten feet between them. He'd no idea how good his aim would be, his hand was shaking so much, but if he opted for the largest target area he couldn't fail to take the piece of scum down.

For half a minute there was a silent stand-off. He could almost see Peter's brain feverishly working out its options.

He waited.

He wanted to savour the moment.

"You won't shoot me in cold blood."

"Won't I...?"

"Please, give me more of a chance to explain. You don't understand. It was either them or me because there was no other way I could raise that money. They were threatening me with serious mutilation if I didn't come up with something fast. They were threatening Mary and the girls anyway. I'd already placed them in danger. I was desperate."

Ben straightened his spine to its full height and felt his eyes blazing. Nothing that Peter could say would ever justify his actions. "You're nothing more than a cowardly pervert. You don't even have the right to breathe the same air as those young women."

"Calm down now, Ben. Let's back up a step. You don't want to use that old thing... it'll probably blow up in your face... and what would happen to your old mum then... eh? Think about it for another minute. Put that old gun down and let's talk this through in more detail. You've had a nasty shock today and I get why you're so upset. But this isn't the answer."

"Have you quite finished?"

Peter opened his mouth to speak but thought better of it.

"But you don't really 'get why I'm so upset', do you? I wanted to give you time to understand that what I'm about to do isn't just about Mary and the girls. It's about what I've witnessed my mother going through, and it's about the suffering that you've gone along with for so many years. I want you to understand why I'm willing to dispense a level of justice that I know the courts can't. I've seen first-hand the despair and the pain that you and your sort cause. You all need wiping off the face of this earth."

"You're being ridiculous. You can't … you'll be locked away… they'll know you phoned me… you're an idiot… a stupid fucking idiot… no… no… no…" His face looked like that of a toddler on the verge of a tantrum, his arms reached out towards Ben, and his hands flapped about in mid-air as if they were practicing how to deflect a bullet, but he didn't move his feet. He was out of ideas.

"If I do go to prison it will be worth it, but I really don't think that I will. I'll admit to seeing the transmitter and taking it, but not to knowing what it actually was. I'll say I thought it must have been something that someone had accidentally dropped. I'm the odd-job man who works with his hands, not at all the sort of person to be messing about with technical stuff. And I'll admit to lying to the police that I'd contacted you this morning to tell you that I'd taken something from your property. I'll tell them I regretted taking it – and that I took it while I was in a state of shock and didn't appreciate that what I was doing was so wrong. I'll tell them that as soon as I realised I might have taken a vital piece of evidence I phoned you to ask what to do with it – but only because I didn't want to get involved in a serious crime. I'll say I was too nervous to take it back to where I'd found it. The police will believe that you came here demanding the article back and threatening me, and that I shot you in self-defence with my father's old pistol that I'd kept in the hallway for decades for personal protection."

"You're talking like a madman. You'll never convince them of all that."

"They'll have to prove otherwise though, won't they?"

*

Forbes had been almost too tired to eat any of the toasted cheese sandwiches Jane had made for the four returning officers, but he'd forced them down and thanked her. The other three had wolfed theirs down, retrieved their sleeping bags from the tent, and then taken up residence on the vacated camp-beds in the garage. The armchair in the living room had beckoned his weary body. He'd always been able to sleep almost anywhere if he was tired enough, and this morning he was definitely tired enough.

He sunk down into the chair.

Adam was outdoors with one large empty tent, two small children, and five women. The inside of the house was quiet. His phone was on the coffee table beside him, and as long as everything remained that way for an hour or so, four exhausted officers would be able to recharge their bodies sufficiently to enjoy what was left of the weekend. With food in his stomach he knew he'd be asleep almost before his eyelids closed.

He allowed his thoughts to drift.

He hadn't officially been on duty, but the moment he'd called in the assaults as a major incident, the case had needed a SIO, and he was already on the scene. Being a detective wasn't a job, it was a way of life, and the officers whose families accepted that fact were the most efficient ones. After thirty years on the force you could retire with a full pension, and that had originally been one of the main attractions of the job. Despite that, he'd questioned his wisdom several times during his early years with the police, usually after attending a gruesome traffic accident, or when thirty years had seemed an impossibly long time.

Time was irrelevant once the body was sleeping.

His mother's face came into sharp focus, as she'd looked when he'd first told her he wanted to be a policeman. She hadn't been thrilled, but his father had talked her round to the idea.

His unconscious mind jumped forward almost thirty years, to the family living room as it looked today, with just his elderly father sitting reading a book, and with the ever present empty chair in the room; the chair where his mother would have been sitting had she not been taken from them.

Something woke him from the half-sleep – something he'd missed – an empty chair – Mrs Allsop

– she clearly hadn't been expecting to be removed from her home this morning without any kind of discussion with her son. And Zelda had been whisked away with her.

Ben Allsop had wanted the house to himself.

Not just that – he wanted his mother, and the dog, to be in a place of safety for the day.

Was Ben expecting a visit from Peter? Had they been working together all along? Had both of them been in league with Richard Meadows?

He looked at his phone. He'd been in a light sleep for less than ten minutes, but it was over an hour since he'd watched Ben driving into the village. Peter Stone had been clocked heading southwards on the M6 about four hours ago. If he'd realised the police were looking for him and changed registration plates, or ditched his car and stolen another, he could easily be back in the area by now.

He picked up his jacket, walked over to the door leading to the garage, and listened. There were distinct snoring sounds. Adam was officially on his honeymoon, but maybe he'd welcome a break from the women and children for an hour or so.

Ten minutes later, after one call to the crime scene manager and another to the station, the two men were in Forbes's car and about to head towards Ben Allsop's cottage.

"Is there any more news on Mary Stone?" Adam was settling into his seat.

"She's lost a lot of blood but should make a full recovery. Her friends in London who triggered the investigation into Peter's internet activities provided contact details for the godparents of the two girls. I understand they're on their way up to Derbyshire today to help out."

"So what are we doing now?"

"You're doing nothing – you are officially on a break. I'm only taking you along for moral support and as someone to radio for help if it's needed. I had an odd thought, and I'm hoping it's not a result of eating too much cheese before going to sleep. It was nothing more than a feeling really, that this morning I'd not picked up on something that I should have and until I've checked it out I won't be able to sleep properly."

They approached the village and slowed. Ben's cottage was the first to be passed but it showed no signs of life. There were about a dozen cars parked along each side of the main street and Forbes looked closely at each one as he drove past.

"The village street looks fairly quiet now, sir, what are we looking for?"

"Anything out of place... I'm going to park up and walk back for a closer look at that dark blue Toyota. It's the same colour and model as the one Peter owns, and was last seen driving. You wait here."

It didn't take a trained observer to see that the registration plates had been changed very recently.

The screws were shiny and the plates didn't quite fit as the originals obviously had. There was a significant colour difference in the paintwork where the sun hadn't reached behind the old plates, and which the new plates weren't quite covering. The vehicle was empty – totally empty, devoid of children's car seats or of any kind of litter. There were immaculate-looking car seat covers in the front and a new-looking rug over the back seat. But the exterior was dusty – very dusty, as though it had been driven several hundred miles recently. Who would clean the inside of a car to within an inch of its life but leave the exterior dirty enough to write on? As much as he wanted to try opening the doors, he couldn't risk setting off an alarm. He hurried back to his Mercedes.

"Anything...?" Adam greeted him.

"He's here... the bastard is here... right under our bloody noses. You call for back-up while I request an armed response unit, and then as long as he doesn't come out we'll sit tight and wait."

*

"Ben... please... you've known me all my life. You took me ferreting, you caught me when I fell from a tree, you taught me how to fish, so how can you now be standing there and thinking of shooting me? Have you really got the guts to squeeze that trigger while looking me straight in the eyes? I don't think that you have."

"Maybe a few days from now you'd be right. Maybe then I wouldn't. We're never going to find that out. But what I felt and saw this morning as I waited outside Dale End Farmhouse is to be the final nail in your coffin." His hands shook, but not enough that he was in any danger of missing his target. "I didn't see inside your house – all I saw were the faces of the people walking in and out while I waited for poor Zelda to be brought out to me. I don't think I've ever seen such expressions of disbelief. I don't think you've any idea of the intensity of the anger in me right now."

"Ben, please put that decrepit excuse for a gun down before one of us gets hurt."

"No, Peter, this ends now – this for all those victims, past and present, and for all those who are being forced to clean up after you. This is for every single sodding one of them!"

*

"Did you hear that?" The woman with the headscarf and wicker shopping basket paused at the side of Forbes's car. Her younger, dog-walking companion turned to look behind them. "Was that a car backfiring... or did it sound more like a shot to you?"

"There are no cars. Someone must be shooting rabbits near the graveyard."

Like something from an old-style comedy sketch, heads appeared from doorways at the far end of the village and two first floor windows flew open. Forbes jumped from his car. "Everyone, please remain calm and go indoors. We may have a situation here. Officers are already on their way to the village. Please… everyone… go inside, remain in your houses, and stay away from the windows. Adam, take my car and block off the other end of the village. Park it across the road and abandon it. Don't get in his line of fire. "

"What about you?"

"I'll phone for an ambulance and prevent him leaving from this end of the street… now go."

32

Fate had brought him to this moment. Years of listening to his mother and her friends, of turning a blind eye to the odd behaviour of Richard Meadows while all the time knowing something was not quite right about the man, and of tramping the fields in the futile searches of so many missing girls.

He sat back down on the sofa and watched the blood seeping across Peter's abdomen. The fact that the bright red stain was still spreading across his sweatshirt meant that his heart was still beating, didn't it? He would have to wait for the blood flow to stop before he could walk away from the cottage and give himself up. Death was the only acceptable outcome.

It shouldn't take too long, but there might be time for a coffee and a slice of toast.

He guessed they'd have to arrest him, take him to the station and question him, and then charge him with manslaughter. It could be hours before he received his next proper meal – maybe he'd melt some cheese onto the toast, and pour a tot of whisky into his coffee.

As he sat at the kitchen table eating and drinking he pictured his mother in her dressing gown, slippers and hair rollers. *'Get your father's gun off the table;'* she'd be shrieking at him, *'that thing has killed people. Have you no respect? Put it back where it belongs.'*

"It's killed one more now, mother." He smiled as he muttered into his coffee mug. Peter should be dead by now. He sounded dead. The irregular rasping breaths had stopped several minutes ago. It was time to face the music.

He got up and walked to the sink.

It wouldn't do for mother to come home to dirty pots. She'd be mad enough at him for making such a mess of her living room carpet.

Maybe she'd be pleased with what he'd just done, or maybe she wouldn't – he didn't really mind either way. He'd lifted the curse from the *'valley of doom'*, as her mother had called it, and that was all that mattered. He was only sorry that he hadn't been able to save Mary and the girls from whatever distress Peter had inflicted on them. He'd had four weeks to realise that they were in acute danger, but the clues had somehow bypassed him. He'd warned her to be careful but he hadn't been insistent. Their traumas were partly his responsibility, but he'd put that right now.

Movement in the garden caught his eye as he dried the plate.

The front door imploded and the little cottage exploded with noise.

The plate hit the floor and shattered, but no one heard it.

"ARMED POLICE… STAY WHERE YOU ARE… ARMED POLICE… DON'T MOVE…"

33

"Well so much for a quiet weekend and an uneventful wedding," Forbes scanned the Monday morning faces of his team in the incident room, "and now for the paperwork."

Yesterday a man – a suspect, had been shot dead right under his nose. It had left him with a sour taste and a lot of questions from the chief constable's offices. He felt overly pleased when his DS walked into the room.

Less than twenty-four hours earlier the two of them had faced a potentially life threatening situation together, and even without the in-depth inquiry which was to follow, incidents like that took time to recover from. "Adam, we weren't expecting you in until next week. Aren't you supposed to be off on honeymoon today?"

"We're booked into a holiday park, but Jane wanted me to call in to the station before we set off and thank you all for the wedding gifts. And she wanted me to check on the condition of Mary Stone."

"She should be discharged from hospital in a couple of days, if all goes well. The knife missed her major organs. Her daughters' godparents are taking the little ones back to London with them today. They're too young yet to understand much of what happened with their mother and step-father."

"Ben Allsop understood," DI Lang added. "He's sticking to his story about not knowing anything about the filming, and he's maintaining that he shot and killed Peter Stone in self-defence. Do you believe him, sir?"

"I think that about ninety-per-cent of what he's telling us is true. The CPS is saying that they want him charged with manslaughter, but I'll predict that the public and the press will be on Ben's side. He hasn't been in any kind of trouble before, so taking his age into account, and his dependant mother, I can't see him getting much of a custodial sentence, if any. It wouldn't be in anyone's interest."

"Is Alison Ransom conducting the post-mortem today?" DC Green asked.

"A Home Office pathologist is coming in to assist her. Stone's business activities and private life are under scrutiny by agents both here and in America. At least that workload has been lifted from this station."

"It just seems wrong that it almost took the deaths of three innocent people to put a stop to his sick practices," PC Rawlings added.

Heads nodded

"We may have lost our suspect yesterday, and he'll never have to answer for his crimes, but we saved three of his victims. And don't lose sight of the fact that because of the skill of this team we saved two young women, also victims of the man, just over two weeks ago. Also we have undoubtedly prevented many future atrocities. We can only imagine what types of suffering may have been inflicted on innocent people in the future had Peter Stone not been stopped."

"Technically speaking, sir, we have Ben Allsop to thank for that," DC Emily Jackson piped up from the back of the room.

ENDS

Thank you for reading this book. If you enjoyed it please consider posting a review on Amazon or Goodreads. Just a few words mean a lot to me and can help other readers.

I appreciate your feedback and if you have any questions or comments please contact me on my email address:
sylviajanemarsden@outlook.com

Thank you for your time in reading this book.

Derbyshire detective DCI Forbes and his team will be back with another Peak District crime to solve.